CATERPILLAR

Kate Oliver

MAB Books
Reston, Virginia

Published by MAB Books, an imprint of Librado Press.
www.MAB-Books.com
www.LibradoPress.com

ISBN 978-1-879571-00-6
Library of Congress Control Number: 2012935184

Page 88: Quotation from *The Catcher in the Rye* by J.D. Salinger
Page 233: Excerpt from *Madam Butterfly*, libretto by L. Illica and G. Giacosa, English translation by R. H. Elkin

Publisher's Note: This is a work of fiction. Names, characters, places, and incidents, either are the product of the author's imagination or are used fictitiously, and any resemblance to any persons, living or dead, business establishments, events, or locales, is entirely coincidental.

For my mother, who always reads every version,
for my father, for keeping a house full of books,
and for Paul, for reasons very big and very small.

I'd like to get away from earth awhile
And then come back to it and begin over.
May no fate willfully misunderstand me
And half grant what I wish and snatch me away
Not to return. Earth's the right place for love:
I don't know where it's likely to go better.

Robert Frost,
from *Birches*

CATERPILLAR

Prologue

A luna moth goes through five instars before it builds a cocoon, which means that it has to grow a new skin five times before it even thinks about becoming an adult. It's a long process, and a dangerous one. At any moment, something might decide the caterpillar looks like bug-sashimi, or the weather might turn bad, or some jerk might come along and flatten it into the pavement. It's a hard life, being a caterpillar.

I know this because when I was thirteen, my seventh-grade science class raised luna moths. We started them from eggs, our teacher hoping we would understand the process of metamorphosis better if we watched it first-hand. Some of the girls in my class were disappointed; they wanted to raise butterflies instead. Something flashy, like monarchs or purple-edged coppers. But I preferred the moths. They have a quieter beauty. They're rarer, harder to find. And who hasn't seen a monarch before, anyway?

We watched the bumpy, fat caterpillars crawl around, and I wondered about them. Did they have any idea, any at all, how sad their little lives were? Or did they dream about the days when they would spin their cocoons and wake up as moths, looking like fairies with their diaphanous green wings, flying softly into the night?

I wondered. What does a caterpillar know about what it will become?

Some of them didn't make it. Some never advanced beyond the larval stage; others never made it out of their cocoons. By the time we were done, only about half of the moths had survived to adulthood, and we released them outside one night, watching as they flew off under the light of the stars.

But I couldn't stop thinking about the ones that didn't survive. What had been different about them? Was it simply inferior health, a case of bad genes? Or was it something else? A lack of willpower? A failure of imagination? Were they afraid?

I thought about them often, my lost caterpillars. But I was thirteen, and I had dreams of my own. That was the year I discovered the romance section of the public library. For two months, I hid in my room, reading. I pined, swooned, and loved along with the characters in every book I could find.

Love. I wondered about it constantly. I wondered what it would be like to feel that pure, perfect bond. To have a man who would risk everything for me; who would want to understand the profoundest depths of my soul.

Then, one day, I came home from school and had an epiphany. I'm not quite sure what sparked it, maybe something somebody said to me. I don't remember. But I knew that day that, somehow, love would never be part of my life.

My sister, the only real friend I'd ever had, was leaving for college. My parents detested each other, and weren't overwhelmingly fond of me, either. And the other people in my life were just passengers in the revolving door that cycled people in and out of my world. Love, attachment, closeness: it was all just a fairy tale … and my life was never going to turn into a fairy tale. I was average-looking, on a good day. I was clever, but not charming. And I was tired of the way my heart ached when I read about soft kisses and warm embraces. Love, I decided, was an unreliable dream—a game for girls who were more desirable or more deluded than I was. So I put the romance novels away.

I decided it was time for me to grow a new skin of my own.

Chapter One

Symbionts

The kid behind me kicked my seat all the way from D.C. to somewhere over Utah, when he finally fell asleep. It was that kind of flight.

I couldn't blame him, though. I would kick the seat in front of me, too, if I could get away with it. But if you do that when you're seventeen, the air marshals come and take you off the plane. There may be waterboarding involved after that—I'm not really sure. So, although the businessman in front of me made a tempting target with his seat half-reclined into my lap, I kept my feet to myself. I consoled myself by ordering an extra glass of orange juice and watching the blandest movie the airline could find for our in-flight entertainment—something about kissing, or ex-girlfriends, or something. I guess this was the closest they could get to sedating the passengers, at least legally. It seemed to be working on me.

I spend a lot of time on airplanes, so I spend a lot of time wanting to kick other people's seats. Of course, it isn't their fault I'm getting dragged around so much. I know that. But still, sometimes I'd like to kick *someone*. Especially those guys who get off on yelling at anyone they think might not be able to fight back: the flight attendants, the women juggling little kids, the

1

old people with walkers. You know the type. Big shots, bellowing their battle cry: "Don't you *know* who I *am*?" I dream of just once standing up and shouting, "Nobody cares, you ass!" But I don't do it. Of course I don't do it. I never say anything that would hurt anyone's feelings, not even when they deserve it. Especially not when they deserve it.

After we landed, I waited for several eons at the baggage claim before my trunk flew down the luggage chute and onto the carousel. It landed with a thud so loud the people around me jumped, and I couldn't help but smirk. My trunk—Old Faithful—always got that reaction. It was a beaten-up, world-weary thing, covered with scuffs and dents from being thrown around in countless airports. I watched as it slowly meandered toward me on the conveyer belt, waiting until it was squarely in front of me before I reached out for the handle.

The trunk was too heavy for me. I knew it. I was pretty sure the businessman next to me, the one I hadn't kicked, had come to the same conclusion, as he stepped forward to get a better look at the circling bags and our eyes met. I didn't wait to see if he would help me. He didn't.

They never do.

With a considerable amount of lumbar strain, I pulled the trunk onto the floor next to me. That was the hard part; dragging it around after that would be easy. It had wheels.

Useless Businessman ogled my beat-up steamer as he pulled up the handle on his tiny Pullman bag. "Looks like that's seen a lot of action," he said, pointing.

"Yep," I replied. I'd had this conversation before. Frequently. A muffled voice on the loudspeaker welcomed us to San Francisco.

"Military brat?"

"Foreign Service."

He nodded. "Must be an exciting life. You should appreciate it. Hell of an opportunity."

I gritted my teeth as I forced a smile. "Yeah."

I'd had this conversation frequently, too, listening to complete strangers extol the wonders of life as a Foreign Service brat. I didn't tell him the truth, that it wasn't the life I'd picked, that it'd been picked for me. What was the point? He'd just peg me as an ungrateful teenager. And I wasn't, really. I knew I had it better than lots of people. I've lived enough places to know what real problems are. Still, it bugged me. Who would want to spend their childhood as a skipping stone, being thrown from place to place, never having any say? And as soon as you start to get settled, someone comes along and tosses you someplace else.

Plunk.

Useless Businessman pulled his phone out of his jacket and walked away as I watched. "Yeah," he said into the phone. "I'm here. I'll be home in half an hour. Did the guy ever show up to fix the cable?"

I watched until he was swallowed whole by the crowd of people in the baggage claim.

I grabbed my trunk by the handle, dragging it behind me as I went off in search of my sister, who was picking me up. I was moving in with her for the year.

My parents were moving—yet again—this time, to Uruguay. I'd been given three choices: go with them—yet again—and spend my senior year at the American School in Montevideo, which offered neither the BC Calculus nor the AP French courses I needed, attend a boarding school, or move in with my sister, Liv.

So there I was.

3

I pulled my trunk over to one of the benches and sat down, hoping that Liv wouldn't be long. I've always hated airports; they leave me feeling raw, like my skin's been stripped away and my insides might fall out. They remind me of moving, and screaming parents, and things left behind.

In front of me, a woman came running through the crowd and threw her arms around a middle-aged man in a sweatshirt, followed by a little girl who latched onto the man's leg, shrieking gleefully. The man bent to kiss his wife's smiling lips, and I had to turn away with a prickling throat. I shook my head, swallowing my irrational sadness back down into my stomach. *Not me,* I thought. Not the little girl with the happy parents, and certainly not the woman with the adoring husband, who was kissing her a second time while I tried not to watch. *Not my life. Doesn't matter. Doesn't matter.*

I'd just decided to find another bench when I heard the sound of my name from within the throng of humanity.

"Cara!" It was Liv, waving like a maniac. As she pushed through the crowd, I could see that she was beaming, and she threw her arms around my neck like I was her favorite person in the world. Which I was.

I closed my eyes against the view of the airport, with its happy families and useless businessmen, its reminders of everything I'd ever lost and everything I'd never had, and squeezed her back.

She coughed against the side of my head. "God, you *stink.*"

I snickered as I pulled away. "Yeah, I know. I think the woman next to me bathed in cat pee before she got on the plane."

I hadn't seen Liv since April, but she still looked the same, with her dark hair pulled back in a disorderly ponytail, her skin

4

browned from working outside. A suntanned, taller version of me. Yet somehow, the features that were so ordinary on me were pretty on her. I'd always thought she was beautiful, though she never saw it herself. She seemed to find the idea offensive.

She gave Old Faithful a pat. "Is this it?"

"Just that and my backpack. I know you don't have much space."

"It's small, but you'll like it," she said. "Come on, I had to park two lots over."

After we hauled my stuff out to her ancient station wagon, we piled in and headed out toward the freeway. "I've got a surprise for you at home," she said, grinning at me and blowing a stray strand of hair out of her face.

"What is it?" I asked.

She laughed. "You'll see. Let's just say the new place has a big kitchen window with a southern exposure."

A southern exposure. The holy grail for indoor gardeners.

Liv was making me a place for a garden.

I love plants. I've loved them as long as I can remember, so elegant in their design, so perfectly self-sufficient. I didn't think I would be able to have any, living in an apartment. I was thrilled. My botanical dreams would not have to be put on hold.

She smiled at me again and looked back to the road. Liv was twenty-two—five years older than me, but it had never seemed like so much. From the time I was born until she'd left for college, we'd been utterly inseparable, a pair of symbiotic organisms clinging to each other to survive in our rootless world. A remora and a shark. An anemone and a clownfish. An oak tree and a rhizobium bacterium.

I'm not sure which of us was the bacterium in that equation.

As the family genius, Liv had finished college in three years, and was starting her second year in the graduate program in Biology at McNair, one of the top schools on the West Coast. This, of course, was exactly what I wanted to do, too. Only Liv's specialty was Marine Ecology, while I preferred the company of my plants, dreaming of the day when I would become a botanist.

When we got back to her apartment, I saw that it was a lot smaller, and a lot messier, than I'd expected. I'd have to find a way to clean up while she was at work. I'd never find anything in the mess of old pizza boxes, library books, and random paperwork.

"Let me give you the complete tour," she said with a flourish.

The first thing she showed me was the tiny kitchen which, as promised, featured an oversized window. Liv had added a shelf to the windowsill to give it extra width, and it made the perfect spot for a tiny indoor garden. On the sill were half a dozen empty flowerpots, which cast long shadows as the sun streamed through the window and into the kitchen. I picked one up and examined it, which was silly because, really, it was just a terra-cotta flowerpot, the kind you can get for a dollar anyplace. But to me, it represented something more. I was the owner of that pot's destiny. I could plant it with whatever I wanted. No one would be able to take it away from me. To that pot, mine was the kingdom and the power and the glory. Amen.

I couldn't run my own life, but I was a fiend with a flowerpot.

Liv smiled as she watched me examine my garden, though I wasn't sure exactly how much she understood. "You can go to the nursery this weekend and pick out whatever you want to plant," she suggested.

"It's fabulous, Liv. Thank you so much."

"Do you want to see the rest?" she asked.

I nodded, and she led me down the hall. I was glad to have my own room, but we would be sharing a bathroom, which, like the rest of the place, was a pigsty. Liv had always been the butt of family jokes for this. My mother often wondered how she'd managed to master Calculus in the ninth grade, and yet was still unable to figure out how to get dirty clothes into a hamper. When she'd left for college, Mom had been worried that she might forget to feed herself for a week and subsequently starve to death. As I stepped over a pile of laundry, I wondered how she'd survived for so long on her own.

She noticed the sneer on my face as I kicked some dirty socks to one side of the hallway. "You can see I cleaned up for you," she said dryly.

"You're disgusting."

She threw a sports bra at my head.

Thankfully, my room was clean. Against the far wall were an old dresser and a twin bed, and there was a small desk under the window, which had a view of the common area between our building and the one next-door in the complex. Other than that, the room was pretty much bare. I was relieved.

"It's great," I said, dumping Old Faithful next to the bed.

"We can go get you some posters, or whatever you want to decorate it."

"No, it's fine this way. Maybe a calendar, but that's it, I swear."

She laughed. "Whatever you say. Just don't tell Mom I made you live in some kind of prison cell, okay?"

7

I put my hand over my heart. "I promise." It was an unwritten rule from our childhoods: don't tell Mom. You didn't tell Mom anything unless you had no choice. It was simply not worth the ensuing histrionics.

"So are you hungry yet?" she asked.

"Extremely."

"Pizza?"

"Please."

Liv had to finish grading her papers—the summer session was just coming to an end—so I spent most of the evening flipping through bad TV and looking at the summer reading list that Liv had picked up for me. No big surprises there. It was more or less the same list they'd given out at my old school in Virginia: Shakespeare, Margaret Atwood, Samuel Beckett. I figured I'd head to the library sometime to see what I could find, so I wouldn't have to wipe out this month's spending money on books. I still had a week before school started. Plenty of time to read three books.

I hoped that the kids at Muro Viejo High—Murray, my sister had said it was called, as if it were some old Jewish guy instead of a high school—wouldn't make my life too miserable. I was not particularly interested in making lifelong friends in the ten months before I graduated and joined the Real World, but I didn't want to spend the year eating lunch by myself in the bathroom, either. My dad had been stationed in D.C. prior to moving to Montevideo, so I'd spent the last three years at a high school in Northern Virginia. My classmates had all been horrified that I would have to transfer for my senior year. It made little difference to me. I was used to moving every few years, anyway. One school was more or less like another.

Things would be better now since Liv and I were together again. Five years apart had been hard on both of us; we'd texted back and forth multiple times a day, but it wasn't the same as actually living under the same roof. I hoped she was as glad to have me there as I was to be there. I would try my best not to make her too crazy since I knew she was insanely busy with school, but I was pretty independent anyway. My father spent most of his waking hours working, and my mother was generally busy fuming about how much she disliked whichever country we were currently living in. She'd liked Virginia better, though, and was not looking forward to being shipped overseas again. I actually felt a little sorry for her.

I was still on East Coast time, so I went to bed as soon as the sun went down. As I closed my eyes, I wondered how I would possibly fill my time during the week before school started.

Chapter Two

Half Moon Bay

The next morning, I woke at the crack of dawn only to discover that Liv had left a note outside my door.

Cara,
Had to get to campus early to get some work done in the lab before classes. Won't be home until tonight—lots of food in the fridge. I've taken my bike and left the car with you, in case you want to go out. There's a map on the floor of the backseat. Keys on hook by door.
- L

Next to the note was a maidenhair fern in a little plastic pot. I popped it into one of the terra-cotta flowerpots, though there wasn't quite enough dirt. I considered heading out to the nursery to work on filling the rest of my flowerpot kingdom, but when I thought about it, I decided that the pots could wait. What I really wanted to see was the beach—I couldn't remember the last time I'd seen the ocean. I thought of driving down to Santa Cruz for the day, but it seemed like a long way to drive on my own when I was still jet-lagged, so I got online and checked out a local map. Half Moon Bay was only a half-hour away. I decided to give that a try after I made a show of taming the mess in the kitchen.

In all honesty, I am not a particularly neat person, but Liv is in a class by herself. I filled two trash bags with empty boxes and expired food from the fridge, and that was without touching the freezer. I figured I would need to hit the grocery store that evening if I wanted some hope of eating a green vegetable in the next few days. Liv seemed to be subsisting on a diet of frozen dinners and breakfast cereal.

I was afraid to mess with Liv's papers, so I left the living room alone, and the bathroom was too scary even to think about first thing in the morning. So I made myself a peanut butter sandwich, grabbed a can of some highly caffeinated soda and a sweatshirt to wear at the beach, and headed out.

The sun was still low in the sky as I cleared the mountains. Everything seemed to be covered in a light fog, and the effect was magical—like I was driving into another world; a world where the sky was invisible and everything was covered with a blanket of mist. The way the light filtered through the fog made me sleepy again, like I was re-entering some long-forgotten dream. I was still lost in my reverie when I heard what I thought was a gunshot.

I'd blown a tire.

I was at least two miles from the main beach entrance—too far to drive on the rim without destroying it. I slowed down and tried to find a place to pull off the road. As luck would have it, there was a scenic overlook about a hundred feet ahead, so I pulled over and stopped. There was one other car already there—a navy-blue Prius. I didn't see anyone nearby. Its hipster owner must have gone for a walk down to the beach.

I popped the rear hatch on Liv's rusty Subaru, for once grateful that in my family, learning to change a tire was considered a requirement for getting a driver's license. When I opened it, I was not pleased (though not entirely surprised) to see that the back of the station wagon was entirely full of Liv's crap. I could feel steam rising off my head as I began taking everything out to get to the spare. The mess seemed to consist mostly of the equipment Liv used to do wildlife surveys: a scale, some camera equipment, a bunch of towels, and a lot of stuff I couldn't identify. As I got to the bottom of the pile, there was one thing that was obviously missing—the jack. There was no way I was going to be able to change this myself. I'd have to call a tow truck.

That's when I remembered that I'd left my phone on the kitchen counter to charge it.

I rolled my eyes and slammed the hatch shut. I would have to walk the rest of the way to the main entrance. There was sure to be someone there who could help me out. But before I walked all that way, I decided to look around for the owner of the blue Prius parked in front of me. I hopped the guardrail and started walking along the narrow footpath that meandered down the hill toward the beach.

I could see immediately that this wasn't a beach for swimming; it was much too rocky for that, and the surf was some of the roughest I'd ever seen. The sound of the waves crashing against the rocky shore was overwhelming, and even though there were gulls circling above, I couldn't hear them. The fog was burning off and the sun was just beginning to break through the clouds, but out over the ocean the sky was still dark. Menacing, like a storm was coming, though the forecast hadn't said so. The air was colder than I'd expected, and my clammy palms were useless as I tried to rub my goose bumps away.

I had to watch my footing as I tried to stay on top of the bigger rocks, not wanting to twist my ankle by falling between them. I was about to turn back when I saw a man—young, I guessed, though I couldn't see him well—standing at the end of a rocky outcropping about a hundred feet out into the surf and about six feet above the water. I couldn't figure out what he was doing; there were enormous waves breaking against the rocks just a few feet from where he was standing. I stared at him, framed against sea foam and the dark sky, and it occurred to me that this was one of the stupidest things I had ever seen. As I watched, he took a step toward the edge. What was he doing?

A wave crashed in front of him, forcing him to take a step back, and it suddenly dawned on me what was about to happen. He was going to get himself knocked against the rocks and killed, right in front of me. I began to shiver as it sank in: I was about to watch someone die.

I scrambled onto the outcropping, trying to get close enough to call to him. As I slipped and fell into a crouch, he took another step forward and leaned toward the sea, his legs tensing as if preparing to jump.

I leaped to my feet, almost sending myself tumbling into the surf in the process. I caught myself on my hands, and looked up to see the man clenching and unclenching his fists, as if he were counting down to something. There was no time for me to get to the end of the outcropping. I'd never make it.

The wind whipped salt into my face as I lifted my head to shout. "Hey!" I screamed at the top of my lungs. "Come back!"

I was still a hundred feet from him, but I knew my voice had reached him as soon as he stepped back and leaned his body away from the waves. But he didn't turn around. Continuing toward him was terrifying with the waves so close, threatening my own drowning with every step. I didn't want to spend the rest of my life with a visual of this guy's brains dashed out on the rocks while I stood there like a moron, so I kept going. I tried not to look at the water, concentrating instead on the man I needed to help.

I could see that his shoulders were heaving, and I wondered if he was crying. Now I was scared—not just that I might fall in, but that he might actually be crazy. I stopped about twenty feet from him and called again. "Are you okay?"

He turned around, and, for the first time, I was close enough to get a good look at him. He was younger than I'd thought before—maybe twenty? It was hard to say. His chest was bare, and his shorts were dripping wet from the cold surf. The first thing that struck me was how outrageously handsome he was. The second was how tired and miserable he looked.

He didn't seem out of control at all, and he didn't look like he meant me any harm, so I held out my hand. "Come on; it isn't safe out here," I called. Even from where I stood, I could feel the mist of cold water from the breaking waves, like tiny droplets of ice burning my skin. I couldn't imagine how cold he must have felt, shirtless and wet.

For a second he just stared at my hand, and the look in his eyes was haunted. I had seen sadness before: my parents', my sister's, my own. But I had never seen anyone who looked so utterly defeated. I knew that I would never forget that look, that pain, for the rest of my life.

He faked a smile. "I'm fine," he called back, shrugging. "Really. I just like to be close to the surf."

I wasn't buying it, but I didn't know what else to say without sounding like a movie of the week. So I just said, "Please?"

He sighed. As he climbed toward me, my eyes met his, and I shuddered.

"All right," he said, smiling in that false way again. "I don't want you to slip out here on my account. Let's go."

As we climbed back to the overlook in awkward silence, I realized that I had no idea what to do next. I was still in the same predicament that had brought me down to the beach in the first place, but how do you ask someone you suspect was in the middle of a suicide attempt for help with a freaking flat tire?

I shouldn't have worried. "Did you know you had a flat?" he asked, pointing at the obvious evidence.

"Yeah, that's why I pulled over. My car's missing the jack and I forgot my phone." *Stupid*, I thought as soon as the words were out of my mouth. Admit I'm alone and helpless to a total stranger. Who might even be crazy.

"I can help," he offered. "Do you want me to put your spare on for you?"

"I can do it myself, if I can borrow your jack."

He smiled, genuinely this time, and opened his trunk. He handed me the jack and reached into his car for a shirt, pulling it over his head as he sat down on the curb.

I changed the tire while he watched, which he seemed to find very amusing. My clothes were wet from climbing on the outcropping, and I was cold and annoyed. What was wrong with this guy? Why was he staring at me? Was he really trying to kill himself, or was he just a huge idiot? I tried to pretend that he wasn't gorgeous, but it was useless. His dark hair was still wet from the sea, and his olive skin practically glowed as the

15

sun started to burn through the fog. Even more startling than the rest of him were his eyes, which were a silver-gray color that didn't seem to go with the rest of his complexion. Like the moon, I thought, or steel. I couldn't help glancing up at him whenever I could. It was like asking a moth not to fly into a flame.

I tried very hard to avoid those gray eyes. I generally avoid making eye contact with people I don't know—it seems like such an intimate act to me. Like kissing someone you just met. I was still trying not to look at him when I pulled the jack out from under the car and, as my eyes involuntarily flicked to his, scraped my hand between the jack and the underside of the car. My breath came out in a hiss, and I quickly wiped the back of my hand against my shorts, trying to ignore the burning. God, I was an idiot. Who hurts themselves trying not to look at a hot guy?

I stood up and handed him back the jack. "Thanks," I said, a little more abruptly than I intended. I was embarrassed by how obviously I was attracted to him, and more than anything I wanted to get out of there before I humiliated myself.

He smiled at me and tossed the jack back in his trunk. "Sure," he said. "Look, I'm sorry you got all wet. I know you were just trying to help. It's not like I don't appreciate it; most people wouldn't have bothered. But I'm fine. Can I do anything to help you?"

"No, I just needed help with the tire, but it's fixed now." I fidgeted nervously. "I'm sorry if I interrupted your, I don't know, communal with the ocean or whatever, but it really did look like you were going to hurt yourself. So, if you do feel like that—and I'm not saying you do, but *if* you do—then I hope you find someone to talk to. I knew someone who did that once, and it was really bad for her family. And her friends, too, you know. They never really got over it." I managed to look up then, and he had that same haunted look.

"I'm fine, really," he said at last, in a quiet voice that wouldn't have convinced anyone. "I should let you go."

I stared at him for a long time, not knowing if I should just go or try to do something else to help. It seemed wrong to walk away and leave him, but how do you help someone who insists nothing's wrong?

But instead of saying something actually useful, I blurted out the first thing that came into my head:

"Would you like half of my sandwich?"

Oh, God, no, please don't let that be what I actually said. Please, please, please …

He burst out laughing. I guess I couldn't blame him, and since there was nothing else I could do, I laughed, too. I was mortified by how stupid I must have sounded to this guy. Finally, he wiped his eyes and said, "I would love to share your sandwich."

I grabbed my lunch out of the car and sat down next to him on the curb.

"It's peanut butter—you're not allergic or anything, are you?"

"No, peanut butter sounds like heaven," he said, taking the half a sandwich I handed to him.

We ate in silence, until I noticed that he was staring at me again. I fidgeted and looked away, and he cleared his throat.

"You're bleeding," he said. I looked down, and, sure enough, the scrape on my left hand was oozing blood down my wrist and onto my knee.

I grunted in disgust. "Great. That's just great."

I let myself look at him again. "I don't … I don't suppose you have a first-aid kit or anything? In your car?"

His lips twitched. "I—uh—no. Actually. Sorry."

I got up and popped the hatch of Liv's station wagon, hoping that Liv had one somewhere in her pile of debris. "Maybe there's one in the back here." I dug around for a minute, and he watched curiously while I pushed things out of the way. I found a red and white plastic bin toward the bottom and pulled it out. By then my entire hand was sticky with blood, and I couldn't get the box open.

He got up and stood next to me, carefully taking the box from my hands. "Here," he said, opening it for me and handing me a couple of sanitary wipes and an oversized Band-Aid.

"Thanks."

I cleaned my hand as best I could, and then looked at the Band-Aid and shook my head.

"Do you need a hand?" he asked.

"No. Yes. It's just—I'm a lefty," I explained holding out my hand as I cringed.

"Oh, okay. Here." He opened the bandage and carefully placed it over the back of my hand. Then he gently held my wrist with one hand while he pressed down on the adhesive with the other. I was surprised by how soft his touch was, despite how large his hands seemed to me, with broad palms and long fingers. They were so warm, too. I was embarrassed by how much I liked being touched by him, and I was sorry when he finally let go. "All done. Does it hurt much?"

"Oh, you know, it's fine," I waved my hand dismissively. "It looks worse than it is."

"So …" he said, slowly. "Can I give you a ride home from the garage? It's going to take awhile to get a new tire put on."

18

"No, thanks, I won't have another way to go back and pick up the car. I'll just wait. It's not a big deal." This time I really didn't know what else to say, so I opened my car door and turned back to look at him. "Well, bye."

"Thanks. For—for the sandwich," he said, and I looked into his gray eyes and felt a jolt that radiated through my entire body.

That jolt was enough to trigger my flight response, so I got in my car, shut the door, and pulled out onto the highway. Liv had always teased me for running like a rabbit anytime I met a cute guy. I never really knew why that was, but I was somewhat relieved that the instinct hadn't left me.

I glanced in my rearview mirror as I drove away, but I could no longer see him. Something squeezed inside my chest—longing or fear or regret, or maybe all three.

I realized that I had never even asked him his name.

Chapter Three

Mistaken

It was a three-hour wait at the garage. With none of my books and no phone. The clerk offered to let me use hers, but I couldn't remember Liv's number since it was programmed into my cell phone and I had never bothered to memorize it. So I spent my time reading *Cosmo* and *Newsweek*, and trying desperately not to think about the boy from the beach and his sad eyes. Just remembering them tied my stomach into knots. I hoped he was okay.

I paid for the tire with the credit card my parents had given me for emergencies, and decided to go have lunch with my sister on campus. Assuming she wasn't busy teaching a class. I knew she was the Teaching Assistant for at least one section of Biology 101.

I heard Liv laughing before I saw her, standing at the bottom of the steps to the Bio building. She was talking to some Euro-trashy-looking guy—an undergrad, I guessed—in a black T-shirt and with so much product in his hair he could have cracked coconuts on his head. Despite all this, he was, unfortunately, devastatingly cute. He leaned in closer and Liv's face colored faintly. I knew the look she was giving him, her lips pursed as if she'd been sucking on a lemon and was getting ready to share the experience. He seemed blissfully unaware of the fact that he was about to be slugged, and persisted in whatever passed for pitching woo amongst the metrosexual set.

I could hear them talking as I got closer.

"… inappropriate. And against department rules. And gross." This was Liv.

"Come on," he said. "No one has to know. Let me buy you a drink. Just one."

Liv smirked. "Gee, I'd really like to, but I'd hate to take the business away from your babysitter."

Uh-oh. I came up behind Liv and threw my arm around her waist. She jumped, and then saw it was me and rolled her eyes hugely.

"Honey," I said, squeezing Liv's middle, "You're fifteen minutes late!"

His eyes flicked from Liv to me, and a slow smile spread across his face. Crap. Time for plan B.

I batted my eyes at Liv. "I thought you were going to meet me at the dermatologist, you know, about that rash on your—"

That did it. He muttered something to Liv about their next class and beat a hasty retreat. She turned around and glared at me. "That was one of my students," she hissed. "You didn't do anything to bolster my professional reputation with that."

"Sorry," I said. "I figured it would be worse for your professional reputation if you punched him in the face."

"I was not going to punch him."

"You were thinking about it."

She shrugged, then smiled. "A *rash?*" she said, raising her eyebrows at me.

"Yep. I've added it to my list. Words that make boys go away."

She leaned down to pick up her books. "Ah. You have a list now. Any other goodies I should know?"

"Well," I said, counting them off on my fingers, "there's commitment, pregnant, shotgun, um, oh! Celibate. That's a good one. Lesbian used to be on there, but that one doesn't work so well anymore."

She laughed. "No, I guess not. So the beach didn't work out this morning?"

Oh, that's right. I was supposed to be mad at her. I told her about the tire incident, and about how I'd gotten help from a stranger. I left out the part about the suicide attempt. "You need to keep the jack in your car," I said, crossing my arms over my chest.

"Sorry," she said sheepishly. "I took it out to make room for the tagging equipment. I'll put it back when I get home. Did you want to have lunch?"

"Yeah, totally, I'm starving."

Liv had to run up to her office, so I followed behind her amused that Liv, with her messy hair, tattered jeans, and baggy T-shirt, was the kind of person who *had* an office. She was really a grown-up now, despite all evidence to the contrary. It was a bit comforting when I saw that her office was almost as messy as her apartment—which is to say, it was two takeout boxes short of a Superfund site.

She emptied her backpack onto her chair while I examined her desk, which was covered with papers waiting to be graded. I picked an exam off the top of the stack. It was marked a C-.

"A little harsh, don't you think?" I asked.

"Ah," she said. "This one belongs to our friend Monsieur Douchebag. I think that's why he was trying to pick me up. Hoping for some grade inflation."

"Oh, well. At least he's cute."

"Glad you think so, since he'll be hitting us up for a three-way later."

"Oh," I said. "Ew."

She laughed. "Yeah, well, unfortunately *cute* and *douche* don't seem to be mutually exclusive." She took the test and tossed it back onto the pile of papers. "Lunch?"

"Absolutely."

We grabbed a few slices of pizza from the dining hall, and I was relieved to see a salad bar, since I hadn't eaten anything healthy since I left my parents in Virginia. We headed outside to eat so that we could avoid the noisy crowd in the cafeteria.

"So," Liv said, stuffing her mouth. "What do you think of the campus?"

"It's big," I admitted. "I got lost a few times. But everything looks amazing. I wish I could just go here in the fall instead of high school."

She nodded. "I know. It's only a year, and then you'll be done."

She unwrapped the candy bar she'd gotten to go with her pizza, and then looked up at me and groaned. "I forgot to tell you. Dr. Yarrow cornered me in the hall this morning, and he reminded me that there's a big barbecue for the science departments on Sunday. Sort of a welcome party for the new grad students. So I'm going, I guess."

"But you hate stuff like that!" I said. Liv was even more antisocial than I was. When we were kids she once spent an entire wedding reception hiding in the bathroom.

"He said he expects me to be there. I think he wants me to meet some of the incoming Bio students. So I have to go."

"Okay," I said. "I can get myself dinner tomorrow night. It's no problem ..."

"No!" she exclaimed. "You have to come with me. Nobody will want to talk to me if I'm there with my teenage sister."

I rolled my eyes. "Thanks!"

She stuck her tongue out at me. "Oh, come on. There'll be free food. We'll stay for an hour, Dr. Yarrow won't have an excuse to freak out on me, and then we'll leave."

"God, Liv, can't you do this by yourself?"

She cocked her head at me and grinned. "I'll clean the bathroom."

"Done."

I spent the rest of the afternoon wandering around campus, trying to get my bearings, while I waited for Liv to finish up for the day. It was nice out and I had a book I'd filched from Liv's office, so I really didn't mind. I felt at peace there. In control. Like I belonged.

It was three-thirty and Liv was going to be done for the day at four, so I plopped myself down on the bench outside the Biology building to wait for her.

As I pulled out my copy of *Lives of a Cell*, a man in a dark suit sat down next to me. He was forty or so, but lean looking, with salt-and-pepper hair and pale-blue eyes. I figured he must have been a faculty member because he was dressed so nicely.

Out of the corner of my eye, I saw him pull a plastic device out of his pocket and stare at the controls, muttering under his breath about what a piece of crap it was. It looked like an XRF scanner—the kind of thing they use to test for lead. I'd seen pictures of them in news stories about how we were all being poisoned by Chinese toothpaste and cheap plastic toys. I wondered what it was for, but of course I wasn't going to ask.

I was risking a furtive glance in his direction when I fumbled my book and dropped it on the ground in front of his feet. He smiled at me, the wrinkles around his blue eyes crinkling, and handed it back.

"Thanks," I said, and went back to pretending to read.

He took the scanner—if that's what it was—and pointed it at his hand, still muttering. This time, he didn't look frustrated with the results. He gasped and turned to look at me.

"Um, is it working now?" I asked.

He shook his head as if to clear it, or to rid himself of an unwanted idea. "Do you take classes in the Chemistry department?"

"Well, no," I said. "Why?"

His eyes met mine, but before I could think to say anything else he reached out and grabbed my hand—the bandaged one, which was closer to him—and scanned it. I cried out and jumped to my feet, pulling my hand back.

"What the hell do you think you're doing?" I screamed.

As he looked from the display of his scanner back to me, I could see that his face was filled with shock and elation, his eyes widening. He was on his feet in an instant. Before I could react, he reached out and grabbed my arm again. His mouth opened slowly, widely, and I thought for a minute that he might scream. Instead, he ground out a single word, in a voice that sent shockwaves of terror down my spine.

"*You.*"

His breathing was hard, and I was suddenly terrified of this man and his crazed eyes. His hand on my arm was so tight that I couldn't pull myself away. There was no one nearby, but it

25

was the middle of the afternoon and someone was bound to walk by in a minute. Was he really going to attack me in public, in the middle of the afternoon?

"Let go," I shouted, trying to pull away from him. His fingers sank so deeply into my skin that it felt like he was crushing the bones in my arm.

"What the hell is going on?"

It was Liv, running toward us. At the sound of her voice, the man let go of me and I stumbled backward. She stepped in front of me and glared at the man in the suit, who looked surprised.

Liv's voice was husky and loud. "What are you doing with my sister?"

He looked over Liv's shoulder at me, and then back at her again. "Your sister?" he asked.

"Yes," she spat. "And I think you'd better explain what the hell you were doing before I kick your ass and call the cops." She continued to stare him down, and he took a step back, though I had a strange feeling that he was probably more than Liv could handle. Though Liv was almost five-eight, he stood half a head taller, and under his jacket lay a set of broad shoulders that didn't belong to a weak man.

"I'm sorry," he said, nodding toward me but dropping his eyes. "I seem to have mistaken you for someone else."

"I should say so," Liv growled.

He turned and stormed away, and Liv spun around to face me. "Are you okay?" she asked.

"Yeah, I'm fine. He just grabbed me out of nowhere. Do you know who he was?"

She shook her head. "I've never seen him before."

"You mean he isn't a professor?"

26

"Not one that I've ever seen."

"But he had this scanner," I explained. "Like he was taking readings of something."

Liv bit her lip. "Maybe we should report this to campus security," she suggested. "Just in case."

Campus security was not helpful. The officer at the desk took my report while watching football on the TV bolted to the wall behind me.

"Maybe he really did mistake you for someone else," he suggested.

"Really? Who *should* he be grabbing and yanking around?" Liv asked.

He shrugged. "I don't know. Just be careful, all right, ladies?"

Liv bristled at his tone. I didn't blame her.

We went home after that, and I tried to blow the whole thing off. I saw how angry it made Liv, and, more than anything, I wanted her to feel better. "Maybe he was just some crazy old guy," I said. "He seemed pretty confused once you said you were my sister."

"Maybe."

I couldn't sleep that night, and I wasn't surprised. I kept thinking about the crazy man, his hand on my arm like a steel trap, and how he'd looked at me like he knew all my secrets, like he could see straight through me. By the time I forced those thoughts out of my head, they were replaced with softer memories of the sad, beautiful boy from the beach. I hoped he was all right. I was sure I would never see him again, but I didn't think I would ever forget the unbearable misery in his eyes. As I replayed the scene in my mind, it seemed to me that

27

there had been something more in the way he'd looked at me when I held my hand out to him. Desire? *Not possible*, I told myself.

I tried to clear my head, to think of nothing, but even in the dimness of my bedroom I could see that the marks on my wrist were darkening into bruises.

The Journal of Will Mallory

August 15
Year 64, day — oh, hell, I don't know.
Forms: Four

I appear to continue being not dead.

I've already discussed here how this came to pass. Though I'm still thinking about it, about her, I'm trying very hard to let it go. I don't seem to have a choice in the matter. I know I won't see her again.

I dreamt of Meris again last night. I always do, whenever I see the ocean. I'm not sure if this means I should go more or less. I do enjoy the dreaming. But then after always comes the waking up.

Things with Kleeman are still not going terribly well. Trying not to think about it. Worse, today was my day for office hours, so I went, figuring that as long as I was going to continue shuffling along this mortal coil, I ought to remain employed. I sat in my office for three-quarters of an hour and tried to explain to unhappy eighteen-year-olds with no hope of grasping relativity that if they were shot into space at the speed of light, their lack of scientific understanding would seem to an onlooker to stretch on for eternity.

I didn't actually tell them that. I probably should have. Would have saved us all some time.

I needed a break, so I went out into the hallway and raised my coffee cup, tapping it with my finger. "Caffeine," I explained to the students who were queued up to talk to me. "I'll be back in ten minutes."

I bypassed the Physics Department's main office, with its coffee maker, not sure where I was going. I wanted to be alone. Not to be surrounded by people I was lying to. Which was unfortunate, because, as I went out the front door, I ran headfirst into Adeep Kumar. Have I mentioned Adeep before? I can't recall.

"Watch where you're going, jackass," he said to me in Hindi.

"Sorry, I didn't see you." Adeep, a native of Seattle, is under the impression that my Hindi—which is better than his—is the result of my spending a summer in New Delhi (a lie), while I was in college (another lie). We've become colleagues, of a sort, as we've begun collaborating on an interdisciplinary research project, though of course he has no idea that our project has any immediate practical applications. Adeep, whose shock of curly, electric-blue hair only seems to accentuate the lankiness of his frame, is a fourth-year grad student in the Chemistry Department. Something of a wunderkind.

He continued to look at me expectantly. "Were you looking for me?" I asked.

"I need more of that powdered palladium."

I nodded. "I'll call." God, I was tired. "Was there something else?"

"Jesus, you're an unfriendly prick," he said. "Aren't you even going to ask how I'm doing? What's new with you, Adeep?"

I sighed. "How are you doing, Adeep?"

He grinned. "I asked the Biology Goddess out again."

"Did you."

"I did."

"And what did she call you this time?"

He ran his hand self-consciously through his hair. "The Barbie Dream-Poodle."

I laughed. "I think that's a no, my friend." Adeep doesn't hear "no" often. I gathered that the Biology Goddess had become something of a challenge for him. From what I'd seen, he was lucky if all she did was make fun of his hair.

30

He shook his head. "Have you seen the Biology Goddess? Legs. For. Days. I'm going to rock her mitochondria, man."

"Please tell me you didn't actually use that line on her."

"The Biology girls love that line," he insisted. "If you weren't such a homo, you'd know that." Adeep is under the impression that my disinterest in "The Goddesses" is due to the fact that I am a closeted homosexual. A notion of which I fail to disabuse him, as it's so much easier—and more pleasant—than the truth.

One lie among thousands. How many have I told? And with each one, some corresponding part of me dies, as if its denial causes it to cease existing altogether. How much of me is left? The real me?

I didn't know. Barely even cared. Then, from somewhere, I heard a shout. A girl. I looked at Adeep.

"What is that?"

He shook his head. "A fight?"

I shoved my mug into his hands and ran across the quad, to the source of the sound, heart racing, feet pounding against the pavement. There was something about the voice—something familiar.

When I arrived no one was there.

Chapter Four

Of Mayonnaise and Men

I spent the day of the barbecue happily transplanting seedlings into my pots: some peperomia, another maidenhair fern, and some sansevieria. Some marigolds for Liv, since she liked them. I was thoroughly pleased with my efforts. They weren't going to turn into anything flashy—the nursery didn't have anything really interesting—but they would do. I surveyed my little green friends with satisfaction. I hoped they were happy to be there, on Liv's sunny windowsill.

I took a shower to get rid of the potting soil that clung to my arms and embedded itself under my fingernails, but I refused to put my clothes on until Liv dutifully cleaned every inch of the bathroom, grumbling at me as she scrubbed that this would make us late. I watched her in my bathrobe with my arms folded.

"I'm done," she said, looking up from the toilet. "I hope you appreciate this."

"More than you know. I'll get dressed now."

I could hear the noise from the party as soon as we parked and got out of the car, and I groaned. Liv didn't look any too pleased, either. "One hour," she reminded me. I hadn't forgotten.

I glanced down at my watch to make sure I knew when we'd be able to leave, to the minute.

The Quad was set up with a long buffet table, and about a hundred people milled around with paper plates in their hands. Liv and I found the line for the food and patiently stood at the end. I passed up the corn on the cob—too hard to eat without making a mess—and grabbed a veggie burger. Liv, of course, got the corn. As we made our way to the end of the line, I heard someone call Liv's name.

"I was beginning to think you hadn't made it," said a middle-aged man in sandals and a Rolling Stones T-shirt. His curly hair was beginning to go gray, but he didn't look like he could have been much more than forty. He gave Liv an annoyed look. "I've got two first-year students that I need you to meet."

"Oh, hi, Steve," Liv said. "Um, this is my sister, Cara, the one I told you about. Cara, this is Dr. Yarrow."

I smiled and held out my hand, which he shook briefly. "Nice to meet you," he said, barely looking at me.

Liv was beginning to freak out, as she realized her plan to hide behind me wasn't working. I nudged her with my shoulder. "Go meet the new students," I said brightly. "I'll be fine here."

Liv looked daggers at me, but Dr. Yarrow, who I was still having trouble thinking of as "Steve," had already seized the opportunity. "Great! Come on, Liv," he said, pushing his way back through the crowd near the food. Liv glared at me and then followed him toward two confused-looking students who were waiting under a ginkgo tree.

The chances of us staying for only the allotted hour were slipping away, so I decided my best bet was to hole up someplace quiet until it was time to go. I scanned the area, my eyes finally coming to rest on a large live oak at the far end of

33

the Quad. If I sat underneath it, I'd still be able to keep an eye on Liv, but I wouldn't have to deal with the crowd.

I flopped down between two large roots, kicking off my shoes. This wasn't so bad. There was free food, and I got to spend the evening outside enjoying the weather. I'd had worse experiences at parties.

As I picked at my food, someone peered at me from the other side of the tree—I was apparently not the only one who was hiding out there. I felt my muscles go tense as I remembered the man in the suit, and prepared to scream. I was trembling as whoever it was came around to my side of the tree.

"Hello."

The fear flew out of me instantly.

It was the boy from the beach.

"Do you mind if I share your tree?" he asked.

"Oh!" I said. "Sure." I scooted over to make space for him next to me, trying to calm my racing heart. As I glanced up at him, he smiled and held out his hand.

"I'm Will Mallory," he said.

"Cara Gallagher." I took his hand, and it felt like grabbing a live wire as a surge of energy shot down my arm. I could have sworn I heard a small gasp escape him as well. He hesitated before letting me go, and I saw his gaze fall on my still-bandaged hand. He chewed his lip as if he were thinking of asking me about it, but was quiet as he sat down next to me.

"So …" I said, trying to figure out what to say, "you're a graduate student?" He looked so young, I wondered how old he actually was. He didn't look more than about nineteen or twenty.

He nodded, saying "I'm in the Physics Department. What department are you with?"

34

Oh. *Here we go,* I thought. I desperately wanted to lie to him. I absolutely did not want him to know I was seventeen. Not that I would have had a chance with a gorgeous grad student anyway.

I opened my mouth, prepared to lie, but when I saw the way he was smiling at me, I couldn't do it. I closed my mouth again like a blowfish. "Actually, I'm not a grad student," I finally admitted. "I'm just here with my sister. She's in the Bio Department."

"Oh, okay," he said. "So what's your major, then?"

Oh, boy.

"Actually, I'm not in college yet," I said miserably. "I have another year of high school. I'll be eighteen in October." I snapped my mouth shut. *Why am I such a moron?*

He looked surprised, but not upset. I guessed that meant he didn't see me *that* way. I shouldn't have been disappointed, but I couldn't seem to help it. "Well, all right," he said. "It must be nice for your sister to have her family living so close by."

"Oh, our parents are in Uruguay right now," I said. "It's just me. I'm living with Liv for the year until I finish high school."

"I guess that explains why I haven't seen you on campus before."

He smiled at me again, and despite my best efforts I found myself staring into his eyes. I felt myself getting lost in his gaze—there was something in the way he looked at me that confused me. I had never been looked at that way by anyone, and I desperately didn't want him to stop. Still, I was embarrassed by how long I was staring at him. I looked away and broke the spell.

"So," I asked hastily. "What are you studying in the Physics Department?"

"Um, well, I'm actually Dr. Kleeman's student."

"Shelby Kleeman?" I had heard of her; she was a famous character in scientific circles. And not for her research. I was surprised that she even had grad students. My sister told jokes about her; the stories went that she was a batshit-crazy old witch that the Physics Department kept hidden in a basement office. Her bizarre experiments never really panned out, but she'd had tenure so long they couldn't get rid of her. Before I could stop myself, I blurted out "The Cold-Fusion Fairy?"

He winced, and I regretted it immediately. "Sorry," I said. "I shouldn't have said that."

"It's okay," he chuckled. "She is kind of eccentric. But she's brilliant. She just has a tendency to get ahead of herself in her research. I could introduce you sometime, if you'd like."

"That would be, uh, great, thanks," I said, forcing enthusiasm. Maybe my sister was exaggerating when she said Dr. Kleeman kept pet rats in her office and flunked people who came to office hours without bringing treats to one Dr. Neutrino and one Professor Wigglebottom.

"Why are your parents in Uruguay?" he asked.

"Um, my dad's with the State Department. Foreign Service, you know? He's stationed at the embassy there." I poked at my veggie burger with my fork. I was hungry but too nervous to eat.

"Why aren't you with them?" he asked, taking a bite of potato salad.

"Well, I didn't want to apply to college from overseas, and the American School there doesn't have all the classes I need. So, Liv was here, and she's sort of an adult, so I moved in with her."

36

I didn't tell him the other reason, the one I never brought up with anyone—that I took the first chance I could to get away from my mother.

"Is that good? Living with your sister?" He looked directly into my face, examining my expression.

"Yeah, we get along great. Anyway, it's nice to have a little more autonomy. That's her, over there," I said, pointing her out. She was across the Quad talking to a tall guy with red hair who kept sidestepping her escape attempts.

Will choked back a laugh, and I wondered if he knew her somehow. "She doesn't exactly look happy," he pointed out, grinning at me.

"She's not really an extrovert." A huge understatement. "Wait, do you know her?"

"Not really. Uh, friend of a friend, I guess. So she's shy?" He bit back a smile, and I guessed he knew more about Liv than he was letting on.

"More like a misanthrope," I said, returning his grin. I didn't admit to him that I was pretty much the same way. People just didn't interest me that much. Most of the time.

"I guess that must run in the family," he said. I turned purple and looked away.

"I'm sorry," he said. "I'm not exactly an extrovert, either. I guess that's why we both ended up hiding over here."

"Yeah, I guess I *was* hiding," I said, hanging my head. I finally took a bite of my burger. "But you don't seem so shy to me."

"I usually am. I just feel like I can talk to you," he said, trying to catch my gaze again. "I guess this is already our second conversation."

I laughed. "I thought we were pretending that first time didn't happen."

He closed his eyes, rubbing his temple. "I'd rather pretend it didn't, if you wouldn't mind."

"Okay," I agreed. "Are you going to tell me what was going on with you that day?"

His eyebrows knit together so tightly it looked like it hurt, and he put his hand over his eyes.

I held my hands up. "Sorry," I said. "Pretending now."

His expression was still pained. "Thanks."

Neither of us spoke for a while after that, and I took the opportunity to finish my dinner. I watched him curiously out of the corner of my eye. He was dressed casually in shorts and a light blue button-down that contrasted beautifully with his olive complexion and dark hair. I noticed that he had a cord tied around his neck, but whatever was hanging from it was tucked into the front of his shirt. I guessed it was a religious medal, or maybe a crucifix. I wondered why he kept it hidden. I'd never thought of myself as the kind of person who had a "type," but I realized that he was definitely it. Everything about him was utterly mesmerizing.

I was mortified when he caught me staring at him, but he just smiled. He wasn't anything like I would have expected— a guy this good-looking, not to mention this smart, ought to have been a self-absorbed jerk. But he was just so *nice*.

I watched the people on the other side of the Quad, and Liv looked like a caged animal. I had to laugh at her, though I knew that I would eventually pay for not rescuing her. Then my eyes fell on a boy with the bluest hair I'd ever seen—like the color of a My Little Pony tail, or blue cotton candy. He was actually pretty good-looking except for the hair, but I guessed the hair went along with the black fingernails. He glanced up and smiled at me. Then his gaze moved to Will, and his eyebrows shot up into his neon hairline. He began walking toward us.

"Oh, holy hell," Will grumbled, leaning forward so that his elbows were resting against his knees. He looked at me through his hand as he rubbed his face. "I apologize in advance."

"What?"

"Just remember that I said that."

The blue-haired boy dropped his backpack at Will's feet. "William," he said.

"Adeep."

"You have a friend."

Will leaned back against the tree, waving a hand at Adeep as if to say, "Do what you must."

There was a moment of silence while Adeep stared at the two of us. "I'm Cara," I said, finally.

"Cara *Gallagher*," Will amended, and the two shared a look I couldn't decipher.

"*No.*"

"Yes."

Adeep's smile spread across his face like melting butter. "So, Cara," he said, tapping my foot with his boot, "you a Biology girl, too?"

"Uh—"

Will shook his head at me, but before I could stammer out an answer somebody grabbed Adeep by the shoulder and pulled him around.

"Dude, what the hell?" Adeep shouted at a pasty-looking guy in Coke-bottle glasses.

"Tell me, Kumar," Glasses-boy said, "why is it, that when I went back and checked the logs for the NMR spectrometer, your name is always the one right before mine?"

"Jesus, Caleb, I don't know. Maybe because I get out of bed before eleven and actually do some *work*?"

Will let out a deep breath and stood up. "Come on, Caleb," he said. "This isn't going to help you."

"You're always in there working with him, aren't you? What the hell are you two doing with the equipment?"

Adeep scoffed. "I'll explain it to you in very small words, you mental midget. Will and I are doing this thing called sciii-ence," he waved his fingers in the air mysteriously. "Occasionally we collect stuff called daaa-ta."

"Adeep," Will warned.

A crowd had gathered behind Caleb, and a middle-aged man with a bad haircut started pushing his way through. "Caleb, this is not how we handle intradepartmental issues."

Caleb ignored him and glared at Adeep. "Maybe if you spent as much time on your research as you spend screwing the freshmen, you'd actually know how to keep the equipment working."

"Maybe if *you* spent as much time on your research as you spend whining to your mommy, you'd actually have your damn doctorate, idiot. How many years have you been in this stinking program?"

Will stepped forward as if to put himself between them, but before he could get there Caleb punched Adeep square in the face.

Adeep went down with blood running out of his nose. Caleb started howling about his hand while two other people grabbed him and pulled him backward toward the far end of the

40

Quad, and a bunch of other people started shouting. Before I could get trampled, Will grabbed my arm and pulled me up. "Change of scenery?" he asked urgently. I nodded.

Welcome to the McNair University Science Division: home of cutting-edge research, hot men, and the occasional geek-on-geek beatdown.

This was so much better than high school.

Will turned back to Adeep. "You okay?" he asked, which seemed ridiculous considering how much blood there was, but Adeep seemed perfectly happy to be receiving the attention of a couple of girls who were stroking his hair and helping him up.

"I'm fine," he said through his pinched nose. "Go do ..." he flopped his hand at Will, "whatever you people do with women."

What did *that* mean?

"What was that about?" I asked, as we cleared the crowd and made our way up the steps and out of the Quad.

"I'm not sure, exactly. Those guys are both with the Chemistry Department. I've heard they've been having some problems over there."

"Wow," I said. "Nerds on 'roids?"

He laughed. "Not exactly. That guy" he indicated Caleb, "is supposed to be running a bunch of NMR analyses for his dissertation. His results keep getting screwed up because all his samples are contaminated, and no one can figure out why."

"What are they contaminated with?" I asked.

"Carbon-13."

My eyes widened. Carbon-13 only makes up one percent of the carbon on Earth—it's not the kind of thing you'd expect to find lying around in large amounts. Or contaminating somebody's research samples. "That's weird. Where would that be coming from?"

"Nobody knows. But he's kind of coming unglued, since he can't finish his work."

"Wow."

"Yeah."

We watched for another minute, as a few people walked the unfortunate Chem student away from the party. Taking him home, I guessed. Will took a step away.

"Do you—I don't know, want to take a walk? Or something?"

"Sure." I glanced back at Adeep. "Is he really okay?"

As we turned back toward the Quad, a bunch of skinny students hoisted Adeep onto their shoulders and began running across the lawn and cheering, while he whooped through the bloody napkin he was still holding against his nose and pumped his fist in the air.

"He appears okay," Will said. "Shall we?"

We started down the walkway. "Have you been on campus much?" he asked.

I shook my head. "Not really. I just moved here this week. I'm still getting lost a lot."

His face brightened. "Oh, well, maybe I can help with that." He pointed to a building on the left. "That's the English Department. History's on the other side of the Quad. The sciences are a little further down."

"Good to know, thanks."

I fidgeted with my hands as we walked. "Uh, so there was something that Adeep said."

He gave me a lopsided grin. "I would advise you not to put any stock in anything Adeep says. Unless it's about Chemistry."

"Um, right."

He stopped and smirked at me. "What did he say that's got you all discombobulated?"

"It was the *whatever you people do with women* thing."

Will laughed, running his hand up the back of his neck as he continued walking. "Oh, that. He thinks I'm gay."

I stopped. "So—are you?" And why did I care so much?

"No."

"And he thinks this *why*?"

"Well, as you just saw, he'll try to pick up anything with a pulse and the appropriate plumbing. I'd rather not get roped into being a part of that."

I felt my face redden. "Right."

He stopped again. "No, I didn't mean—"

"No, really, it's fine. My plumbing and I have never been more flattered."

"Oh, God."

"It's nice to know that people realize I have a pulse, too," I said, though I couldn't help smiling at him.

"I'm sure your pulse and your plumbing are equally lovely." He snapped his jaw shut, and then went bright red and turned away.

"Oh," I said, mortified. I suddenly found myself very busy admiring the grass, while he noticed something interesting in the sky and stared up at it. We basked in the awkwardness for an unbearable eternity, while I tried to think of anything I could say that would make things less gross.

Then I felt vaguely sick and doubled over.

43

"Are you okay?" he asked, putting his hand on my shoulder.

"Yeah," I wheezed. "Fine. Ugh." My stomach was definitely not okay, and I felt a stab of nausea. "Oh. Think the plumbing and I could use some Drano."

Will put his hand sympathetically on his own stomach. "Did you eat the potato salad?"

"Yeah."

"Me, too. Not sitting so well."

"Do you know where it came from?"

"The Math Department, I think."

I rolled my eyes "Figures." I straightened up, ignoring the complaints of my innards. "Must have been the mayonnaise. I should have known better."

He nodded. "It seemed like such a good idea, at the time."

"As is often the case, with mayonnaise."

He chuckled. "Will you be okay?" he asked.

"Yeah, I'm sure it'll pass in a minute." I took the last swig of my water and threw the bottle into a trash can. "You?"

"It's not too bad."

"Famous last words."

"Mmm."

He grinned broadly and we walked down past the Economics building, the Sociology building, and the Women's Studies annex. It was there that I saw something under a bush.

"Oh, crap," I said, getting down on my hands and knees for a better look. "It's a fledgling."

I couldn't tell what kind of bird it was, but it didn't have its adult feathers and it squeaked in anger about being stuck down on the ground. "It must've fallen out."

Will looked up at the catalpa tree next to me. "I think that's the nest," he said, pointing upward. "I don't think we can reach it without a ladder."

It was about ten feet up, and the branches were large. "I can get to that," I said.

"Are you sure? It's pretty high."

I patted the branch next to my shoulder "I was the tree-climbing champion of my neighborhood in Falls Church two years running." I kicked off my shoes. "Can you give me a boost?"

"What? Oh, sure." He bent his knee slightly, and I pushed off of it and shimmied my way onto the lowest branch. Then I pulled myself to a standing position and climbed to another bough on the other side of the tree.

"Okay," I said. "I can reach it now. Can you pass him up?"

He carefully scooped the baby bird into his cupped hands and then handed him up to me. It was hard to balance without holding on, but I managed to plop him back into his nest. "He's in!" I called down.

Will's smile was so dazzling that I nearly fell out of the tree.

I'm not sure what my face looked like, because his smile fell. "Are you okay?" he said.

"Oh, yeah," I said, shaking my head. "I'm coming down."

I climbed back down to the lowest branch and jumped down, and Will handed me my shoes.

"That was really nice, what you did," he said. I was completely, totally aware of his eyes on me.

"It was nothing," I said. "Anyone would have."

"No. I don't think so."

Then he seemed to change his mind about something and looked away. My heart was still pounding as I put my shoes back on.

We walked a bit further and he pointed out several other buildings, but truthfully, I wasn't paying much attention, focusing instead on the low sound of his voice as he described the layout of the campus. I breathed in the cool evening air; the sun was just beginning to sink on the horizon, and the light was an incredible shade of gold. It was a glorious evening. I stopped in front of a bench near the Modern Languages building. "Do you mind if we sit awhile?" I asked. "The sun is nice here."

He sat down next to me, and I liked having him there. I had to remind myself again not to get my hopes up. He was out of my league, and, even if he hadn't been, he was too old. From his perspective, I was jailbait, at least for another two months. As if it would have mattered, even if I were twenty instead of seventeen. Guys like that always ended up with Barbie dolls; I'd seen it a million times. Still, I couldn't help but appreciate the way the sunlight filtered through the trees, leaving a pattern of light and shadow to dance across his face. The effect was so beautiful it was hard to resist reaching out and touching it.

"So, you know my story," I said finally. "Where are you from? Where did you go to school, you know, as an undergrad?"

He dropped his eyes from mine, and his smile vanished. "Um," he said, still not looking up. "Delaware. I did my undergrad at the University of Delaware."

I didn't miss the change in his tone; he was flat, devoid of emotion, and his face was tense. I wondered what was wrong with this kind, gentle boy; there seemed to be some kind of dark cloud that descended over him sometimes. I thought again of the sight of his heaving shoulders at the beach, his eyes looking

46

toward my hand like it was some long-forgotten memory. "You didn't like Delaware?" I asked, trying to catch his eye again.

"Oh. No, it was fine," he said, refusing to meet my gaze. "Should we start heading back now?"

I was hurt, and I knew it was all over my face. I couldn't imagine what I had done to shut him down like this. "Okay," I said, getting up. "I need to find a ladies' room first. Can I go in there for a sec?" I asked, indicating the building behind us. Geology, apparently. How fitting. Full of rocks to match the ones in my head.

"Do you want me to wait outside for you?" he asked.

"I'm sure I can find my own way back," I said, starting in the direction of the building. To my annoyance, he followed me anyway.

There was an awkward silence as we walked, and more than anything I wanted to say something about that day at the beach. I wanted to blurt out "So, I'm glad you decided not to kill yourself," or something, *anything* that would acknowledge what had happened between us before, but I couldn't bring myself to spit it out. What was wrong with me? What was wrong with *him*? I could feel my frustration rising, but just then I saw something moving out of my peripheral vision, just barely. My feet stopped and my head snapped around.

He was gone, but I'd seen him—I was sure. It had to be him.

"What's wrong?" Will asked, walking back to where I'd stopped.

I could feel myself trembling, and I shook my head. "It was him," I whispered. "It had to be."

Will reached out and curled his hand around my elbow. "Who?" he said suspiciously.

47

I shook my head again. It was too crazy. But he persisted, and pulled me closer to him. "Why are you afraid? Who was it?"

I kept my eyes focused on the building I was sure he'd stepped behind, and I told Will about the man who'd grabbed me, and about the scanner he'd used on my hand. As I described him, Will's face blanched with alarm.

"Which hand was it?" he asked urgently.

I held up my left hand.

Chapter Five

Hide and Seek

Will's eyes went from mine to my hand and back again. "Damn," he said. *"Damn."* He grabbed my other hand and began pulling me along the path so fast we were almost running. "We have to get out of here."

"What?" I said, keeping my voice low. "Who is he?"

"I don't know," he said. "I haven't got a clue. But if he's really following you ..."

I glanced back again. He was there, no longer bothering to hide. And he was gaining ground on us.

"He's there," I whispered.

Will yanked me closer to him, and threw his arm around my waist. "We have to get out of here," he repeated.

He pulled me onto a walkway between two buildings, which dead-ended into a brick wall. "This way," he said, nodding toward a door in the Geology building. "We'll go through here."

"Will!"

He didn't answer, but when he reached out to try the door, I could see fear on his face as he realized it was locked. "Damn it!"

"Are you going to tell me what this is about?" I demanded.

He let go of the door and looked back at me. "Listen to me, Cara," he said. "That man back there—if he's—" he trailed off and shook his head. "It would be very, very bad if he caught us together. Do you understand?"

I didn't understand, but I nodded anyway. "But he's coming," I whispered.

"I know. I'm—I'm going to have to leave you."

"No! You can't leave me alone with him." I yanked up my sleeve, showing him the bruises that encircled my arm.

His face darkened. "He did that?"

"That's what I've been trying to tell you."

He let out a breath. "Okay. I'll just …" He reached out and held his hand against my face, looking dead into my eyes. "Do you trust me?"

"I don't even know you!"

He winced. "I know. I know you don't. Please, trust me. Trust me, okay?"

I looked into his eyes, and his face was so earnest, so honest, that I just nodded. "Okay," I said. "I trust you."

His hand fell from my face, and he stepped away, lifting the cord from his neck. Attached to it was a small pouch made of dark brown fabric, like something Harry Potter would use to carry his eyes of newt. He weighed the pouch in his hand before he looked back at me.

"What the hell is that?" I asked. "Your *magic crystals*? Are you crazy?"

"That's not—" he began, as I looked back over my shoulder, to see if the man in the suit was still coming. I couldn't see him, but I heard footsteps from the side of the building, coming fast. He was running.

"I'll come back for you," he said. "Don't tell him about me."

"But—" I flipped my head back around to ask him where he was going, but he was already gone.

His clothes lay in a pile at my feet.

I did the first thing I thought of—I kicked the pile of clothes behind a bush. Just in time, as the man rounded the corner. I was backed against a wall, and I was alone. Was there anyone close enough to hear me scream?

I stood mutely as he approached, taking his time as he sized me up. I felt dizzy with fear, as tears began to rise in my eyes. As he saw my fear, he smiled.

He was about twenty feet from me when he stopped, and crossed his arms as if deciding what to say.

"I wanted to apologize to you for our misunderstanding the other day," he said.

"I—okay."

"Sometimes I take my work a little too seriously. You understand."

I stared at him silently, but he continued anyway.

"I'm doing some contract work for the Chemistry Department, to determine the source of some difficulties they're having. Do you think you'd be willing to answer a few questions for me? It won't take more than a few minutes." He smiled warmly, and suddenly, he was just a middle-aged man. I saw no trace of the anger that had been on his face earlier. He reached out his hand for me.

"Let's go someplace where we can talk, shall we?"

I looked at his friendly face and outstretched hand, and wondered if maybe this had just been a big misunderstanding. But just as I started to relax, I saw something familiar flash

51

across his eyes. It was gone almost before I'd recognized it, but it was too late.

It was a gleam of rage.

Then the door next to me flew open.

I didn't know the man who stepped through it; he had to have been at least seventy, and his polyester suit was so out of date it looked like he'd been in stasis somewhere, waiting for 1978 to come back. I was speechless as he reached out his hand for me.

"I'm available for office hours now, Miss," he said.

I looked up at him, and saw the urgency in his face. I took his hand and he pulled me through the door, locking it again behind me against the man in the suit.

"Who are you?" I asked.

"Dr. Gordon," he said, dragging me up the stairs. "Head of the Geology Department. Will sent me."

Will. I remembered the pile of clothes, and I pulled my hand away. "You saw Will?"

He hesitated. "Yes, that's what I said."

"Was he *naked*?"

He stammered for a minute. "No, of course not."

I stopped mid-step, putting my hand down on the banister to steady myself. "What's going on? Who are you? Where is Will?"

"Do you think that man was close enough to get a good look at him?"

I shook my head. "At Will? I don't think so."

"Come on, up to my office. We'll wait until he leaves."

"Why should I trust you?"

He stopped and looked at me for a while, and then reached out for my arm. He slid my sleeve up with one finger, exposing my bruises. "Because I've never hurt you."

I looked up at him for a minute, and the way he looked back at me was strange, like he knew me and was just waiting for me to realize that I knew him, too. Only I didn't. He was right: between him and the man outside, there was no real choice. I followed him up the stairs and into his office. I flopped down into a chair next to the window.

"Are you going to start talking now?" I asked.

He rubbed his wrinkled forehead, then dropped his hand and swore.

"What?" I asked.

"Another problem," he said, pointing to the window.

I followed his gaze. The man in the suit was outside the front of the building, talking to someone.

It was Liv.

I flew out of his office and down the stairs before he could stop me. "Wait!" he called.

"I can't! That's my sister!"

I stopped at the front door. I could see Liv talking to the man at the bottom of the steps about fifteen feet from where I stood, but I couldn't hear what they were saying. Liv, at least, didn't look like she was about to kill anyone. I wasn't sure if this was a good sign or not, though. I remembered that he had been trying to get me to talk to him, too.

"Don't go out there."

I turned and looked at Dr. Gordon. "Why?"

"I—"

Before he could continue, the man outside was walking away. Liv walked up the steps toward me.

53

I went out to meet her. "What are you doing in here?" she asked, obviously annoyed. "I've been looking all over for you. Somebody called and said you were hurt."

I blinked. "Somebody called?"

"Yeah, some professor from the Geology Department. Said you needed help. Are you okay?"

I started to tell her the truth, but then something caught my eye from the other side of the path.

It was Will, standing between the eucalyptus trees across the walkway. My eyes met his and he shook his head, just once, and gave me a pleading look.

I looked back over my shoulder for Dr. Gordon. He was gone.

This was getting annoying.

I looked back at Will, who was wearing the clothes he'd left in a pile at my feet. Across his forehead was a single bloody scratch.

He mouthed, "Please."

I shifted my weight onto my left leg. "Um, yeah," I said to Liv. "I came in to use the bathroom and tripped on the stairs. I just twisted my ankle a little. It's not too bad."

Liv slung her arm around my waist, taking the weight of my right leg. "Well, come on, you big baby. Let's go home. At least you got me away from that crazy redhead. I swear, it was the worst case of verbal diarrhea I've ever seen."

We started down the steps, and I looked up to meet Will's eyes as he watched me.

"Liv, why were you talking to that man out here?"

"Oh, yeah," she said. "He was apologizing to me for the other day. Said he got carried away."

"Did he say who he was?"

"Some guy from Cal Tech. The Chem Department brought him in to help fix some problem they were having."

"The carbon-13 contamination?" I asked.

"Yeah. You knew about that?"

"Somebody mentioned it to me at the barbecue. Did he say anything else?"

"Not really, just that they'd found the source of the contamination, and that he was leaving on Monday."

"So what was it?"

"What?" She struggled with my weight and grunted. "The contamination? Some anomalous ore deposit they were looking at, he said. People not keeping the lab clean between tests."

"Oh."

We were at the bottom of the steps, and as we walked by Will, I saw him take a step back and turn to go. I watched his back for thirty seconds before I stopped. "Wait a sec," I said to Liv, and hobbled away from her.

I called to Will and he stopped, his eyes wary. I caught up to him as quickly as I could with my fake limp, and stood close enough so that I could talk to him without being overheard.

"Why are you limping?" he asked with the tiniest grin.

"*Apparently* I hurt myself," I said. "And I'm not the only one." I slowly reached up and brushed the hair out of the scratch on his forehead.

He pressed the back of his hand against the scratch, and then quickly wiped the blood off on the back of his pants. "It's just a scratch," he said and then smirked at me. "You threw my clothes into a holly bush."

"You want to explain to me why you weren't wearing them?" I reached into my pocket for a tissue and held it up to the scratch on his forehead. "Here, press on it—it'll stop in a minute."

He gave me a rueful look and complied. "It's, uh, complicated."

Before he could say anything else, I heard Liv calling me. "Cara!" she shouted. "You can hop home by yourself if you want. I'm leaving."

Will grinned. "I think you're needed elsewhere."

I gave him an exasperated glare and let my hand fall against my thigh with a smack. I glanced over my shoulder at Liv, who was already walking away, and then back at Will.

"You told me to trust you, and I did," I said quietly.

He didn't answer.

I snorted with disgust. "Yeah, that's what I thought," I said, turning away.

"Wait."

I turned back, and the look of longing he gave me took my breath away. He reached out for my hand and held it on top of his, palm against palm. He ran his finger down the back of my hand all the way to my fingertips.

"The first time I met you, you had dirt under your fingernails."

"So you're going to criticize my personal hygiene now?" I jerked my hand back, but he held it firmly.

"No. No. I've been wondering what you were doing, before." He looked at me earnestly.

"Repotting a maidenhair fern, actually."

When he looked at me quizzically, I explained, "I like plants. Kind of a lot."

"Ah."

"Science geek."

"I gathered that."

"So," I said.

"So."

I should leave now, I thought. *This is ridiculous.* But I couldn't bring myself to let go of his hand.

Finally he cleared his throat. "Are you free Tuesday?"

I hesitated, but only slightly. "Yes, but I don't have a car."

He glanced sideways at my sister. "Would it be terrible if I picked you up?"

I bit my lip. "It might."

"Could you meet me in front of the Biology building? Say at five?"

"The Biology building?"

"I might have something to show you."

I looked around, scanning for the man in the suit again. "What about—"

"I'll check out his story with Adeep; he'll know if he was really working with the Chem Department. And if he's really leaving."

"I'll be there," I said firmly. I would just have to find some way to make it happen.

From a distance Liv screamed, "CAROLINE!", and I jumped.

"I've got to go," I said, pulling my hand away. As my hand slid out of his grip, I realized he was as reluctant to let go as I was.

I had to run to catch up with my sister, remembering I was supposed to be limping at the last minute, which turned into a ridiculous skip-hop maneuver that made me look like a hyper four-year-old instead of someone with a twisted ankle. I turned to look back at Will, and he was laughing to himself as he walked away.

"Are you really okay?" she asked once we were both in the car.

"I'm fine. It's really not that bad."

Back home, I settled down on the couch with a bag of frozen peas over my ankle, wondering how long I needed to keep faking this. Liv finished making herself a drink and came and sat next to me.

"So what was it with that guy today?" she asked.

"Will?" I said innocently. "I was just asking him about something. He helped me when I fell down the stairs."

Her eyes narrowed. "You were sitting with him before that. At the picnic."

Oh. I hadn't realized that Liv had seen that. She had seemed so preoccupied at the time. I tried to figure out the best way to spin this. "Um, well, we were both just hiding from the mob. He's shy, too."

"Uh-huh," she said. She was not convinced. I was never very good at lying to Liv. She'd known me too long. "He's with the Physics Department, right?"

"Yeah. Physics. I think he said he was with Dr. Kleeman," I said. I was giving out too much information and I knew it, but I didn't seem to be able to stop myself.

"Dr. Kleeman?" she said, making as if to pull her own hair out. "The freaking Rat Lady? Nobody *normal* would choose her for their major professor."

Well, maybe she wasn't wrong. I laughed at the truth of her statement, but managed to save myself. "Neither of *us* should really be commenting on *normal*."

"That's not really the point."

"What is the point, then?" I said, my voice rising. Who did she think she was?

"The point is that he's, what, twenty-three? And you're seventeen," Liv said, pointing a finger at my chest. "Not only is that illegal, it's gross. And a guy—like that—shouldn't have trouble getting girls his own age to go out with him."

"In the first place, nothing like that is going on," I shouted. "He was just being nice to me, which is more than I've been able to expect from *you* lately. And in the second place, what do you mean a guy *like that*?"

She shook her head. "You've seen him. Please, I'm sure the only reason Kleeman's classes are all full this semester is because he's the T.A."

A small, irrational lump formed in my throat. "You're saying he's out of my league."

"Cara—"

"That's what you meant. Because nobody that good-looking would ever go out with a troll like me!" I turned and stormed out of the kitchen and into my bedroom—slamming the door for emphasis—and threw myself down on my bed. I was exhausted. Between being scared to death by the hand-scanning nutjob, seeing a hot guy vanish sans clothing, being rescued by an ancient relic in a bad suit, and having Liv insult me, I was done trying to keep myself pulled together. I just wanted to be alone. The worst part was that I knew what she was saying was true. A guy like Will would never be interested in me. It was just a biological fact: The alpha male does not go after the gimp.

I could hear Liv outside my room. "Cara," she said through the door, "look, that's not what I meant. He's just too old for you. I want you to be careful."

"It doesn't matter. Nothing like that is going to happen, anyway." I said into my pillow.

I could hear her sigh through the door. "You know you're not a troll."

"Please," I said. "I should just move in under a bridge and start harassing billy goats."

Another sigh. "Can I come in?" she asked.

"No."

She came anyway, and sat at the foot of my bed. "I'm sorry. You know, I'm not good at this. You were supposed to be kind of a 'hands-off' project for me."

"I didn't realize I was a project," I said, rolling over to glare at her.

"Do you think Mom and Dad didn't say anything to me about taking care of you?'

"I guess I didn't think about it," I admitted.

"Cara, this is hard for me, too. I don't like playing the heavy. But you still need someone to look after you."

"So do you," I countered.

She laughed. "Well, it's a good thing I have you, then." She reached out and mussed my hair, and I smacked her hand away. "I know it's been boring for you here so far, but you'll start school in a few days, and you'll have lots to do."

"God," I groaned. "You sound like Mom."

"Vicious! Well, it's true anyway. Maybe you can go out for cheerleading this year!" she giggled maniacally and shook her head from side to side, smacking herself in the face with her ponytail.

I hit her with my pillow.

"Do you need a bedtime story?" she asked.

"Hit me."

"Once upon a time, a protist formed a symbiotic relationship with a cyanobacteria and became a chloroplast and we all lived happily ever after with lots of carbon and fixed nitrogen. The end."

"God, no wonder I'm so screwed up."

She kissed my forehead. "You're not screwed up. You're just unusually neurotic for a great big sack of bacteria."

After she left, I lay awake for a long time, even though I was exhausted. What was going on with Will, really? Was he really going to tell me the truth? Despite what I had told Liv, I couldn't deny the way he had looked at me tonight—it was the same look of yearning that he'd given me at the beach the first time we'd met. The memory gave me butterflies, not just in my stomach, but everywhere.

Tuesday was still two days away, and I wondered how I was going to stay sane until then. There was only one thing I was sure of: I needed to figure him out. I had never done well with unanswered questions, and he was a total enigma.

But not for long.

The Journal of Will Mallory

Memory is a funny thing, how certain events can come back to haunt you, years later. How certain conversations can suddenly work their way fully formed into your conscious thoughts, bidding themselves to be acknowledged. A discussion with a friend, a joke shared with a colleague. An argument. Rather, the *argument.*

Remember this one, Will? it says.

Yes, I remember.

I thought I'd been in the right during that particular argument, all those years ago. I really did. It was only later, after it was too late, that I'd realized I should have listened. I thought they were being silly, overprotective of me as the youngest member of a dying race and all that.

"He's too young," had been the conventional wisdom. "He isn't ready for this yet. He can barely hold himself together."

"It's only a two-year mission," I'd responded. "I'll be fine. It'll only be an issue if someone tries to kill me, and who's going to try killing me? I'm not going there to fight."

"There may be complications you can't foresee."

"Look," I'd said. "I'm the most qualified person for this mission. I have the highest linguistic aptitude of any of the scientists here. There are seven thousand languages! You're going to send someone who won't be able to communicate?"

In the end, I'd won. I'd had help—my oldest friend was on the selection committee, and he called in some favors for me. So, despite my age, I was selected for my stellar communication skills. And they are stellar. I can learn a new language in a matter of hours. I'm as fluent as a native within days. Among the best linguists in the universe, I'm the best of the best.

I realized later how useless those skills could be. And as I long for the company of a girl I can barely speak to, I truly feel younger than ever.

So, yes, I remember. I was wrong.

I was too young. I still am.

Chapter Six

Honesty

By the time Tuesday arrived, I was little more than a raw bundle of nerves, having spent the previous two days with nothing to do except water my plants, read, and watch Liv study. As we sat in the kitchen finishing breakfast, my leg was jiggling so violently under the table that she kicked me.

"Will you knock it off?" she said, not looking up from the article she was reading while she ate her cereal. "What's up with you this morning? You're so hyper."

"It's nothing," I said, flustered. I was trying to keep my plans for the day under wraps, "I'm just thinking about some errands I need to run today."

"Well, I hope you didn't plan on using the car. Steve and I are helping tag elephant seals down at Año Nuevo. I'll be gone most of the day."

"He's going with you?" I asked. "Does he usually do that?"

She shook her head. "Not usually. It's supposed to be nice out, and the conference he was going to was canceled." I stared at her for a while. She had that look she got when she was keeping something back; she pressed her lips together, and she kept her eyes firmly on her reading. I wondered what she was thinking, but I didn't want to engage her any more than necessary that morning. If I talked to her too much, I was bound to end up saying more than I should.

"Okay," I said, turning back to my cornflakes. "Well, I can take the bus anyway, so don't worry about it."

"Can you pick up a gallon of milk while you're out?" she asked, finally pushing herself away from the table.

"Oh. Sure. Are you leaving now?"

"Mm-hmm. We're meeting at Steve's house before we head out." She stuffed a couple of water bottles and a tube of sunscreen into her backpack, and turned to me one last time before she opened the front door. "Don't forget your phone this time, okay?"

"Right," I said, getting up to grab it off the charger. "Thanks. I'll see you tonight. Don't piss off any bulls. Or run fast, if you do."

"I'll do my best," she said with an eye-roll. Then she shut the door behind her and I was alone.

I caught the No. 8 bus to campus, spent most of the morning and early afternoon in the library, and then left at four-thirty for the Biology building. I realized that I would be way too early, and I wondered briefly if I should walk around for a while. I didn't want to appear over-eager. But I was terrified that he would lose his nerve and leave, and I wanted to make sure I saw him before he got the chance to chicken out.

It turned out that I wasn't the only one who was early. Will was standing in front of the building in shorts and a T-shirt, when I arrived at a quarter of five. "You're early," he said, clearly surprised.

I was insulted. "Did you expect me to be late?"

"Actually, I'm a little surprised that you came at all."

65

We stared at each other in silence for a minute, until I broke away and turned to look at the building. "Why the Biology building?" I asked.

"The greenhouse is up on the roof," he said. "I thought—I thought you might like to see it."

"Isn't it locked?"

He pulled a black lanyard out of his pocket; there were half a dozen keys attached. "Somebody owed me a favor."

He held the door open for me, and I took a deep breath and walked inside.

"Are you sure you're okay with this?" he asked, his face concerned, as we walked up the steps to the fourth floor. "I don't want to take you anyplace you don't want to go. And if you don't feel safe ..."

He had noticed my apprehension. "I don't feel unsafe," I said quickly. "But just in case you did have any ideas, my sister knows I was planning on meeting you today."

"Really?" Now he looked surprised and a little amused. "You told your sister? How did that go?"

"Oh, she was fine with it," I said, keeping my eyes focused on the steps. With a sideward glance, I saw him trying to force a grin off his face. I was lying and he knew it.

When we got to the top floor, I could see it was divided in half; the front of the building was entirely encased in glass, while the rear appeared to consist of typical office space. "The faculty offices are back there," he explained, as he unlocked the door to the greenhouse.

"So," I said, as the lock opened with a *snick*, "was that man the other day—was he looking for you?"

"I don't think so," he said. "Adeep told me he was visiting from Cal Tech. Richard Leaf, or somethingorother. He left yesterday."

"Why were you so scared of him?" I asked. Will either ignored the question or didn't hear me, because he didn't turn around.

We walked inside, and I was blown away by the size of the room. I'd never been in a greenhouse that size. My eyes didn't know where to look first.

"Wow."

He cracked a smile, the first real one I'd seen that day. "Liv hasn't brought you up here before?"

I shook my head. "She's busy."

"Well, let's take a look."

We did, but mostly he followed me around as I read labels and looked at all the specimens. There must have been fifty different experiments going on there: genetic splicing, traditional hybridization, and some other things I wasn't sure about. I stopped in front of a table full of orchids. "What are they doing with these?" I asked.

He looked over my shoulder. "It's not labeled. Probably just someone's pet project."

There must have been twenty kinds there, arranged on a rolling plant cart. I inhaled their fragrance, closing my eyes, and then coughed.

I laughed, and pointed toward the culprit, which had dark-red blossoms. "Smell that one," I said.

He did, and then gagged.

I laughed at his disgusted face. "Carrion orchid," I explained. "They smell like rotting meat, to attract flies for pollination."

"How lovely."

"Hey, you can't argue with success." I reached out and touched the edge of one of the dark-green leaves with my fingertip. "I love these," I said.

"The smelly ones?"

"All of them. They're just—I don't know. Magic."

He smiled at me, and I realized that we were standing shoulder to shoulder now, though I didn't know if I was unconsciously moving closer to him, or he to me. "You think so?"

I waved my hand around the room. "Well, they all are, aren't they?" I pointed to a bag of potting soil that was left on the ground. "I mean, look at it. It's dirt. It's nothing. But out of it comes everything." I squatted down next to the bag. "It's not dirt. It's a bag of endless possibilities."

I glanced up at him. "You probably think I'm crazy."

"No," he said, holding his hand out to me and pulling me to my feet. "I think you go through your life with possibilities stuck under your fingernails." He looked at me hard for another minute. "I have something to show you."

Still holding my hand, he led me to a microscope on a rolling cart that someone had set up in the greenhouse. We sat down in front of it, and he pulled a small packet out of his pocket and unwrapped it. It was a slide.

"What's that?"

"A pet project of my own."

"You do a lot of biology work in the physics lab?"

He smiled at me. "There's no physics in this." He positioned the slide for me. "Take a look."

I looked at him, confused, and he nodded. "Go ahead."

68

I leaned forward, and as I put my eye to the viewfinder, he reached over and pulled my hair behind my ear.

I couldn't understand what I was seeing. "What is this?" I asked, not looking up from the microscope. "It looks like a cell, but not."

"It's a cell," he said.

"I can't see a membrane."

He handed me a pipette. "Take the cover slip off," he said. "Touch it."

I took it from him, and looked through the viewfinder as I gently touched the cell with the pipette. "Whoa," I said. "It just goes right through it. I can see the cytoplasm moving—wait—"

I looked up. "What is this?"

"What do you think it is?"

"I don't know. I thought, at first, animal cell, but there's stuff in there that doesn't look right. I'd like to see what it looks like under the electron microscope. Some of these organelles don't look right, either. I can't tell what they are."

I looked back to the microscope. "The nucleus is *huge*. I wonder how many chromosomes this thing has."

"Two thousand."

I scoffed. "Nothing has two thousand. Even adders-tongue ferns only have twelve hundred. And this is definitely not a plant cell."

"No," he said. "It isn't."

"What is it, then?"

"Me."

I laughed, not even bothering to look up. "Funny."

He reached over and turned off the light on the microscope, forcing me to look up.

"Cara," he said quietly. He took the slide from under the microscope and wiped it against his pants. Then he snapped it in half and threw it into the trash.

A chill ran over me. "What are you doing?"

He looked at me for a long breath. "Okay," he said. "You're a scientist. Do you believe that life exists only here on Earth? That the rest of the universe is simply stars and dead hunks of rock?"

"No. It wouldn't make sense. The universe is a big place. For life to have begun here and nowhere else, nowhere at all … it's just impossible." He looked at me hard, and the meaning behind his words began to sink in. "But—you're not saying—"

"I'm saying."

I shook my head. This was ridiculous.

"I'm not from Earth."

Silence.

"I'm from a world very far from your solar system. My people don't naturally have a solid form, like this," he said, holding out his hand for me to see. "We evolved in our lower atmosphere, and our bodies are more like what you would consider a gas."

He paused and I buried my face in my hands. "This is some kind of joke," I said. "Did Liv put you up to this? Does she really think I'm this gullible?"

"It's no joke," he said wistfully. "You've seen me transform before."

"I didn't *see* anything except a pile of clothes."

He gave a small smile, and reached out his hand for me. I waited to see what he would do, but he just waited patiently, with his hand outstretched. Tentatively, I reached out and took his hand in mine.

He closed his eyes, and a shimmer ran over his body in a way that didn't seem humanly possible—it was like looking at ripples running under the surface of the ocean. What happened next was so quick, so instantaneous, that I'm not sure what I actually saw. I felt the hand holding my own change as it became smaller, softer, more feminine. The boy in front of me was gone. I was looking at a mirror image of myself.

I jumped up, knocking my chair over, and managed to stumble backward until I was against the wall. I'd lost all the feeling in my hands, but I was pretty sure they were shaking. I may have screamed, or cursed, but doing so was so incidental that I didn't remember later exactly what I'd done.

"How—?"

"I just can. It's what I am."

I crouched a few feet away from him, watching him sweep his hair—my hair—out of his face.

"You see now?" he asked.

I nodded and slowly crept forward. He held perfectly still while I reached out and touched his cheek, his hair. Everything felt exactly like mine, although he was still in his own clothes, which were too big for his new body. He closed his eyes when I touched him and I pulled my hand back.

He pulled the brown pouch out of his shirt and reached inside, looking for something. After a minute he seemed to find it, and he shimmered, and was himself—or at least the "himself" that I was used to—again.

He looked at me, his eyes almost pleading. "You aren't afraid of me?"

Good question. I felt like I should have been, but I wasn't, and I wasn't even sure why. The gentle hands? The soft voice? I didn't know. I shook my head. "Should I be?"

"No," he breathed, and it was as if the word came from somewhere deep inside him, like some kind of universal truth he was desperate to communicate. "Never, Cara. I would never hurt you. We don't hurt people. We're just curious."

"Who is *we*?"

"My people. We're curious about other races, other worlds. I'm what you would call an anthropologist." He looked at me hard and repeated, "I would never, ever hurt you. Or anyone else."

I let myself look into his eyes, so that he would know I was telling the truth. "I believe you."

I could see the relief wash over him.

I was dizzy with wonder and ravenously curious. "What is in that bag, exactly?" I asked, pointing at the pouch around his neck.

He emptied the contents into his hand—there were a few of the dark, wavy hairs that I recognized, a small, black feather, and a few other hairs that were unfamiliar to me. "I'm still relatively young, as my people go. I need to have contact with the genetic material I want to emulate. I keep a few spares around, in case I need to change form for some reason. Think of it like a chameleon changing color, except that I change my entire genome."

I reached out and took the bag in my hand, turning it over a few times. "What is it made of?"

"It's just oilcloth, to keep everything dry. I made it years ago, after I first became human. I was in France at the time."

I looked at him sideways. "How many years are we talking about here?"

He took the pouch back from me and hung it around his neck. "This was around 1950, give or take."

I startled. "How long have you been on Earth?" I asked.

"I was stranded here in 1947."

"Oh," I said, doing the math; he'd been here over sixty years. I was thunderstruck. Then the key word in that sentence finally sank in. "Stranded? What does that mean? You can't leave?"

"No," he murmured quietly. "I can't leave. My navigation controls were set wrong, and I came out of my FTL wormhole too close to the planet."

FTL, I thought. Faster-than-light, he must mean. These people—or whatever they were—had far more sophisticated technology than we did. It was like meeting a member of some advanced race from *Star Trek*.

He continued, "When I hit your atmosphere, my power source overheated and I had to jettison it before it exploded and took the ship with it. I was able to land, barely, but I can't go FTL again unless I can get a replacement. I can still move the ship from place to place on Earth, but I can't use it to go home."

"No one ever came to look for you?" I asked. Stranded for sixty-five years. I couldn't imagine. I was beginning to understand the haunted look he got sometimes.

"If they did, they never found me. My ship has a distress beacon, but if the navigation controls were off, that could have been calibrated wrong as well. After the first couple of years, I gave up hope that anyone was coming to get me. They probably assume I've either died or that my mind has gone, in which case they might as well leave me here. Either way, they won't send anyone else."

He looked tired now, like telling me this had taken all the strength out of him, and he turned his face back toward the rest of the greenhouse and closed his eyes. I leaned my cheek against my hand and stared at him, trying to find a hint of anything that wasn't human. I couldn't find a single thing, except that he was almost too beautiful to be real.

"What do you call yourselves? Your people?" I asked finally.

"In your language the closest word for us is the Eolian."

"Eolian," I echoed. I remembered from my Earth Science class that it meant something that was borne of the wind. I tried to imagine what a creature like that would look like. The only things I could think of were ghosts.

"Why are you here, now? Doing grad school, I mean."

"Well, our ships are powered by a kind of cold-fusion technology. It takes a lot of power to generate a temporary wormhole through space, which is what allows us to go faster than light. Dr. Kleeman has been working on cold fusion for twenty years. I've been hoping that her research might help me find a way to fix my FTL drive."

"And how is that going?"

"Very badly," he conceded. "But it's the best lead I've had in sixty years. I keep trying to nudge her in the right direction, but it doesn't seem to be helping."

"I'm sorry, Will," I said, and I was. I reached out and carefully put my hand over his, and he looked at me with that longing look again. I finally realized what it meant—he didn't want me, he was just incredibly lonely. The thought hurt, but I tried to shrug it off. He had confided in me alone. He needed a friend, and I could be one for him, if nothing else.

I squeezed his hand. "It's okay," I said. "You can talk to me about anything, any time you want. I'll be here for you. I promise."

He turned his face away from me, and I could see him trembling. I realized after a minute that he was crying, silently, and I moved closer to him and carefully draped my arm over his shoulders. He reached out and took my other hand in his and squeezed it, hard. As I held him, I realized that there were tears falling from my eyes, too.

I thought I knew what it felt like to be alone. I knew then that I was wrong.

Finally, he let out a breath and lifted his head, wiping his eyes with the back of his hand.

"Are you all right now?" I asked, sitting up again.

"I am," he said. "I'm sorry, I just got a little overwhelmed. I've been starved for friendship for so long." He looked at me and cocked his eyebrow. "I can't even begin to imagine what you must think of me."

I didn't know what to say, so I played with my hands as I looked down at the ground. "I think you are the most amazing person I've ever met," I said finally.

"Person," he repeated, his lips beginning to show a smile.

"Isn't that what you said? That while you're in this form, you're essentially human?"

He nodded. "Yes, while I'm human I have human needs, human desires, human feelings." He gave me a long look and I turned away, embarrassed.

"Well, that makes you a person, as far as I'm concerned."

"I'm glad to hear you say that. I don't know what's going to happen with Dr. Kleeman. I don't know if I'll be able to fix my ship or not. But if you'll be my friend, I think I can muddle through somehow."

"I'll be there," I said. "I promise." I reached out and took his hand again, and he closed his eyes and smiled.

75

"What is it?" I asked.

"When I touch people, I can feel them, like I can get a sense of them through their DNA. It's hard to explain—it's what my body does. It absorbs DNA so that I can mimic it. Every person feels a little different."

"Can you feel me? Right now?"

"Yes."

"What is it like?"

He closed his eyes again. "Like hearing a familiar voice in a crowded room."

I smiled and squeezed his hand, and he let out a slow breath. Then he opened his eyes and grinned at me. "Would you like to see something else?"

"There's more? What are you going to show me now?"

"Home."

Chapter Seven

Stardust

I called Liv from the car and told her I would be home late, and then Will and I drove an hour up through the mountains, climbing the oak-covered hills as we climbed into the sky. We were headed for Fremont Peak, which Will explained was the best place in the area to see stars, and had a small observatory that the local astronomy clubs used for meetings and demonstrations.

"It's not the world's best observatory," he explained. "But they do have a 30-inch telescope. It's so dark up there you can really see the stars. We'll get there early enough to see the sunset."

I worked on the sandwich we'd picked up on the way out of Muro Alto, and he glanced at me frequently as he drove. "You must have a million other questions."

"I do," I said. "But I can wait. I want you to be my friend, not my science project."

He laughed. "I appreciate that. I'll tell you anything, really. I want you to know me."

"Okay." I thought for a minute. "What is it like to be ... not solid?" I asked.

He thought for a few seconds before he answered. "It's very different than being human. We have cells and DNA; that part is the same. But we're held together by energy, and we aren't exactly physical beings in the way you are. Our life cycle is very different from yours. We don't age in the way that you do. When we first come into being, we can't transform. It's an ability we acquire as we mature. When we grow old we lose the power to transform, and then, over many centuries, we even lose the ability to stay cohesive. Our cells drift farther and farther apart until we die."

"Many centuries?"

"Yes, our lifespan is many, many thousands of years."

I was stunned. "How old are you, actually?"

He hesitated. "It's hard to say, we don't mark time the way you do."

"Give me your best guess."

He squeezed his eyes shut, as if he was deciding whether to answer this one or not. "I was about two hundred when I arrived on Earth. Very young, by our standards."

Two hundred and sixty years old. I suddenly felt very insignificant.

He saw my discomfort. "I don't want you to think of me that way," he said gently. "I've been human for a very long time. Right now, I *feel* human. That other life, that's over for me now."

"If you really think so, then why are you working with Dr. Kleeman?"

He looked ahead at the road and shrugged. "I have a duty to try to get back if I can. This is my last effort."

He was quiet again, and I stared out the window, looking up at the vast vault of darkening sky ahead, and trying to imagine the stars beyond. How far had he come?

"Can I ask you one now?"

"Of course," I said.

"Is our being friends going to cause you a problem?"

"A problem?" I was confused.

"With your sister."

I chuckled. "Honestly, I think it would bother her less if she knew you weren't human. Right now, she just thinks you're a pervert."

"Really?" he said, laughing. "What did I do to earn that label?"

I blushed. "I'm sorry! It's like things just fly right out of my mouth before my brain can stop them."

"It's okay," he said. "I like that you do that. But you still didn't answer my question."

"It's the age difference," I admitted. "She thinks it's a little creepy for a guy in his twenties to want to be friends with a seventeen-year-old girl."

"I see," he said. "I guess that makes sense."

"It doesn't mean she's right."

"Still, I don't want to cause any problems between you."

"Well, that's easy enough to deal with," I said cheerfully. "I just won't tell her."

We arrived at the top of Fremont Peak just as the sun touched the horizon, and we parked the car and walked up the short road to the observatory. When we got to the top, we stood and looked down the mountain at the most amazing sunset I'd ever seen; the sky was totally clear, and we could see down the mountains and into the surrounding areas for miles, all the way to the sea. The dark blue of the sky bled down into the purple nearer the horizon, and the last light of the day reflected off the orange poppies that littered the hill below us, making the ground itself seem to glow.

He smiled at me. "Magic?"

"Magic," I agreed.

The air chilled as we waited for the last bits of daylight to ebb away, and we walked back to the car to find a sweatshirt, where we were greeted by swarms of little red lights coming toward us.

"What's that?" I asked, before I heard the voices. The red lights were tinted flashlights.

He frowned at me in the dark. "They must be having a program tonight," he said. "I should have checked."

I pulled Will's sweatshirt over my head. It smelled like the beach. "Do you need the telescope, to show me?"

He took my hand. "I think I can show you, anyway. Come on." He led me to a grassy area, which was full of people drinking hot cocoa from thermoses and chatting about their hobby telescopes, and we flopped down on the cool grass. He scanned the sky for a minute.

"There it is," he whispered in my ear. "Way over there in the east."

Astronomy was never my strong suit. "Which constellation is that?"

"Andromeda. The main star has six planets."

"Do we know this?"

"You've found four. It's very far."

I followed his eyes toward the eastern part of the sky, but I couldn't make anything out. "Show me again," I said. He reached out his hand, pointing, and I rested my cheek against his shoulder so that I could see exactly where he was indicating. "Oh!" I said. "It's the one that looks like a V?"

"That's the one."

I lay back on the grass with my hands behind my head, and he lowered himself down next to me.

"What's it called?"

"Meris."

"What is it like?"

He waved his hand from one side of the sky to the other. "A giant ocean. Very little land. There are two races that live there: us, and the Livan. We lived in the atmosphere for thousands of years before we learned how to become solid. It happened after the Livan colonized our world. They were the first solid-form creatures we'd encountered. We've co-existed with them ever since."

"Is it very beautiful?"

"In some ways, yes. The oceans on Meris are a hundred different shades of blue, depending on where you are on the planet. The cities are lovely. Peaceful. Clean. But the landscape isn't so varied as here." He smiled at me and tapped my arm with his hand. "And no orchids."

I held my hand up, blotting out a hundred stars. The sky was full of them—I'd never seen so many, never lived any place dark enough. The air was cold, but Will's shoulder was warm next to me, and I didn't care. I glanced over at Will, who had stars reflected in his eyes.

"I read somewhere that everything in the universe is made out of stuff that exploded out of dying stars," I said.

"That's true. You, me, the dirt." He gestured behind us at the stargazers who were talking quietly. "The hot cocoa. We're all made of stardust."

I looked up. "We all came from up there, then."

"Yes. We did." He rolled toward me, propping himself on his elbow. "What are you thinking, right now?"

I held my hand against the sky again. "I feel absolutely tiny." I laughed. "How far is it?"

"Forty-four light years. Sometimes it seems farther than others."

"What about now?"

He held his hand up next to mine. "Right now, it doesn't feel far at all."

He drove me home not long after that; it was late, and I was about to lose my excuse of the library, which closed at ten. As we sat in his car outside my building, I was paralyzed by my reluctance to go inside.

We were both silent, and I wondered what he was thinking. All I could think was how sad I was that the day was over, and I wondered how much time we would be spending together—as friends—from then on. Or if this has just been some big cathartic thing for him, and now that it was over, we'd just go back to talking about potato salad.

"I …" I stammered, "um … are …"

"When can I see you again?" he said, saving me. "Are you busy getting ready for school?"

I took a deep breath. So he did want to be friends. Real, non-potato-salad friends. "I start on Thursday, actually."

"Thursday?"

"It's a short week," I explained. "It's some weird thing they're doing this year. Maybe—maybe Saturday?"

He nodded. "Dr. Kleeman's used to having me in the lab seven days a week. I think she can manage without me if I decide to have a life now and then, though. Saturday it is."

"That sounds great."

"Where would you like to go, then?"

82

"Anyplace. I don't care."

He gave me a hard look. "That doesn't make things any easier for me, you know."

"Sorry." I stopped to think it over, but I was getting hungry again, and that drove my answer. "Okay. I would like to eat in a restaurant that serves something that won't clog my arteries."

"All right," he agreed. "One non-artery-clogging restaurant. Anything else?"

There was one other thing, but I had to summon the courage to ask. "We could go to your place for a while. I'd like to see where you live."

He pressed his lips together firmly as he thought about this. I was sure I had overstepped my bounds with him.

"I'm not so sure that would be a good idea," he said finally. "It's not that I don't want you to come, but I live on campus—"

"—and it wouldn't be good if I were seen going into your apartment."

"Not if you aren't ready to tell your sister that we're friends."

"No. Not yet."

"Are you sure? I think it would be better if you told her," he said. "Lies can have a way of coming between people."

"Let's wait until after my birthday. I think once I'm eighteen she'll be less worried about things."

"All right, then. Should I pick you up here? Say at six?"

Six in the evening. This was starting to sound like a date. Well, I *had* asked to be taken out to eat. I wondered if I had anything decent to wear. "Sure," I replied casually. It was a big apartment complex, and I doubted that Liv would notice me getting into Will's car.

"Saturday then?" he asked, flashing me a beautiful smile.

"Saturday," I agreed. He got out and opened the car door for me, which was silly and romantic at the same time. "Thanks," I muttered.

I started up the stairs, but then I remembered one other thing. I ran back to the window.

"Does Dr. Gordon know about all of this? The Geology guy in the bad suit?"

His eyes crinkled. "You've never met Dr. Gordon."

Oh.

"That was you," I said. He gave a sly, lopsided grin that made my insides weak.

"He's kept the same suit in his office since the seventies," he explained. "He wears it to budget meetings. Kind of famous for it, actually."

I laughed and started up again. This time it was his turn to stop me, and I turned back to him as he called my name.

"I had a wonderful day today," he said.

I couldn't stop the smile that spread across my face. "So did I."

I was giddy as I climbed the stairs to my apartment. Saturday. I wondered how many Saturdays I would get to spend with Will.

For the first time, I was genuinely excited about my life— not just my future, but my present. Suddenly, tomorrow was not just another day to endure. It was something to look forward to.

The Journal of Will Mallory

She held me while I cried.

She put her arms around me and, for a few minutes, it felt like home. I remember that, long for it. For the quiet surrender of sharing myself with someone else.

It's been over sixty years since I merged with another Eolian, that gentle way we have of coming together in our natural state and sharing our thoughts. I miss it, the way any thought, any feeling, any memory can be instantly, completely given over to someone else. There's no chance of miscommunication, no lies, no subterfuge. Only however much of yourself you feel like sharing.

I think, now, that this sounds terribly romantic, but of course it isn't. We have no romance. I suppose romance is the human answer to merging, borne out of a need to be close to someone else, in a more meaningful way than by simply mating. Though humans seem to do plenty of that, too.

I cried, and she laid her cheek against my shoulder, pulling me to her. I found her hand and squeezed it, hoping she knew, somehow, what she'd done for me. What she was doing, at that very moment, by touching me. I wanted so badly to tell her everything about myself, to make her know me, to tell her every thought I'd had rattling around in my head since I'd become human. And I realized that I would tell her; and she'd tell me, too, all her secrets, and we'd be friends, and I would never, ever, be alone again.

She was soft against me, and I realized that the pain had all worked itself out, and I no longer felt like a man split in two, between my shell and my spirit. I was whole. I was free, healed by her touch and my reconciliation with truth.

She hasn't left my mind for an instant. And I think this could either be a very good thing, or a very terrible one.

Chapter Eight

The Education of Cara Gallagher

Liv was sitting on the couch with a tub of ice cream and a spoon when I walked in. She glared at me while I set my keys down on the counter.

"What are you reading?" I asked.

"*The Social Amoebae,*" she said acidly.

"Wow, you sound happy," I said. "Elephant seals chase you away?"

"Where's the milk?" she replied curtly.

Crap. "I forgot. Do you want me to go back out?"

She gave me a dirty look. "Nah. I'll go in the morning."

"Sorry."

"So, what did you do all day, when you weren't buying milk?" she asked.

I wished I had thought this through better—I didn't have a good alibi. "I was at the library."

"*All day?*"

I coughed. "Yeah."

She grunted and turned back to her ice cream, and I went into the kitchen to scrounge up something to eat. I discovered half a pan of dayglo-orange macaroni and cheese on the stove, and decided to close my eyes and finish it. It tasted about as good as it looked, and I reminded myself that in a few days I would get to eat a real meal. With Will.

I told Liv I was going to bed and flipped through my closet to find something to wear for my—dare I even think it—date. I hadn't bothered to bring any of my nicer dresses—the formal-wear I was required to wear for embassy events was all in storage back in Virginia. At the back of my closet, I did find one lonely sundress: blue-green, like the sea, with white batiked flowers. I hoped it didn't make me look any younger than I actually was.

I got into bed and tried to finish *Hamlet*, but I kept thinking of all the questions I'd like to ask Will. There were so many that I wondered if I should start writing them down, but I didn't want him to feel like I was interviewing him. I reminded myself that I had been drawn to him even before I knew who he was. I tried to focus on that instead. He was a man, not a specimen.

My alarm went off at six the next morning. Liv was already gone, but before she'd left she'd stuck her well-worn copy of *The Catcher in the Rye* upside down on top of my backpack.

It was a little tradition of ours, from when we were kids. She would find the perfect "inspirational" quote for the beginning of the school year. For the last few years she'd just e-mailed them to me.

I flipped to the page she'd marked, and read the starred passage.

I'm always saying "Glad to've met you" to someone I'm not at all glad I met. If you want to stay alive, you have to say that stuff, though.

I'm so lucky to have such a great sister.

At seven sharp, I started school.

There are several things in the universe with gravity so intense that you would be lucky to escape them alive and uncrushed. A neutron star. A black hole. High school.

At least the black hole crushes you fast. High school does it in slow motion, over four years. Assuming you last that long.

By all accounts, Murray (though it made me cringe to call it that) was one of the best high schools in the state. Possibly in the country. The test scores were off the charts, they offered every extracurricular you could imagine, and the campus itself was a beautiful, mission-style oasis. None of that mattered to me. I would have hated anyplace I went, simply because it was high school.

It was a big enough school that I expected some small measure of anonymity. The reality, unfortunately, was that the kids in my AP classes had been tracked together since middle school and I stuck out like a sore thumb. Since everyone else was busy catching up with people they hadn't seen over the summer, I was mostly ignored that first day, though I wasn't sure how long that was likely to last. It wasn't until I got to my AP English class that anyone went out of their way to speak to me.

"Hey, you're new, aren't you?" asked the girl sitting next to me. She was pretty, with long black hair pulled into a ponytail, big gold hoops in her ears, and a face full of artfully applied makeup. Over the back of her chair hung a very expensive purse. I recognized the logo as Hermès. My mother had gotten a similar one for my parents' twentieth wedding anniversary. I was pretty sure it cost more than Liv's car.

"Yeah," I said. "I'm Cara. I just moved here."

"I'm Morgan," she said. "So where are you from?"

"Virginia, most recently. My dad's in the Foreign Service, so we move around a lot."

"What is he doing here?" she asked.

"He's not, actually. I'm living with my sister this year; she's a grad student at McNair."

Her eyes lit up like it was Christmas morning. "Your parents don't live with you? No adults at all?"

I didn't like where this was going. "Actually, my sister's twenty-two, so she's technically an adult."

She rolled her eyes. "That's even better. You have someone to buy beer for you. *You*," she poked my shoulder conspiratorially, "are going to be *so* popular. Don't worry, I'll totally help you plan your parties. We'll have all the best people."

I groaned inwardly. "Actually, my sister's got me on a pretty short leash. If I cock up, she'll bounce me back to my parents."

"That sucks," she said, giving me a disgusted look. I was not living up to my promise as the cool new girl, and I could see her quickly losing interest. Which was fine with me.

"I know," I agreed. "It's too bad, right?"

At that point the teacher started class, and I got to spend the next ninety minutes listening to people discuss their impressions of *Hamlet*. Morgan didn't look at me for the rest of the period.

Lunchtime came around, and no one else had bothered to speak to me. I loaded up at the salad bar and then tried to find someplace quiet to sit. I wanted to get as much of my homework done at school as possible, so I'd have more time to live my real

90

life once I got home. As I entered the cafeteria, Morgan waved to me vigorously. I cursed to myself. I had the feeling that if I ignored her, she might have the power to make my life very unpleasant. I smiled and headed to her table, which crowded with a noisy group of about ten people, all of whom appeared to be seniors.

"Have a seat!" she said, pointing out an empty chair. "Everyone, this is Cara. She lives with her older sister."

Why did she have to bring that up? Everyone said hello, and I waved nervously. I got the impression that Morgan was something like the queen of this particular clique. I recognized several of the other kids from my classes earlier. A group of overachievers, it appeared, of the type who come from money and are expected to generate more of it once they leave college. I hunched over my tray, determined to eat as fast as possible and make an excuse to get out of there.

The girl on my left leaned over my shoulder to catch my eye. "Hey," she said. "I'm Molly. Do you really live with your sister?" She was a short, blond girl who hadn't yet lost all her baby fat. Her slightly round face was friendly.

"Yeah, I do," I said, "but she won't let me have any parties. Sorry."

She laughed at me, much to my surprise. "I guess Morgan already got to you. Don't worry about her too much. She puts on a front, but she's nice once you get to know her."

I had met girls like Morgan before, and I was pretty sure she was one of those girls who actually got *less* nice as you got to know her, but I didn't think pointing that out would make me any friends. "She seems nice," I said, redoubling my efforts to finish my lunch.

"So is this, like, totally different from the school you went to before?" she asked.

"Um, well, they didn't offer a glass-blowing class at my last school," I said.

She looked slightly offended. Thankfully, she seemed to respect my desire to be left alone and didn't talk to me again. I was sure she thought I was very unfriendly, but I just wanted to get through the day—well, the year, really—with as few entanglements as possible. I'd already been assigned an essay on Hamlet's feelings of alienation, and I wanted to get at least half of it done before the end of the day. After I finished my lunch, I looked over at Molly. "I'm supposed to meet with my guidance counselor now, so I've got to go," I lied. "It was nice to meet you."

"Oh, do you need help finding the office?" she asked. "I could take you."

"No, it's okay. I'll find it." I knew I was being rude. I waved at the rest of the table and left quickly before anyone else could talk to me, dumping my tray on the way out.

I found a quiet corner on the grass behind the science building and pulled out my notebook and my copy of *Hamlet*. I had written half a sentence when I realized there was someone standing in front of me, blocking the sun.

I looked up and saw a tall, athletic boy that I recognized from Morgan's lunch table. I probably would have thought he was cute, if I had never seen Will. He had his arms crossed and was staring at me. Had he followed me from the cafeteria?

"Why are you hiding out here?" he asked. "I thought you said you were going to the office."

I swallowed hard. "Well, the counselor wasn't there, so I thought I'd come out here and start my homework."

He grinned. "Doing homework in school on the first day? Aren't you adorable."

"I just want to get it done. I have stuff to do after school."

To my horror, he sat down on the ground next to me. He was close enough that I could smell his aftershave. I fought the urge to move father away.

"I really do need to get this done," I protested.

"Why?" he asked, leaning in closer. Too close. I scooted away a few inches.

"I have plans later."

"I don't believe it. I don't think you have anything planned at all," he said, and his half-sneer coupled with the edge to his voice made me uneasy. He reached out and flicked a blade of grass off my jeans, and I flinched as his finger grazed my thigh.

I felt a bubble of anger form in my stomach and rubbed the place where he had touched me. "Why do you think this is your business, exactly?" I asked.

"Hey, I'm just trying to be friendly."

Whatever he was being, my gut didn't register it as friendly. The main benefit of being a Foreign Service brat is that you meet an unusually large number of people in a very small period of time. You learn to trust your instincts. My instincts about this guy—had he even told me his name?—were not good.

"I appreciate that," I said, "but I have a date later, and I need to finish this." It was a lie; I'd made no plans with Will, and even if I had, we weren't exactly dating. But this guy didn't need to know that. I hoped his simply thinking I had a boyfriend might be enough to get him to back off.

"Oh," he said, raising his eyebrows. "A date? Did you meet someone during first period?"

"He doesn't go to school here," I countered, and then wondered why I was still even having this conversation. I stuffed my books back into my backpack and got up to leave.

"Okay, okay, I get it," he said, standing up and backing off with his hands up. "You're one of *those* girls. That's fine." He snickered. "I'll see you later." He looked at me in a way that made me feel dirty and walked away.

I briefly considered what he meant by "one of those girls," but I already had a pretty good idea: I was one of those girls who didn't think I owed something to any random person with a Y chromosome. I doubted he would have put it quite that way, though. I wondered what Liv would have done in that situation, and the scenarios I came up with all made me smile. Liv didn't give a damn about offending people, but deep down, I still wanted people to like me. As if she were with me, I heard Liv's voice in my head, reminding me that there are some people you actually *don't* want to like you. I was pretty sure I had just met one of them.

I was angry about the whole encounter and even angrier that I didn't have any time left to work on my essay. AP Biology started in five minutes, and I didn't want to be late. I got up and walked around to the front door of the science building.

I was standing at the back of the room, looking at the empty lab tables, when Molly came through the door. As she saw me, she gave me a smile and waved me over. "Would you like to be partners?" she asked.

She seemed nice enough and I didn't know anyone else, so I agreed, hoping that she didn't turn out to be a complete idiot. As we sat down, she asked, "Did you get to see your counselor?"

"Oh," I said. "Yeah, I took care of everything. By the way, the guy at lunch, the tall guy with the UCLA shirt—what was his name?"

She smiled knowingly and I knew she'd gotten the wrong idea. "Oh, that's Adam Douglass. He's cute, right?"

"He's not really my type, actually," I said. But I could see that she wasn't buying it.

"Sure."

"I'm kind of with someone," I explained. Maybe if I put this out on the grapevine, Adam would believe it and leave me alone.

"Oh, really? You have a boyfriend back in Virginia?" she asked.

"Oh, no, actually, he's in Muro Viejo."

"Wow, you work fast," she said with a laugh. "Does he go here, or to Murray North?"

I paused, trying to decide how much she needed to know. "Actually, he's at McNair," I said, hoping I wouldn't regret it later.

She blinked at me. "Wow," she said.

"He's really nice."

"You should totally get him to pick you up from school sometime. Morgan would die."

"Isn't she your friend?" I asked.

"Of course she's my friend," she said, not understanding, and I wondered what she thought the word *friend* actually meant.

I opened my mouth to say something back, but it was time for class to start, and Ms. Maliki, a teacher in her early 30s, began handing out course objectives and outside reading lists. I glanced over it. There was nothing on the list I hadn't already

95

read or studied, since I used to read Liv's textbooks on her summer breaks while she was in college. What a colossal waste of time.

My last class of the day was French, which was also likely to be a piece of cake since I'd spent two years in Geneva when I was younger. I saw with some disgust that Adam was in that class with me. I made sure I sat on the other side of the room.

I was relieved that I'd asked Liv to pick me up that day so that I wouldn't be stuck waiting for the bus. As I walked out of the foreign-languages building, I repeated my silent mantra: *It's only high school. It's not real life.*

Liv was already waiting when I got to the kiss 'n' ride, and I was amused by how much her old, mud-covered car contrasted with the BMWs and Lexuses (*Lexi?*) that filled the rest of the lot. I got in and threw my arms around her.

"That good, huh?" she said with a laugh.

"Do I really have to do this? I already know everything."

"I know you do, Care-bear," she said, mussing my hair. "If I could get you out of it, I would. Do you have a lot of homework?"

"Just some reading and an essay, but I have two days to get it done," I said. Murray was on a block schedule, which meant I didn't have the same classes every day. Of course, this meant that I would have to start all over again tomorrow. I tried not to think about that—it made my head hurt.

"Do you want to go out?" she asked. "I don't have to go back to campus until later."

I did. We got milkshakes from Foster's Freeze and then headed out to the Sierra Baja park for a walk.

Neither of us was dressed for actual hiking, so we walked out to the lake and sat on the grass near the dock. The lake was placid, and the trees growing up around it made me feel like we were up in the Sierras rather than a few minutes from downtown Muro Viejo. It was so beautiful, I had to admit that I liked Muro Viejo better than anyplace else I had lived before, even after today. I stretched and lay back on the grass, with Liv lying next to me, looking up at the clouds. I let myself relax into the ground, filling my lungs with the clean, fresh air.

Liv, at least, seemed to have had a good day. Her face was slightly browned from the sun, and she sighed contentedly as she stared up at the sky. I couldn't help but feel jealous.

"How did you get through it?" I asked her.

"What, high school? I didn't have much of a choice. You just get through it. Don't worry, though, in a few years you won't even remember how much it sucked," she said. She ran her fingers through the grass and sighed again.

"You remember it," I said.

"Well, yeah. But I'm weird, remember?"

I laughed. "What's so great about being normal?" I asked, poking her in the side with a twig.

"Well, it would make high school a lot easier, for one," she said, snatching the twig from my hand and poking me back.

I turned back to the clouds, and wondered what Will had been doing while I was living my teenage-angst horror show. I thought about what Molly had said, and wondered if he actually would pick me up sometime. After I became legal, that is. I didn't want to get him into any trouble. The thought of Morgan watching me climb into Will's Prius made me smile, even though I knew it was shallow and petty. It was okay to dream, right?

I watched the clouds blow across the sky, and thought about my stargazing trip with Will—about what it had been like

97

just to talk to him, to be close to him. The memory left me feeling warm and jittery, like I'd had too much coffee. I wished I could see him, but I couldn't very well abandon Liv, and anyway, he was busy with Dr. Kleeman that week. I wrapped my arms around myself and let all the air out of my lungs.

"Do you need to go soon?" Liv asked.

"Yeah, I have an essay to write."

"Okay," she agreed. "Ugh. Mom left a bunch of messages today. I probably have to call her back."

"She called?" That was a shock—she hadn't called since I'd moved in. I figured she was busy getting settled in Montevideo. Or that she'd forgotten about me. One of those.

"Yeah." She didn't move.

"Liv?"

"Mmm."

"What do you think she wants?"

"Not thinking about it. I refuse to live outside of this one perfect moment," she said raising her face to the sky and closing her eyes.

Despite her words, I could see that her hands were clenched tightly into fists. As if in a sympathetic maneuver, my stomach tied into a giant knot.

I called Will after dinner, while Liv was out running errands. I was pretty sure she hadn't called our mother.

"Hi," I said sadly, as he picked up the phone.

"What's wrong?" he asked.

"Nothing, really. Just a bad day,"

"I'm sorry. Is there something I can do to cheer you up?"

"I miss you," I whispered.

98

"So do I," he whispered back. Then, returning to his normal voice, he added, "I don't want to get in the way of your schoolwork."

"Get in the way," I begged. "Please."

He laughed. "Are we still on for Saturday?"

"Saturday."

Saturday, Saturday, Saturday.

Chapter Nine

Dark Matter

I was up before Liv on Saturday morning, and decided to surprise her with a full grocery run, including two gallons of milk. Of course I had to put everything on the floor of the back seat, since the trunk of the station wagon was still inaccessible. I began to fantasize about getting my own car.

When I went to get the groceries out of the car, I noticed that the bread had fallen out of the bag and landed on top of a T-shirt that was balled up on the floor. I picked it up to bring it inside, assuming it was Liv's, but upon closer inspection realized it was much too big for her. This was a man's shirt.

Liv was just getting out of the shower when I came in with the groceries. "Hey, thanks," she said, giving me a big smile. "Guess we won't have to have raisins for breakfast after all."

"No problem," I said. I finished putting the last of the food away, and then remembered the shirt. "Oh, I found this in your car. Someone must have left it there the other day." I tossed her the shirt, and she grabbed it and turned away.

"Oh," she said. "Um, thanks. There were a bunch of people in my car. I'll have to see whose it was."

"Did a lot of them go home topless?" I said with a laugh.

"Um, no, but, you know, we got wet. Someone probably changed and forgot their old shirt in the car."

100

Liv was obviously hiding something, but I had secrets of my own and I didn't want to pry too much. The shirt hadn't been remotely damp when I got it out of the car. I wondered if Liv might have a secret boyfriend, but the idea was so ridiculous I couldn't believe it.

I was trying to decide what to do for the day when my phone rang. I looked at the number and saw that it was Will calling, and my heart was suddenly in my throat. I ran to my room and answered.

"I hope I'm not calling too early," he said.

"No, not at all. I just got home from the grocery store."

"Oh, good. Well, I just got the day off from Dr. Kleeman, and I was wondering if you might want to get together earlier? I thought maybe we could go to Santa Cruz for the day and have dinner down there."

A whole day with the object of my fascination. I was trembling with excitement.

"That sounds great! Oh, when did you want to go?" I asked.

"Can I pick you up in an hour?"

I paused. Would Liv still be here in an hour? "I'll meet you down at the bus stop in front of my complex."

He did not sound happy. "Cara, I don't like doing this. I don't think you should be lying to your sister."

"It's just for a while," I said quickly. "Trust me, okay?"

He let out a frustrated sigh. "All right, I'll see you in an hour."

I stuck my phone in my purse and tried to decide if I should wear the dress or something more casual, since we would be spending the day in Santa Cruz before dinner. I remembered vaguely that my mother had once told me that, when in doubt, you should always go dressier. I normally never listened to my mother, but this time, I grabbed the dress.

Now I only had to deal with Liv, who was in her bedroom with the door shut. I called to her as I walked by her room, hoping that if I kept moving, she wouldn't pay too much attention to me. "Hey! I'm going out today. I'll be home late tonight."

To my horror, Liv stuck her head out of her room. "What?" she asked. Then she looked at me. And my dress. "Why are you all dressed up? Where are you going?"

"I thought I'd go to Santa Cruz for the day," I said. No point in lying more than I had to.

"By yourself?"

"Um, yeah."

Her eyes narrowed. "How stupid do you think I am, exactly? Who are you going with?"

"Nobody," I squeaked.

She folded her arms and glared at me. Okay. I could play hardball, too. I walked into the kitchen and grabbed the mysterious shirt off the counter, where Liv had left it. "Whose shirt is this?" I demanded, thrusting it in her direction.

"Nobody's. Well, nobody important. I told you, there were a bunch of us on that trip."

I raised my eyebrows at her.

She glared at me. "I'm twenty-two and you're seventeen."

I stared back at her. Finally she grabbed the shirt out of my hand and stuffed it under her arm. "Fine," she said. "If someone tries to ax-murder you, don't come crying to me."

"I won't. See you later."

Fifteen minutes later I was getting into Will's car. His face was almost wistful as he held the door for me. "You look wonderful today."

I wasn't used to receiving compliments, and I cast my eyes down in embarrassment. "Thanks," I said quietly.

"Oh," he said, "was that inappropriate? I'm sorry."

"No, I'm just—not used to it." It was a strange feeling, being complimented by him. On the one hand, it was amazing, thinking for a second that he might actually mean it. On the other hand, I didn't want to fall for him any more than I already had. I knew who I was. I knew it was impossible for him to feel the same magnetic pull that made me want to throw myself at him, like a bug hurtling toward a speeding windshield. I waited for the inevitable splat.

"I find that a little hard to believe." He got back into the car and pulled away from the bus stop. "Did you really want to go to Santa Cruz, or is there something you'd rather do?"

"No, I've been wanting to go there. I haven't been before."

"Well, I was thinking you'd like to see the kelp forest, but have you ever been ocean kayaking before?"

"I haven't," I said. "And I didn't bring anything to wear under a wetsuit. But I've read about it, and I've always wanted to see it." I was disappointed; the kelp forest was supposed to be amazing—a giant underwater ecosystem based on a dense canopy of seaweed. It's one of the most unique ecosystems in California.

"We could do an easier trip," he suggested. "If we go to Loch Lomond, we can do some flatwater paddling, and you wouldn't have to worry about getting your clothes wet. It's really beautiful there; I think you'd like it. We could still have dinner in Santa Cruz."

103

We drove the hour down, and he asked me about all the countries I'd lived in, my schoolwork, and what I hoped to study in college. I told him about the small greenhouse my parents had let me keep when we lived in Sumatra, and how I'd grown five kinds of orchids. I'd had to leave them behind when we'd moved again.

We parked our car near the entrance to the Loch Lomond recreation area, and found the boat rental. Will paid for a double kayak, and the man at the dock gave us a wet-bag for my purse and Will's wallet. I'd lived too many unsafe places to feel comfortable leaving my stuff in the car. He reminded us very firmly that this was a drinking-water reservoir, and that there was absolutely no swimming. How he thought I would swim in my dress was beyond me, but we agreed.

The scenery was amazing, and I was glad we had come. A dense cover of trees came right up to the edge of the water, which reflected a perfectly blue sky. As we set out, we passed a canoe carrying a father and son on a fishing trip, and I had to smile at the excitement in the young boy's face. I noticed Will looking at them, too. His eyes were sad, and I wondered what he was thinking.

Will was a fast paddler, and we were quickly moving across the lake. "Do you do this a lot?" I asked. He was sitting behind me in the kayak, but when I looked at him over my shoulder I could see that he had his sleeves rolled up, revealing a set of toned arms that moved the paddle through the water with ease.

"I do," he said. "I love to be out on the water. I've got a single kayak that I keep in my apartment, and I take it out whenever I can. Well, whenever Dr. Kleeman lets me."

I laughed. "Lets you? Does she keep you locked up someplace?"

"It feels that way sometimes. She's just really demanding."

"So how long have you been with her, at McNair?"

"This will be my second year. Either way, it's probably going to be my last."

"What do you mean, *either way*?"

He stopped paddling and put his oar across the kayak. "I'm not really a physicist, Cara. Actually, I'm not very good at it at all. I know the basics of how my ship works, and I can recite things I've read in books here on Earth, but I've got no talent for it, and Dr. Kleeman knows it. I won't make it through another year of the program."

I was surprised to hear that—I couldn't imagine him being bad at something. I wasn't used to having people admit their deficiencies to me. "How did you get into the program, then?" I asked.

"I faked my records. I've been here a long time, and I've got a pretty good network of people who can do things like that. When you have to change identities as often as I do, it comes in handy."

I thought about that for a while, and he began paddling again. He was taking us closer to shore, and I could see some tiny secluded inlets lining the lake. "What will you do, then, if you haven't gone home?" I asked, and my voice faltered on the last word. I had known Will for such a short time, but already I felt miserable at the idea of him leaving. Well, it was no big deal. Nobody stayed in my life for long, anyway.

"I don't know," he answered sadly.

Just then, a great blue heron flew in front of us, not more than ten feet in front of our boat. "Look!" I shouted with delight.

105

"Did you see! Oh, he's beautiful!" The bird circled back around and flew down the shore. "I've never seen one so close."

I turned to look at Will, who was smiling at me. "What is it?" I asked.

"Nothing," he said. "It's just nice to see you get so excited. It seems like every time I see you, you let more of yourself out."

I turned back, and he leaned sideways to try to get a better look at me. "I'm embarrassing you again."

He was, but I couldn't bring myself to mind. "It's not always a bad thing."

"Do you want to take a break for a while?" he asked. "There are some little inlets where we could pull out."

"Sure, my arms could use a rest."

We paddled to a tiny, sun-filled oasis amid the trees. An enormous sycamore tree stood back from the sandy area surrounding the shore, shading out most of the smaller plants, and the ground was bare. Will paddled the kayak as far as he could, and then kicked his shoes off, waded in, and pulled the kayak out another few feet, so that it was perched most of the way on the sand. He offered me his hand as I kicked my own shoes off and got out.

I knew I'd landed on something the instant my foot hit the sand. Before I could react, I felt a sharp pinch across my big toe. I yelped and tried to pull my foot up, losing my balance in the process. I fell into Will, who struggled in vain to keep us upright before he slipped and fell, too. We both went into the water with a giant splash.

I sat up, sputtering, and Will did the same. "I'm sorry," he said, "I think I slipped on some algae. Are you okay?"

"Yeah, I must have stepped on a crayfish." I held my foot out of the water to examine it. It was red where I'd been pinched, but it hadn't broken the skin.

We sat in the water for a second, and then Will started laughing. "What is that quote about the best-laid plans of mice and men?"

I laughed, too, and then he helped me to my feet. The water was only about a foot deep where we had fallen, but we were still both completely soaked.

"Well," he said with a grin, "the way I see it we have two choices. We can either paddle back to the dock, drive home, and miss dinner, or we can hang our clothes out in the sun for a while and hope they dry before we get too hungry."

I blushed scarlet. My dress was already clinging to me in ways I considered mortifying, and I didn't know the etiquette for hanging out with one's theoretically platonic male friend in one's underwear. As I considered this, he unbuttoned his shirt and hung it off the end of one of the sycamore's low branches, laying it carefully so that it would catch the breeze. He then did the same thing with his shorts. Stripped down to his boxers, he flopped down on the ground, and then gave me a triumphant smile, as if daring me to do the same.

Well, I couldn't really see any more of him than if he'd been in a bathing suit, and I rationalized that it would be the same on my end if I were sitting on the beach in my bra and underwear. If anyone passed by, it would simply look like I was sunbathing in a bikini. Not that I owned one of those. I turned away from him, slipped out of my dress, and hung it carefully over a branch.

"I hope we don't get arrested for swimming," I said. When he didn't answer, I glanced over my shoulder to see what he was doing. He was staring. Hard. If any guy had ever looked at me that way before, I couldn't remember it.

I was torn between feeling extremely flattered and extremely embarrassed, but I didn't think I could handle much more of it. I carefully picked up my sopping dress and, turning sharply, flung it at him. It hit him in the face with a loud smack.

"Oof," he grunted. "What was that for?"

"Liv was right," I chided, and I took my dress back and re-hung it. "You're a pervert."

He mumbled something about "stupid hormones," and I sat down next to him carefully, so that nothing important would fall out.

I had seen him shirtless that day at Half Moon Bay, but I hadn't really looked at him closely. His skin shone like bronze in the sun, and his body was lean and muscular. I tried not to stare.

He, on the other hand, wasn't trying quite as hard, and I was glad that my mother had forced me to buy new underwear before I left for Muro Viejo. I wasn't quite sure what to make of his attention—he had used the word "friends" so many times to describe us, but I was feeling less like his friend all the time, and more like something quite different. I tried not to think about it; I didn't need to get my heart broken on top of everything else.

"Have you thought of anything else you wanted to ask me about?" he asked, finally blinking and looking up at my face. I got the distinct impression that it was taking some serious effort for him to tear his eyes away from whatever he was looking at. I hoped it looked good, whatever it was.

"You don't mind?"

"Not at all. I like talking to you about this."

I thought for a minute. "Okay, here's one. Why did you choose to come to Earth?"

He laughed. "Well, there was some controversy about whether we should risk studying humans at all." He shot me a nervous glance, and I nodded to encourage him to continue.

"The original recon team came back with some interesting data. Humans are pretty different than most of the life we've studied. You're sort of, well, primal."

"Primitive, you mean," I said, poking his arm.

"Well, okay, yes. You have a bunch of characteristics of less-intelligent life—instinct, hormonal urges that interfere with rational thought, extreme emotions, that kind of thing. But you also have reason and intellect and curiosity. I found the idea of the human condition fascinating, and I wanted to experience it for myself."

His stomach growled and I laughed. "Sounds like you're experiencing it right now."

He shook his head. "I didn't think we'd be out this long, or I'd have brought us something to eat. Are you hungry, too?"

"Starving, actually."

"I'm so sorry. Do you want to go back?" he asked.

"I might have something in my purse. Hang on." I carefully waded back to the kayak, feeling the silt with my toes before putting my foot down to avoid stepping on anything. I grabbed the wet-bag and brought it back to Will, fumbling for my purse as I walked. I pulled out the library book on top, and found the Hershey bar I'd bought that morning and forgotten to eat. I broke it in two and handed half to Will.

"It's not much," I said, "but it's something."

"Thanks."

I went to stuff my book back inside, but before I could he picked it up. He held the cover toward me. It was *The*

Handmaid's Tale, another of my summer reading books. "Is that any good?" he asked.

I sniffed disdainfully and took a bite of my half of the chocolate bar. "Oppressed women. My mother would love it."

"Is your mother oppressed?" he asked. He caught my tone and was smiling.

"She likes to think so."

"But you don't."

I lay back on my elbows again, surprised that my first instinct was to answer him. This was not the kind of thing I usually talked about with anyone, except maybe Liv. But there's something about knowing someone else's secrets that makes you want to share your own. So I continued. "Here's the thing about my mom. Before she met my dad, she was all set to become a chemist. A really good one, too. Here's the story: She's in college, at Georgetown, and then she meets my dad, who's in the School of Foreign Service, and she falls totally in love with him, and when he takes his first assignment overseas, they get married and she never even goes to grad school. And she has Liv, and then me, and then at some point she realizes she has made a Huge Mistake, but she feels like it's too late for her to fix it, so she's just bitter and angry all the time, and she blames my dad for ruining her life."

"Wow."

"Pretty much."

"I guess you don't get along with her too well."

"Not especially. I guess I'm just tired of the whole *poor oppressed woman* routine. She made the decision to get married," I held up one finger. "She made the decision not to go to grad school," I held up another. "She made the decision to have kids, and she made the decision to stay married after she realized she'd screwed up. Nobody did anything to her, but it's easier to blame other people for your problems than to try to fix them."

"Is that why you're always insisting that you don't need anyone? So you don't end up like your mother?"

"Um, well, I guess that's probably part of it." I said, looking away from him. It was easier to talk about how mad I was at my mom than to talk about how screwed up I was.

"What's the other part?" he asked. He scooted over so that he was sitting right next to me, and our shoulders were touching. It was strange to have him so close; except for the occasional hug from Liv, no one ever touched me. I had to admit that I liked the way it made me feel, having him pressed gently against me. I leaned back against him, feeling his warm skin against my bare arm, and was glad when he didn't move away. He seemed to enjoy being close as much as I did.

I shrugged. "Well, you know, when you move all the time, after a while the people you meet stop feeling real. It's like they're props or something. They're there, and you talk to them, and you might even hang out or eat lunch together or whatever, but you don't really know them, and they don't really know you, and you both know you're leaving in a year or however long anyway, so nobody really cares. Then you leave and you never think about them again."

He was so quiet that I couldn't help looking up, and in his face was the look of anguish I had seen on the beach the day we first met. My heart ached, as I realized how close I was getting to the truth of his own pain. "Is that what it's been like for you, too?" I asked quietly.

He nodded. "Yes, just exactly that way. Props. I never thought of it like that."

I reached out and carefully put my hand on top of his, half expecting him to pull away. He didn't.

"That day at the beach," I said, my voice barely above a whisper, "what were you really doing? Please tell me the truth this time."

He turned and looked into my eyes, sliding my hand between both of his. "You felt lonely, moving around so much and never making any real friends?"

"Yes."

"Imagine living that life four times over, only without your sister, and without any hope of anything ever changing. Imagine knowing, with complete certainty, that you would never have a true friend, or feel love, or any kind of real connection to another person. Never."

I felt like I had been punched in the chest, and I could feel tears rising behind my eyes. "I can't really imagine. It sounds awful."

He reached up and tucked my hair behind my ear, and I was starting to realize how much that small gesture must mean to him, how much it must mean for him just to have a shoulder to lean against, a lock of hair that needed tending, a hand to touch. "The day at the beach, I was coming from Dr. Kleeman's lab. She's published some controversial things lately, and she had just told me that she might be losing her tenure. Working with her was my last effort to go home, and I saw it slipping away. After sixty years of solitude, I couldn't stand it any longer. When you saw me, I was preparing to shift into my natural form. I was going to let myself disperse into the waves."

I couldn't speak for a few seconds. I understood, then, the look on his face that day. The look that has stayed with me every

112

day since. "You were going to kill yourself," I said, choking, and I felt the tears spilling over my eyelids.

"No, no, no," he murmured, wiping my cheeks with his fingers. "It's all right; I think it had to happen that way. Because there you were, like my personal guardian angel, with your sandwich. And you really seemed to care what happened to me, even though you didn't know me at all. So I thought, maybe this was a sign, and maybe I should just try to push on a little longer. Then there you were again, and I realized that maybe meeting you wasn't an accident; maybe I was *meant* to meet you that day."

I blinked the tears out of my eyes and forced a smile. "I would never have thought that you believed in fate."

"I never did. Not until now. But like you said, the universe is a big place. I just can't accept that our paths would cross that way by accident, not when I needed someone the most. Once they did, though, I realized that maybe I couldn't go home, but I wouldn't have to be alone, either. That's when I decided that I had to tell you everything. It didn't matter whether you panicked, or even if you turned me over to the FBI, because I had already been to the lowest possible place. For the chance to have a friend, it was worth the risk."

"Well," I said, squeezing his hand, "I didn't panic, and I don't plan on turning you over to the FBI."

"No," he laughed softly. "Your reaction has been better than anything I could have possibly hoped for. You can't imagine what it means to me, to have you want to know me. Thank you for that—for letting me share myself with you. And for sharing yourself with me."

I was blushing again, but I didn't want him to see, so I leaned forward and put my arms around him, feeling the

113

muscles in his back tense slightly as I rested my hands against his bare skin. He pulled me into a close embrace, and he was so warm, so strong, that I couldn't believe he was anything other than a real man. We stayed in each other's arms for a long time, and I felt so strange and so wonderful at the same time, I hardly knew what to think.

It was scary, realizing that there was so much of me that I'd never noticed before. It was like finding out my insides were full of dark matter—endless quantities of material I couldn't see, couldn't describe, but couldn't deny, either.

You can only detect dark matter because of the way it responds to gravity, making galaxies spin. It seemed like the dark matter in me was set spinning by Will. I was filled with wanting and needing and feeling, with all kinds of irrational debris that made me want to touch and be touched, and not just physically, either. It was like finding out the Cara that I thought I knew was only the tip of an enormous iceberg.

And it was even scarier because I hadn't wanted to choose him, hadn't wanted him to be the gravity that pulled me in. It was like something inside of me, something in that big vat of dark-Cara-matter, had chosen him all on its own.

That was the moment I knew I was going to let him break my heart.

After we returned the kayak we drove into Santa Cruz and decided to have dinner on the wharf, looking out at the ocean. As Will parked in the lot at the entrance, I was surprised by how far the wharf extended out into the water.

"How far out does this go?" I asked.

"About half a mile. Pretty, isn't it?"

I nodded. The wharf was lined with a mix of eclectic shops and restaurants. Since it was a Saturday and the weather was beautiful, it was bustling with people shopping and sightseeing. It was early for dinner, and most of the restaurants we passed were still empty.

As neither of us had ever eaten there, we decided to pick whatever looked good as we made our way down the wharf, out toward the sea. Walking next to Will was a wonderful feeling. I wondered briefly if I had earned some incredible karma in a previous life that I deserved to be with such an amazing creature.

We came across a pan-Asian fusion restaurant, and decided it looked promising. Our table sat next to a floor-to-ceiling window that looked directly out onto the ocean, and we watched sailboats lazily coming into the harbor after a day on the water. It was beautiful and serene, and I was already feeling relaxed and a little sleepy from our day of paddling.

He reached out and took my sun-browned hand. I looked at him and smiled. Being with him was so comfortable, so easy, like slipping into a pair of shoes that fits you perfectly; it was like being with him was just *right*. I wondered if he felt the same way about being with me.

"Would you like to split one of the assorted platters?" he asked. "Is it okay if we get the vegetarian one?"

"That sounds great," I said. "I didn't realize you were a vegetarian. I guess it makes sense."

He smiled warmly at me. "It's hard to eat a cow, once you've been one."

"You've been a cow? What was that like?"

"Pretty boring, actually," he admitted. "But still."

115

We didn't talk much after that; we were both tired and far too happy for serious conversation. He was delighted with the food, though, and eager to try each new dish. He took a bite of the paneer mahkni and gave a delighted moan, and then speared another piece and held the fork out to me.

"Try this," he insisted. "It tastes like flowers."

I opened my mouth and let him press the contents of the fork onto my tongue. It did taste like flowers.

"It's wonderful," I said. "You've never had Indian food before?"

"Sure I have," he said, "but I've never had anyone to share it with."

We spent the rest of the meal analyzing the smells, flavors, and textures of every dish on the plate. In all my life, I don't think anything had ever tasted as good, and I knew it wasn't because of the food.

By the time we arrived home, I was so exhausted that I could barely keep my eyes open. I was just starting to doze off when Will stopped the car in front of my building.

My eyes snapped open, and I looked over to Will. "We're here?" I asked sadly.

"We are." He looked somewhat amused.

"What's funny?"

"Nothing. It's just that it's been a long time since anyone missed me. It's a nice feeling, being wanted."

"Will you miss me, too?" I asked softly.

"You know that I will."

"Tell me anyway," I challenged.

"Okay." He chuckled. "I *will* miss you. I will miss the ridiculous things you say when you're not on your guard. I'll miss the way your eyes light up when you're asking me about

116

myself, like I'm the most interesting thing in the world. I'll miss how kind you are, even to a featherless bird or a poor, lost Eolian. But," he added, with a twinkle in his eye, "I think most of all I'll miss the fact that I can't tell if you actually enjoy hearing how much I like you, or if you are, in fact, getting ready to smack me."

"If I wanted to smack you, I would," I said, but I was fighting a losing battle not to smile. I could feel my lips curving despite my best efforts.

"Oh, I don't doubt it," he said. "When can I see you again?"

"My classes only go until two. I'm sure your schedule is more difficult than mine."

"That's probably true," he said. "Dr. Kleeman has some new experiment she's been getting ready for. I'm supposed to help her set up for it this week."

"I'm surprised she gave you the day off, then."

"She didn't, actually," he admitted. "I called in sick."

My mouth fell open. "Why? That work means everything to you. It's your chance to go home."

He turned away from me, pursing his lips as if he were trying to decide what to say. When he turned back to me, his voice was softer than I'd ever heard it. "Let's just say that things aren't as clear to me as they used to be." He reached out and gently stroked my cheek with his fingertip, and I shivered. He looked into my eyes, as if gauging my reaction to his touch, and I felt like whatever bond was between us had suddenly become more serious.

Someone nearby slammed a car door, and I jumped. "I should really go in," I said apologetically. "I'm going to get an earful from Liv as it is."

117

"I'll call you tomorrow," he said. "And Cara?" he added as I opened the car door.

"Yes?"

"You know you can call me whenever you'd like."

I laughed at his earnestness. "Good," I said. "Because I intend to." Then, before I even knew what I was doing, I leaned over and kissed his cheek. I felt him inhale sharply as my lips met his warm skin. For my part, my heart was in my throat.

He leaned his head against the seat and looked at me longingly as I closed my door. I pressed my hand against the window briefly. He reached out and put his fingertips on the other side of the glass, and I could have sworn that I could feel the heat from his hand. I mouthed "goodbye" one last time. Then I ran upstairs to face Liv.

Liv was in her pajamas already, though it was barely after eight o'clock. As if that wasn't odd enough, she was staring at the television, which she almost never watched. The phone sat on the floor by her feet. Had she been calling our parents to rat me out? Maybe she'd changed her mind since this morning.

"Hey!" I called as I closed the front door, hoping my positive mood might be contagious.

Liv glared and said nothing. I swallowed hard.

My sister rarely lost her temper with me in a serious way, but when she did, it was not pretty. I recalled one incident that occurred when I was about eight: I'd accidentally downloaded a virus onto her computer, and she lost an entire quarter's worth of schoolwork. She didn't speak to me for a week. I never did find the head from my Cabbage Patch Kid.

I threw myself into the chair across the room from her. "Okay, Liv. Let's have it."

To my surprise, she laughed. And laughed. To the point of hysteria. I was starting to freak out, and she was starting to tear up, when she calmed down enough to speak. "Oh, Cara, Cara, Cara, you idiot. I'm the least of your problems." She held up the phone. "Mom called."

"So what?" I said. "You *told* on me?"

Liv ignored me. "She's in Lima."

"Lima, like Lima, Peru? Why?"

"Because that's where she caught her connection. She'll be here in the morning."

Liv laughed again and I buried my head in my hands.

The Journal of Will Mallory

I am acutely aware, always, of any part of Cara's body touching mine—her skin, her hair. Today I leaned toward her and her eyelashes brushed my face. I thought I might die as they left little trails of bliss across my cheek.

It's such a comfort to me, the increasingly familiar touch of her. I think of every moment of solace I'd had these last years: hot soup after a day in the rain, a kind word from a stranger, a soft bed after a hard day. She puts all those feelings to shame with the brush of a fingertip. I want to run my fingers through her hair, my hands over her skin, press myself against her and feel her breath, her heartbeat. I want to drink her up, to feel her against every part of me. She feels soft and warm and like no one else I've ever touched. My body responds to her like a tongue to honey.

But it isn't just comfort, just sweetness, that I find in her. The man in me is feeling something else completely.

I am trying very hard to force away these feelings, which are growing increasingly potent, increasingly urgent. I hoped they would pass, that it was just a natural reaction to her beauty. But that isn't it—and my feelings are growing stronger with every touch, every glance, every time I catch the scent of her hair, hear the sound of her voice. I want her in a way that I've never wanted anyone before.

120

This is a mistake. I've been down this road before, and I know where it will lead for me. I've decided never to ask Cara for anything but her friendship. But my resolve is weakening every second.

Chapter Ten

Mommy Dearest

There was a lot of screaming the next morning, as Liv and I struggled to get the apartment presentable. At least I'd been to the grocery store, so if Mom decided to inspect the fridge, she'd find it well-stocked. I was scrubbing the bathroom grout with an old toothbrush when there was a knock at the door.

I cursed under my breath. I'd changed into my bathrobe to clean, and now there wasn't time to change into anything else.

"She's *early*," whispered Liv, who was wearing an old T-shirt that seemed to consist mostly of holes and unidentifiable stains.

"You'd better answer the door!" I hissed back.

We pasted the sincerest-looking smiles we could muster onto our faces and opened the door.

Standing in the doorway was our mother, looking far too elegant for the amount of time she had just spent on an airplane. I was flooded with relief when I realized that she didn't have any luggage—she must have already checked in at her hotel. I wondered how long she was planning on staying. I'd forgotten to ask.

"Ah, my girls," she said as she walked through the door. She hugged Liv and then me, looking us over. She then walked into the living room and surveyed the apartment.

"This is a nice little place," she said. "I was a little worried I might find you drowning in pizza boxes and old papers."

Liv laughed nervously. "Of course not, Mom. We're doing great."

"Have you eaten yet?" I blurted out. I knew my mother was more likely to give us a hard time if she was hungry. Plus, heading out to a restaurant would get us out of the apartment, and it would only be a matter of time before she found something to criticize there.

"No, just the horrible breakfast they gave us on the plane. I'd love to go out, but it doesn't look like either of you is ready to go yet. It must be nice to be able to sleep so late."

"We can be ready in five minutes," I said, as Liv did what appeared to be some kind of yogic breathing exercise. I grabbed Liv's sleeve and pulled her down the hallway.

"Oh," I asked before I went into my room to change. "How long are you going to be in town?"

My mother sighed dramatically. "Well, I'm not really sure yet."

I stopped short. "What do you mean?"

"Well, I'm divorcing your father."

Breakfast was long and awkward. Our mother explained, as if we had ever missed it before, how she had given up all her dreams to marry our father, how she hated being a Foreign Service wife, and how she had missed out on everything she had ever wanted to do.

"I feel like this is my last chance," she said, "to live life on my own terms."

"That's great, Mom," Liv said flatly.

"You aren't upset?" she asked, missing Liv's tone.

"Nope," Liv said, taking a bite of French toast. "You should do whatever makes you happy."

"I appreciate that, Olivia."

"So," I said, after a long silence. "What are you going to do? Now that you won't be in Uruguay anymore?"

"I'm trying to figure that out. I'm thinking of getting a teaching credential, so I can teach high school chemistry."

"You could go back to Virginia," Liv suggested. "I know you liked it there."

"Maybe. I was thinking I might stay here in the Bay area. You know, so I could be closer to you. I just need to find a big enough place for Cara and me. I'm going to meet with a Realtor next week."

I concentrated very hard on chewing my omelet so that I wouldn't hyperventilate.

After breakfast, Mom was tired from her trip and went back to her hotel to take a nap. Liv and I collapsed in the living room, and Liv buried her face in the back of the couch and emitted several fake sobs.

"Well, that sucked," I said. "Do you think we should call Dad?"

"He didn't call us," Liv reminded me. "I wonder if he's noticed that she's gone yet. Maybe he'll finally take some time off now that he doesn't have to hide out at work all the time."

"Dad works all the time because of his job," I protested. It was true; everybody we grew up with had parents who worked long hours—though maybe not as long as our father.

"He worked that much because he wanted to. To get away from her," Liv said, looking at me as if I were a complete moron.

"You don't know that."

"It's the truth, Cara. Look, there are a lot of workaholics in the State Department, but he worked every chance he got. Every weekend, every time he got a chance to take a trip without us, he took. Of course, that just made everything worse, since she was stuck at home with us while he was off at the office or hanging out at state dinners, which only made her more pissed off. So he'd come back, and there would be more yelling, and then he'd run back to work again."

"You're saying it's *his* fault?" The idea that my father's obsession with work had contributed to my parents' train wreck of a marriage hadn't occurred to me. It was my mother who always instigated the fights. My mother who was the constant critic. My mother who would never let Dad forget exactly what she had given up to be with him.

"It's both of their faults," Liv said. "Take your pick: bitter or self-involved."

I just shrugged. I had to admit, I was a little sadder than Liv. I knew my parents hadn't gotten along, but still, divorce seemed so final. I wondered where Liv and I would go for Christmas, but that thought was selfish, and I knew it.

"Do you think they'll really get divorced?" I asked.

"Probably not." Liv shrugged. "I don't know. I guess it depends on whether she's more fed up than she is scared of being alone. 'Cause you know what *that* would mean."

"Yeah," I agreed. "There'd be no one left to blame."

125

Chapter Eleven

A Waltz

My second week of school was pretty much like my first. Morgan was in my U.S. government class and said hello to me, which was nice. I still couldn't recognize most of my other classmates, but I had to admit that there were probably only a handful of people in the school I could even identify.

The homework load was a little more than I'd expected. I wasn't thrilled about that. I figured if I worked through lunch every day, I could still have a few hours every day to spend with Will and Liv. Though with my parents' marriage headed down the tubes, I wondered if I should be looking for a part-time job to help pay for college. I was sure that my dad wouldn't cut me off, but if he suddenly had to start paying alimony, I didn't know how much he'd be able to help out. Mom was heading out of town again this weekend, sorting through things back at our home in Virginia, and I tried not to think about the fact that I might be moving in with her when she got back.

At lunchtime on Monday afternoon, I was headed toward the cafeteria when I was surprised by the sight of students leaving campus in droves. Then I remembered that at Murray it was okay to leave for lunch, after the end of the first week of classes. Just as well, I thought. The campus would be quieter, and it'd be easier for me to start my homework without being hassled. Before I could head into the lunchroom, Molly caught up to me.

"Hey!" she said, her short, blond hair bouncing against her shoulders. "We're headed to Los Olivos for lunch. You should come!" I had to think for a minute before I remembered that Los Olivos was the shopping center across the street from the high school. There were a lot of small shops and restaurants there.

"That sounds great, but I didn't bring enough money to pay for a real lunch," I said honestly.

"I can loan you a few dollars—you can pay me back tomorrow. Come on!" She grabbed my arm and began pulling me toward the parking lot.

If there was a way out of this without making an enemy out of the only person who had been really nice to me so far, I couldn't see it, so I resigned myself to going along.

In the parking lot we met up with most of the people I'd seen at lunch the week before. I was not thrilled that Morgan and Adam were among them. Morgan, at least, waved at me. Adam looked at me with contempt and said something under his breath to the guy standing next to him—Ethan, I think—who looked at me and laughed.

Molly and I piled into Morgan's very expensive car, along with a few people I thought I had classes with: Allison Feng and her boyfriend, Tristan, who didn't seem to talk much. The rest of the group was in Adam's three-row SUV.

We met up at a pizza place at Los Olivos, which was swarming with students enjoying their lunch breaks. I didn't think it was possible to get sick of pizza, but after living with Liv for a week, I'd had enough. I could hardly go against the group, though, so I ordered a slice and choked it down.

127

"How's your sister?" Morgan asked, as everyone finished their pizza. "She's at McNair, right?"

"Oh, she's fine," I said. I couldn't fathom why she would ask about her.

"Isn't your *boyfriend* at McNair, too?" she said

I glanced at Molly, who smiled apologetically. Everyone at the table was watching me, and all the other conversations had stopped. I realized that this was not good.

"Um, yeah. He's there," I said.

"So is he a freshman?" Morgan asked, twirling her finger in a loose lock of hair.

I hesitated as I thought of the best way to answer that. I figured the safest bet was to make our age difference look as small as possible. "Yeah, he's a freshman."

Morgan grinned triumphantly. "But the freshmen haven't come to campus yet," she said with a smirk. "The dorms don't even open for another two weeks."

I groaned inwardly as I realized that she had been leading me into a trap, and was angry at myself for not seeing where she was going until it was too late. Afterward, I thought of a million things I could have said to save myself. I could have said he was local and wouldn't be living on campus. I could have said he was living off campus with relatives. I could have said he was a space alien who would be orbiting the campus in his flying saucer. *Anything* would have been better than saying nothing.

So, of course, I said nothing. I could hear the others snickering to themselves, and I felt sick, knowing I would spend the rest of the year living this down. I had invented a fake college boyfriend, and I couldn't even correct the mistake at this point. No matter what I said, I'd look like a liar.

"So," said Adam. "Will your boyfriend be taking you to homecoming?"

"Of course not," said Morgan. "Why would a college guy want to go to a high school dance?" The group laughed again, louder this time.

I'd had enough; I could see I was just going to be the butt of their jokes now, whether I stayed or not. I resigned myself to the fact that they would be making fun of me behind my back for at least the next week, and I got up to go.

"Oh, where are you going?" Morgan asked.

"Back to school," I replied, as coolly as possible. "I have some work to catch up on."

"Oh, another hot date this afternoon?" Adam said. He bumped Ethan's shoulder and everyone laughed some more. I grabbed my things and left.

Molly followed me. "Cara, wait!" she called. I paused briefly to let her catch up, once we were out of the earshot of the group who was still at the table. "I'm really sorry," she said.

"Why did you tell her?" I demanded.

"Because, I thought he was real. I didn't realize you'd made him up."

"He *is* real!" I said, and started walking again.

"But—"

"Look, it's just complicated, okay?"

"Please don't be mad at me," she said, almost running to keep up. "I had no idea she'd do that, I swear."

Why didn't I believe that?

"I'm not mad at you," I said. "I just don't want to talk about it anymore."

The walk back to campus was not far, but I still had to run to make it to my next class, and I had trouble concentrating. The teacher had to ask me the same question three times, and I could have sworn the entire room was watching me. When I looked around, I saw that there were two girls from lunch in my class, and they were whispering behind their hands while they stared at me. I knew then that this would be all over school by the end of the day. I breathed deeply and reminded myself that I would be seeing my not-quite-imaginary friend in just a few hours. That was the important thing, I told myself. What happened at school didn't matter.

After school I practically ran to the bus stop, and when I got off in front of the McNair library, I was so relieved to see Will that I threw myself into his arms. I only stopped myself from crying by sheer force of will.

"Hey," he said, "What's wrong? What happened today?"

"Nothing important," I said into his shoulder. "Just another bad day."

"Two in a week hardly seems fair," he said, pulling me closer. "Do you want to tell me what's going on?"

"It's all so stupid and juvenile. I just want to forget about it," I said. I pulled away, remembering where we were. I didn't need to make a huge PDA spectacle when Liv might be around the corner.

"Maybe I can help," he offered.

"I don't think so. High school just stinks. But it's only a year, and then I'll never have to think about any of this crap ever again. Anyway, I don't want to waste my time with you by thinking about it."

He looked a little sad, though I couldn't understand why. Why would anyone want to hear about the trials of being the high school outcast?

I reached out for his hand, and mine slid effortlessly into his, like it was meant to be there. He lifted our joined hands and looked at them for a minute, curiously, as if he were thinking the same thing.

"I just need some ice cream," I said.

"I think we can manage that," he said, letting our hands fall again. "Anything else?"

I thought about that for a minute, and from somewhere deep inside me came a memory—a flash—of my thirteen-year-old self. I remembered a fantasy that I had nurtured back then, one I had ordered myself to get rid of because it was so childish, so silly. Somehow, with Will looking at me like I was a beautiful woman instead of a scraggly seventeen-year old girl, I couldn't help but think of that dream again.

"Do you know how to dance?"

He blinked at me in surprise. "Um, well, I did, a little, but that was more than fifty years ago."

"I can show you. Can we do that? Can we dance?"

He laughed softly. "Cara, I would love to dance with you, but I don't think anyplace is going to be open at three in the afternoon."

"Let's go someplace else, then. Someplace with just us."

He smiled. "Let's go to the beach. Pescadero, maybe? I just need to stop at my apartment first."

"That sounds perfect."

We walked across campus together, and I was almost giddy, I enjoyed being with him so much. As we passed the Physics building, he stopped, frowning.

"What's wrong?" I asked.

131

He shook his head. "I'm not sure. That man over there," he said, indicating a dark-suited older man coming out of the building. "I feel like I've seen him before."

The man turned around, and as I saw his face, I froze. It was the same man who'd grabbed me my first day on campus— the man who had followed us the day of the barbecue. I clutched Will's arm and pulled him around the side of the building.

"That's him!" I said. "The man who chased us across campus."

"I didn't really get a good look at him that day. Are you sure it's the same man?"

"Positive."

He leaned back and peered around the corner. "Get back," he said. He pushed me against the wall and pressed himself against me, making it look like we were just a couple making out next to the building. I buried my face in his neck and closed my eyes.

After a few seconds I felt Will's muscles relax and he stepped back. "He's gone," he said.

"Did he see me?"

"No. I don't think so."

He took my hand and we started in the direction of his apartment again. "He scanned the hand you bandaged, after I cut it changing my tire," I said.

He nodded. "I've been wondering if this might have something to do with me. My body contains the same amount of carbon as yours, but it's possible our world contains more of the 13-isotope than Earth. There's no way I can do an analysis without drawing attention to myself."

"What should we do?"

He looked at me seriously. "If you see him, get away. Don't let him touch you again. But he's probably just trying to find the source of contamination in the Chemistry lab. It's a pretty big jump from that to *alien*."

"What if he tries to scan you?"

He grinned. "I won't let him—that's why I ran that day. Try not to worry too much. This may not have anything to do with me at all. Just keep your eyes open."

I ground my teeth together. I knew Will was just trying to make me feel better, but his explanation didn't hold up, and I figured he knew it. Because if the contamination really had been caused by random ore deposits, why had he come back?

And if it hadn't been, then why had he left in the first place?

We walked up the steps of his building in the grad-student complex. It was a fairly new building, decorated tastefully, if rather blandly, with contemporary furniture. Will lived in an efficiency on the second floor.

I was a bit surprised by how sparsely it was outfitted; I'd have thought someone would accumulate more stuff over sixty years. Practically the only thing in the place that wasn't standard-issue was the kayak leaning against the wall by the front door.

"I guess you don't keep much from one identity to the next," I said, looking around.

"I'm used to leaving things behind," he explained. "But there are a few things I've become attached to." He gestured to the wall across from the sofa, upon which hung two paintings. The first was of the ocean, looking dark under the cover of storm clouds. The second was of a woman holding a child.

"Did you paint these?" I asked.

133

"I did, a long time ago. When I first became human, I worked as an artist for a while."

I stepped closer to get a better look. "In France?"

"No, this was before that. I was in New Orleans."

"They're so beautiful." I reached my hand out, wanting to touch them, but pulled back at the last minute. "The light is so real."

"I'm glad you like them. My people don't have a culture like yours, with art and music and literature. We eventually learned from the Livan after we started adopting a solid form, but theirs is nowhere near as sophisticated or varied as yours. It's one of the things I admire most about humanity."

I gazed at the paintings for a long time, admiring the beauty, the serenity of them. "Who is the woman?" I asked.

"Just someone I saw in a park. She was there with her child, a little boy, and he fell and hurt himself. She picked him up to comfort him, and there was such tenderness, so much love in the way she held him and talked to him. I guess you could say it touched me. I didn't want to forget it."

I continued admiring them while Will grabbed a few things out of the kitchen.

"Do you still paint?" I asked.

I looked over my shoulder and watched him stuff a few things into his backpack. "No. I— the man I was then, the form I had—it was different. It had a talent for painting. These hands," he held them up, showing me, "they don't have the knack for it."

"But you loved it. I can tell. You couldn't have painted like this, if you didn't."

He came back and stood next to me. "I did love it, but that was in another life."

134

I reached out and stroked his palm, admiring the hands he had, and wondering if his old ones could possibly have been any better. These seemed so perfect, it didn't seem possible. "You should try. You might surprise yourself. Your hands might be different, but your spirit's the same."

"Maybe you're right," he said. "I'm just so busy these days, it's hard to remember that there used to be a life outside of the lab. Are you ready?"

I eyed his bag. "What do you have?"

"A little surprise."

We drove down to the beach, and walked down the sand together, hand in hand, and kicked off our shoes. The sky was turquoise, the water a perfect blue-green, and the sand a smooth caress of white punctuated only by our own footprints.

The air was unusually warm that day, and the sun was hot on my face and my arms. I wanted to dig my toes into the sand and root myself there, savoring that moment for a lifetime.

Will was staring ahead at the waves, lost in their rhythm, and I had to stand up on my tiptoes to catch his eye.

"You like it here," I said.

He nodded. "All Eolians love the sea. There's just something about it—I don't know. It calls to us." He put his arm around me. "I'm glad you're here with me."

I leaned my head against his shoulder. "Dancing?" I asked hopefully.

"Surprise first," he said, opening his backpack. "Here's the first one." He pulled out a plastic box, holding it up so I could see what was inside.

"Cannolis!" I exclaimed. "I love these."

"I figured you would. I was saving them for you. I hope they aren't too soggy."

135

"I'm sure they're great."

He handed me a plastic fork and set about trying to get the tape off the outside of the container, trying not to smile as he struggled with it. It was nice, somehow, knowing that all the little annoyances of being human were just as annoying for him. Finally, he gave up and took a Swiss army knife out of his pocket.

"Ow," he muttered.

'What's wrong?"

With a slightly embarrassed look he held up his hand, palm out, so that I could see. A trail of blood ran from the tip of his finger.

"Oh," I said. "Here." I grabbed a napkin out of his backpack, folded it in half, and pressed it over the cut on his finger. "It'll stop in a second."

I looked up at him and saw that his expression was very warm—tender, even. But behind that was an undercurrent of humor that he wasn't able to hide completely.

I looked at his hand and shook my head. "It's completely stupid, what I'm doing, isn't it."

"Not stupid, no," he said.

"But unnecessary."

He smiled, reaching out with his other hand to stroke my face. "Depends what you mean by unnecessary."

His fingers were hot on my cheek. "You like this?" I asked quietly.

"Yes."

I hesitated before I looked up into his eyes. "Why?"

"Life for Eolians is different than for humans. I never had any parents, never had anyone—like you. No one ever cared for me before. Or looked after me."

"You like being cared for?"

A slow smile spread across his face. "Oh, yes."

It was ironic that the very feeling that made me the most uncomfortable—the feeling of being dependent, in any way, should give him so much happiness. I was beginning to understand those feelings now, in the way it gave me a secret thrill whenever Will did something for me, not because he had to, but because he wanted to. I thought that if Will wanted to look after me, just a little bit, it might not be so bad.

I was still cradling his cut hand in my own, and I looked down at it. "I've been wondering about this since the science picnic," I said. "You scratched your forehead that day."

"I remember. It hurt."

Can you really get hurt? As a human?"

"Up to a point. If I'm confronted with any kind of pain that my mind perceives as life-threatening, I won't be able to maintain my solid form. I'll revert to my Eolian body. It's like a genetic fail-safe mechanism to keep us from dying when we're in another form."

"I guess that makes sense. But you can bleed?"

He grinned. "Sort of."

I hesitated before I asked the logical next question. "What happens to your blood?"

He looked down at his hand. "Take a look and see."

I glanced up into his eyes before I pulled the napkin away. There was a bright red stain on it from his cut finger, and I looked up at him quizzically.

"Just watch," he said.

I looked back to the napkin, and the blotch of red began to glimmer as it rose, as if it were evaporating. As I watched with wide eyes, the blood rose into the air as glimmering droplets of

137

mist. They hung there for only a breath, and then faded away as they dissipated.

I looked back to his cut hand, and as I watched, he shimmered and the cut was gone. He looked down at my face and laughed. I could hardly contain my delight, but then I clapped my hand over my open mouth.

"I'm a terrible person," I said, "getting this excited about seeing you bleed. You're just so amazing."

He laughed again, shaking his head. "You're not a terrible person, but I'm glad you think I'm amazing, anyway."

We ate the soggy cannolis out of the box. "So, if you dissipate like that, how did you get that cell that you showed me?" I asked through a mouthful of pastry cream.

"Some of my cells are still on that towel," he explained. "If it was cold enough, they wouldn't dissipate at all."

"So if you cut off your finger—"

"Please tell me you aren't thinking of making me do that."

"No! No, of course not. I'm just wondering."

"It would hurt. A lot. I'd most likely end up with a small amount of self-contained gas. It wouldn't be solid, but it wouldn't go anywhere, either."

We went back to chewing and then, satiated with saturated fat, decided it was time to dance.

"Surprise number two," he said with a grin, and took a small sphere out of his bag.

"What are they?"

"Speakers," he said with a grin. He scanned through his IPod until he found some classical music. "A waltz?" he suggested.

Starting at the beginning seemed like a good idea. I nodded.

"When did you learn to dance?" he asked. "It isn't exactly an activity for an introvert."

"No, it's not," I admitted. "My dad made me learn when I was a kid. He said it was an important thing for kids in the diplomatic corps to learn, for social events. I hated it."

"You did? Then why do you want to do it now?" he asked, though I was pretty sure he already knew the answer.

"I *think*," I said, "that I wouldn't hate dancing with *you*."

"I'll try not to prove you wrong," he said, smiling. He held out his arms for me and I was in them in a second, as he very carefully laid one hand on my back and folded his other hand around mine. I maintained a discreet distance between us, still too shy to close the gap, although I desperately wanted to.

"Okay," I said. "Now, this is a three-step dance—"

"I think I remember the basics," he said, and, waiting for a break in the music, he nodded to me and we began to dance.

It was not like dancing with the clumsy, gawky boys in my "Intro to Ballroom" class. Not that he was Fred Astaire, but there was no awkwardness to his movements. And he actually led, which was a strange sensation, I had trouble following him, and he laughed as my feet stuck in the sand.

"I've read that dancing is all about trust," he said. "If I'm going to lead, you have to let go a little bit."

"That isn't easy for me."

"I know," he said. "But being strong doesn't mean you have to be in control every second."

I laughed, but I knew he was right. I breathed and relaxed, and then we were dancing together.

It was better than I'd imagined, being in his arms and moving synchronously. After we got the steps down, I looked up into his eyes, and he was beaming. We danced like that, staring into each other's eyes, for what felt like a tiny bubble of eternity. Until I felt cold water rush over my feet.

The tide had come in around us while we danced. We grabbed Will's things, running farther up the beach to avoid the rushing water, and collapsed into the sand, laughing as we held each other.

"When you do dance, I wish you a wave o' the sea, that you might ever do nothing but that," he said.

"Shakespeare?"

He nodded.

"That was amazing," I said, still breathless. "When did you learn to dance?"

He was quiet for a few seconds, and then let his hands fall from me. "That's a bit of a long story." He turned off the music. "I do need to tell you, though. You should know."

I scooted closer to him, nervous by how serious he'd become. He had never told me much about being human, other than that he was very lonely. I supposed I should have expected that there was more to the story.

"A long time ago, not long after I first arrived, I lived as much like a human as I could. I wanted the whole experience," he said.

"Is this when you were an artist?" I asked.

"Yes. I worked, and I tried to do everything other humans did, like dance. I had a home, and even friends."

He paused and I suspected what was coming. "And you were with someone?" I asked quietly.

He nodded. "Once. I don't want you to misunderstand; she did mean a great deal to me, but it wasn't love. And … when we were together … things didn't go so well." He looked away from me, but I could see the pain in his face.

"By together," I said slowly, "You mean ..."

"In flagrante delicto."

"Oh. *Really* together. Like, Biblically."

"Yes."

"What happened?" I asked. My voice grew quiet; this was a subject not terribly familiar to me. I felt even younger than usual.

He fixed his eyes on the ocean. "Well, it started off all right, but then—I, um, couldn't contain myself."

I managed to disguise my laugh as a cough. "Ohhhh," I said, patting his arm. "You know, I think that's a pretty common problem. I mean, you must have heard that guys—"

"No, no, no" he protested, but at least he was smiling now. He turned and looked at me at last. "Not that. That would have been normal, at least. I reverted. To my normal state. I told you that we can't maintain solid form when faced with any severe physical pain. It turns out, we also revert when faced with anything so intense that it overwhelms us. Human emotions are stronger than anything else I've ever felt. So, one second we were ... together, and then ..."

My mouth fell open. "Oh, God. She didn't know? What you were?"

"No. I never told anyone before. No one but you has ever known the truth. So there we were, together, and suddenly I vanished, and when she looked up for me, there was only a mist."

"What did she do?"

"She screamed, and she ran. I was terrified—I'd never reverted unintentionally before, and I didn't realize what was happening to me. I almost dispersed completely before I understood what was going on; I was lucky I survived. I couldn't re-integrate, so there was nothing I could do except to run and hide. I went looking for her afterward, but she had told everyone that I was a demon. She even spent some time in a mental institution. I felt horrible about that. I never saw her again."

"I'm so sorry," I said softly. "That must have been awful. Is that when you stopped trying to be with people?"

He nodded. "That's when I realized that it wasn't worth it. If I couldn't be honest, everything that happened between me and everyone else in my life was simply a lie. I was just an actor, not a real friend, or a lover. What was the point? I was better off being alone."

We were both quiet for a long time. I was so sad for him, having spent so many years— no, decades—alone. It hurt to think about it. Finally, I asked the one question I couldn't get out of my mind.

"Do you regret it?" I asked. "Being with her. I mean, I know it ended badly, but at least you got to see what it was like."

His eyes were thoughtful. "Yes." He paused and reached for my hand. "I regret it. I wanted the experience, to feel close to someone. To know what it was like to experience that, as a human. And I did care about her, but it wasn't love. The intimacy wasn't real, and I can't take it back. Given how things worked out, it looks like it won't be something I'll get to experience again, so I'm left with this one flawed memory. And it hurts."

My heart ached for him. I knew that, as a human, he had the same desires, the same needs as any other man. What must it be like to know that sex, that ultimate level of physical intimacy, wasn't possible for him? I'd read that the average

142

human male thinks about sex every five minutes. I wondered if those thoughts tormented him constantly as well.

But he hadn't always been human. "Weren't you ever with any of your own people? Before you were human?"

"We don't really have anything like sex. Well, the Livan do, but they view sex as pretty much only for reproduction. Eolians merge with one another in our natural form, but it isn't really a selective process. It's how we all interact with each other."

"How do you—you know—reproduce?"

His expression was pained. "We don't, actually. At least not anymore."

"I don't understand. You said you were young."

"I am young," he said. "I'm one of the last Eolians to be born on Meris. You see, I told you that when we take another form, there are some inherent risks. We might forget things, for example. And that's what happened to us. When we became solid, we forgot how to reproduce. The minds of the Livan, the first solid beings we emulated, were not sophisticated enough to understand the process, and we lost it."

I was stunned. "You forgot—how? Didn't you realize it was happening?"

"Not until it was too late," he said. "We're a long-lived species, and we don't reproduce often. By the time we realized what was happening, there wasn't a single Eolian left that hadn't taken a Livan form. The only ones to be born after that were the ones who were still fetal at the time of the colonization. I was one of those. "

"Can't you reproduce in solid form?"

He shook his head. "It just doesn't work for us. We're a dying race, Cara. In another ten thousand years, there won't be any of us left."

"Oh, Will," I said sadly. "I'm sorry."

"Don't be," he said, and he took my hand in his. "I don't think there's an Eolian alive who would give up the ability to transform, to take solid form, even knowing what it would mean for us. We're still hopeful that our scientists will come up with a way for us to be able to bear children again. There's always hope."

"Yes," I agreed. "There's that, at least."

We sat quietly holding hands while Will's eyes focused somewhere far away. "I promised you ice cream," he said.

"You already gave me a cannoli."

"That's true, but ..." he trailed off. He turned his face away and swallowed hard, and I could see the edges of a dark cloud forming in his face. I felt my chest tighten.

I threaded my fingers through his. "Come on," I said. "Let's go find you something that tastes like flowers."

He closed his eyes and leaned his forehead against the side of my face. "How ..." He shook his head. "You're wrong, you know." He leaned in closer, resting his free hand on the back of my neck. "You're the amazing one."

We sat on the patio outside of Vivoli's, my favorite gelato place, and shared a scoop of orange-chamomile with pink spoons. The patio was empty except for us, and we watched the back-to-school shoppers walk up and down the street with their bags on the opposite side of the sidewalk. The sight of them made me depressed, as I realized that the school year was really underway now, which meant my teachers would be ramping the homework up soon. My last days of freedom were ending, and I could see the minutes slipping away from me like leaves on the wind. I poked the table with my spoon so hard it snapped in half.

"What's wrong?" he asked, reaching out to take my hand. "Is it what I told you before, about my past? Does it bother you?"

I shook my head. "That's not it. Not really, anyway. I'm just thinking that school's started, and I'm going to be miserable, and I'll never see you."

"Oh," he said, stroking my hand with his fingertip. "Is that it? Well, I hardly think they're torturing people over at the high school. You'll be fine."

I looked at him sadly, and he laughed. "And you'll still be able to see me whenever you'd like. Most of the time."

"At least until you start getting embarrassed by me," I muttered under my breath.

"What? Because of your age? From my perspective, the difference between seventeen and twenty-two is hardly more than a microsecond. It's meaningless to me."

"That's only part of it," I said. "You're gorgeous."

He shook his head. "Cara, this is a mask. I only look this way because I chose it."

"Exactly. So you can't tell me that you don't value beauty, because if that were true, you wouldn't have picked this," I said, gesturing at his face.

"In the first place," he said, flipping my hand over to caress my palm, "I chose this because I've discovered that physical beauty opens a lot of doors in this world. And in the second place, you *are* beautiful. Heartbreakingly so."

I pulled my hand away. "Don't do that, please. It only makes it worse than it already is."

He looked at me quizzically then, as if I'd said something that didn't make sense. He reached out and put his hand under my chin, bringing my face up to look at him. "What happened to you?" he asked.

My eyes were stinging, which only made me feel more embarrassed, and I was sorry I'd brought it up at all. This was not something to cry about. I refused to cry about it. I looked away and bit my lip.

"Someone told you that once, and you believed it," he said.

I pulled away from him. "It doesn't matter. This is stupid. I need to go home, anyway."

"No," he said firmly. "I won't let you run away this time. It *does* matter because it's making you unhappy." He pulled his chair around the table so that he was sitting right next to me.

"Tell me what happened," he urged.

I didn't want to tell him. It was stupid, and embarrassing, and more embarrassing because it still upset me so much. "I really don't want to."

"You don't want to, but I think you need to," he said. "It couldn't possibly be any worse than the things I've told you."

I could see he was not giving this up, and dragging it out only made me feel more ridiculous. Better to get it over with and hope he didn't think any less of me afterward. "I'll tell you," I said, not looking up at him. "But you're just going to laugh at me when you hear how stupid it is." I glanced at him, but he just looked at me expectantly. "When I was thirteen, right before we moved to Sumatra, I went through this phase where I really wanted to be more grown-up. I wanted to be beautiful, like my mother. I made her take me out and buy me a bunch of fancy clothes, and dresses, and jewelry, and I started dressing up for school, and trying different things with my hair. Stuff like that."

"Sounds like most girls that age," he said. "So what happened?"

"Well, there was this one boy, Andrew Rollins, he sat behind me in English class, and one day when I went to sit down he turned to the guy sitting next to him, and he said *Cara's just one of those girls that thinks she's pretty, but she's not.* And I realized he was right. I was so embarrassed that I'd been making a fool of myself that I went home and packed up all my new clothes, and everything else, and just went back to the way I was."

Will exhaled sharply, and I looked up to see that his eyes were closed and he was muttering some choice four-letter words under his breath.

"I told you it was stupid," I said, as he looked back to me.

"You're right. It was stupid that you believed him then, and even stupider that you still believe him. You really don't know why he said that?"

"Because I'm not very pretty," I said, shrugging. "It's not the end of the world."

He slapped his hand on the table so hard the couple walking by with a Pottery Barn bag stopped and stared. "No!" he said. "Get rid of that right now. He wanted to tear you down, that's all. And it worked. He was just some screwed-up, little snot-nosed kid, and you believed him! But why do you *still* believe him?"

I couldn't answer.

"Cara, if you had any idea what I feel every time I look at you, we wouldn't even be having this conversation. You are exquisite. The first time I saw you on the rocks at Half Moon

Bay, I thought I was having some kind of vision. So you think, what, that you should look like all those other dime-a-dozen girls who are all trying their best to be carbon copies of one another, too afraid to stand out? *Why*? You are beautiful because you *don't* look like them; you have your *own* beauty. You just can't see it because you have this ridiculous voice in your head that keeps telling you otherwise."

I chewed my lip and tried to pretend my eyes weren't filling with tears. He watched me for a long time before he spoke again.

"This was around the time Liv left, wasn't it."

I looked down at the ground. "Right before that, yeah."

He groaned very softly, so quietly I almost missed it. "Human beings have a remarkable talent for kicking each other when they're already down, don't they?"

I nodded. "I just … I just wanted …"

"You just wanted someone to love you. And he made you feel like you didn't deserve that. He was wrong, Cara. You do deserve it."

He shook his head and reached into his back pocket, pulling out a small, black book.

I tried to ignore my quavering voice. "What is that?" I asked.

"My journal," he said. "I've kept one, on and off, since I became human. It helps me, sometimes, to write things down. I never planned to show it to you, but maybe you need to see it." He flipped through the pages until he found the one he wanted, and handed it to me.

I looked down at the page; it was marked "August 15." The day after I'd moved in with Liv. The day we'd met at the beach.

I looked up at him and he nodded at me. "Read it."
I read it.

August 15

Year 64, day 154

Forms: Two

I went to the sea searching for death.

Instead I found kindness. Beauty. For fifteen minutes, a friend.

I know I will never see her again, the goddess with the windblown hair and eyes like the night. Who ever dreamed that such a creature could exist? She looked at me, and saw not a stranger, not an alien, but simply a man in pain. I cannot stop thinking of her, her lovely brow creased by worry. For me. For me! As if I am real.

I will go back to Kleeman. I will endure a little longer. Somewhere, there is a goddess with a face like heaven and a filthy car who, for a quarter of an hour, was my best friend in this world. I will pretend that she thinks of me, too. That I am her friend. Oh, that I could be.

But she exists. That's enough. I will go on.

I reflexively turned the page and saw my name.
"The rest are all about you," he said quietly.
I closed the book and looked up at him, my heart stuttering. "Why?"

"I think you know why." When I didn't answer, he continued, his voice very soft. "I needed to give a voice to the things I was feeling. To make sense of them." He put his journal back in his pocket and reached for my hand. "You see now?"

I nodded. The tears were spilling over my eyelids, and I didn't know what to say. I reached for Will and he pulled me onto his lap and held me close. It was warm, being in his arms. And safe. I felt something stir deep inside me, and I realized it was hope.

"You are real," I said, sniffling. "And you have terrible handwriting."

He laughed and pulled me closer. "I'll try to be neater next time."

"No," I whispered. "It's perfect."

The Journal of Will Mallory

Reading the works of Confucius today, I came across this:

If language is not correct, then what is said is not what is meant; if what is said is not what is meant, then what must be done remains undone

And I wonder, with increasing frequency, whether the limitations of language make true understanding among humans impossible. Can a true understanding ever take place when communication is so imprecise? When one can never take at face value the words of another? Perhaps this is the heart of true friendship: a promise never to lie.

She saw my home today, or what passes for it these days. I didn't expect to be so self-conscious of my living space, of how empty and sterile it was. It was so pathetic I could hardly bear for her to look at it.

I contrast my empty, cold apartment with Cara, so full of life it practically bursts from her. Her calloused hands, with nails that are never entirely clean. The brightness inside her that makes each new discovery shiny and new and hopeful.

I find that I've come back to the work again, to my real purpose, understanding humanity. Only now, everything comes back to Cara.

I look at her, and I wonder what it is that draws me in. All her features are just a fraction too large for her face, and the effect gives her

151

a kind of otherworldly beauty. Her eyes, overlarge and so dark that at first I thought they were entirely black, are completely at odds with the current fetish for light eyes among her people. Yet something inside me seems to recognize her kind of beauty instinctively, wanting to see more, wanting more images of her imprinted inside me. It's a strange kind of hunger that humans have for beauty. It's something for which I appear to have no immunity.

I've fallen down the rabbit hole, and I never want to stop. She's made me remember who I used to be, when the universe was filled with the promise of endless wonders.

Chapter Twelve

Bob

It was a few days later when I sat in Bio, thinking that I was going to get to see Will again after school. It made it hard to concentrate, and as I waited for class to start, I closed my eyes and tried to think about meiosis instead of Will's hands. Or his arms. Or his face.

Gah.

I leaned back on my stool, and Molly looked at me and squealed.

"Ohmigod, what is in your hair?"

Crap. There was something there; I could feel it moving. I stuck my fingers through my hair to see what it was, and it squished, barely. *Oh, God.*

"What is it?" I hissed.

"I don't know. A caterpillar?"

"Could you get it out, please? I can't see it."

She reached out and then pulled her hand back. "I can't. It's too gross."

"Too gross?"

"Yeah, it's got all these giant spiny things. Do you think it might sting?"

"Just. Get. It. Out."

She didn't move. I turned and looked at the guy at the table behind us. Matt. Something. I think. "Can you do something about this?"

He didn't look overwhelmingly happy, but I guessed he figured he'd lose his guy cred if he wimped out. I felt him carefully working the caterpillar out of my hair, and then he set it on the table.

"Dude," he said. "That's like the mother of all caterpillars. It's like the Darth freaking Maul of caterpillars."

He wasn't wrong. It was huge—bigger around than my finger, and twice as long. And bright blue, with a half a dozen red horns sticking out from the top of its body. It did look like the kind of thing that might sting. A lot. "I've seen these before," I said. "We had them in Virginia. I can't remember the name."

It thrashed on the table, angry about being handled so much. Ms. Maliki, who had just entered the room, came and stood next to me.

"You found him!" she said. "We've been looking for him for days."

"What is it?" asked Molly.

"A Hickory Horned Devil. The largest caterpillar in North America. My sister lives in North Carolina and brought these in for my freshmen to look over while she was here last week. This one got out."

"Do they bite?" asked Molly.

"Nope. Impressive, though, isn't he?"

"He's amazing," I said, watching him crawl across my notebook. "I didn't know they got so blue."

"He's in his final instar," she said. "He'll be pupating soon. I guess I'll have to take him home. I can't very well mail him to North Carolina."

I watched the giant blue caterpillar, looking every bit his name, crawling toward Molly, who pulled her stool back from our lab table and squeaked. "I'll take him," I said.

"Are you sure? He won't be eating any more, but you'll have to have a safe place for him to overwinter. They pupate underground."

"I've got some potting soil at home."

"Great, Cara. I've got a leftover terrarium. The freshmen are raising anoles this quarter."

Molly gave me an odd look. "What, are you going to keep him as a pet?"

I picked him up and set him inside the little glass box Ms. Maliki handed to me. "I just think he's cool," I said. "Plus, this way maybe I'll get to see him transform."

"You should totally give him a name," Matt-Something suggested. "How about Dragonslayer, or Skullcrusher?"

Molly gave him a disgusted look. "Do you do *anything* besides play *World of Warcraft*?" She looked at the caterpillar, a little less freaked out now that he was safely behind glass. "Is it a male or a female?"

"No way to tell until it reaches the moth stage," Ms. Maliki said. "The females are bigger."

I smiled as the caterpillar tried climbing the glass walls of the terrarium, getting halfway up only to slide back down again.

"Bob," I said.

That afternoon I sat doing my homework at the kitchen table, waiting for Molly to call. She'd asked me to talk her through some stuff for her lab report. Bob was climbing a twig inside his terrarium on the counter next to me, and I looked over at him and wondered what he was thinking. Caterpillars must

155

think about things, right? They do have some kind of rudimentary brain. I wondered if he knew it was almost time to burrow down into the ground and start his transformation.

Or maybe he was just pissed that he'd literally puked out his guts and couldn't eat anymore tasty leaves.

Blech.

I'd looked Hickory Horned Devils up after I'd come home from school. It takes them at least eleven months to pupate; virtually their entire lives. Bob would only have about a month as a caterpillar, and then a few days as a full-grown moth. I wondered what that was like—to spend more of your life becoming than being.

Or do they even know they're becoming, while it's happening?

He was already in his last instar; probably today or tomorrow he would burrow down into the ground and start his change. I wondered what that was like. Did it hurt? It must. How could it not?

I was still watching Bob when I noticed something small and gray scurry across the floor and under the table. I jumped up on my chair as soon as I realized what it was.

It was a rat. A big one. And it was looking at me.

Why wasn't it running away? Aren't rats supposed to do that?

I stared at it for a long time before I squatted down to get a better look. He didn't move.

"Will?" I whispered.

He stared back. I slid off my chair and got down on the floor next to him. "Is that you?"

He nibbled at my sock.

"You could have just called," I said. "Is everything okay?'

156

I stared into his beady little eyes and he stared back. I reached out and patted his soft fur.

I didn't see the broom coming until it was too late, and he squeaked in protest as it came down hard on top of him.

"Gotcha, you little disease vector!"

"Liv!" I screamed. "Stop it!" I wrenched the broom out of her hands and the rat scurried under the couch.

"What is *wrong* with you?" she shouted. "Do you want to get hantavirus? What were you doing, trying to play with it?"

"I—uh—no. I just didn't want you to hurt it. Do you think it's okay?"

She looked at me incredulously. "We've got to find you some friends."

I went over to the couch and started to pull it away from the wall.

"Have you totally lost it?" Liv said.

"I just want to see if it's hurt—"

"Cara, oh my God!"

I didn't see him on the floor back there, so I guessed he got away all right. I pushed the couch back against the wall while Liv started talking about traps. I wasn't listening all that carefully, but I'm pretty sure she also called me a psychopath. Then I heard my phone ringing in my room and I went to answer it.

"Hey," I said, flipping my phone open. "Sorry. So do you need me for this?"

I was greeted with a low laugh. "I always need you."

It was Will.

I threw up a little bit in my mouth.

"Um, were you just here?" I asked in a shrill voice.

"What? No, I'm at home. Why?"

I gagged, kicking off my rat-chewed socks and throwing them into the trash. "No reason."

I could hear the laughter in his voice. "What did you think I was?"

I was still dancing around the room, waving my hands in the air as if that could somehow rid me of rat cooties. "I'd rather not say."

"Oh, no." He laughed. "Did you want to get together?"

"Sure, but I need to shower first."

He picked me up outside my apartment building half an hour later. "Did you have anything in mind for today?"

I smiled at him. "I want to do nothing."

"Are you that tired from school already?"

I bit my lip, unable to say what I meant; it was just too embarrassing. I just wanted to be alone—just Will, and me, in a room, with no distractions.

He looked at me for a minute, and then shrugged. "All right," he said. "Where should we go to do nothing?"

"Your place?" I said hopefully.

"Okay," he said, pulling out of my parking lot. "I have a surprise for you in my freezer."

"That sounds like the best kind of surprise to me."

The surprise, as I had hoped, turned out to be a tub of chocolate ice cream. We ate it sitting on the couch, looking out the window at the people walking to and from their apartments. I was alone with the most amazing man on the planet, or, possibly, in the universe. The happiness practically oozed out of my pores.

"Oh," I said, setting my empty bowl on the coffee table. "I thought of another question for you."

"Hmm," he said, eating the last bite of his ice cream. "Okay. Go ahead. I hope it's a good one."

"Well, I was wondering, who was this?" I asked, gesturing at his face and body.

He looked a little surprised. "The actual human who looks like this? He was a college student in Maine. A chemistry major, I think. Oh, you'll be happy to know that he was actually a little younger than I'm pretending to be, he was just twenty. James Napolitano, if I remember right."

Napolitano. Italian, then. That explained the Mediterranean appearance. "Why did you choose him?" I asked.

"Well, I needed someone in his early twenties, who was intelligent and didn't have any congenital health problems, and I needed someone who couldn't be connected to McNair."

"And you wanted somebody good-looking," I pointed out.

"Well, I've been in this form for a while now, and you're the only one who's noticed so far," he said, grinning at me.

"Maybe you just weren't paying attention before."

"That's possible," he admitted. "Anyway, I was in Maine last, so I had one of my contacts pull some names for me, and when I saw him it seemed like a good fit."

That sounded reasonable. I had to admit that I did like his choice. "So have you always been, you know, male?"

He laughed nervously. "Mostly," he said, rubbing the back of his neck and looking up at the ceiling. "I've been a woman exactly twice. I was not very good at it."

"Really? Was it that different?" I asked, the age-old question.

"For me, yes, it was that different. Being a woman is more socially complicated than being a man. You can't get away with as much. It's like your mistakes stand out more, and, of course, I

159

still don't understand all the human social conventions, so I really made an ass out of myself. I found it exhausting." He looked down from the ceiling and grinned at me. "And there's the fact that I seem to be more drawn to women. I guess you could say that I love women, but I hate being one. So, mostly I've always been male."

I thought about that for a while. "There must be things about being a man that are harder."

He nodded. "Yes. Men are supposed to feel less."

"They don't?"

"No. Not at all. They just spend a lot of time hiding it. Or getting drunk to cover it up."

"I'm glad you don't do that."

He pursed his lips. "Who says I don't?"

I didn't really know how to answer that one.

I looked up into his eyes, and he leaned toward me, just a bit. We were sitting hip-against-hip, arm-against-arm, and my body was so tense I thought I might scream. I tried not to think about it.

"There's something else I've been wondering," I said. "Why me?"

"Why you?"

"Why did you decide to tell me the truth? You could have told anyone. You could have told Adeep, or the girl in New Orleans. Was it just because I was at the beach that day? Because I stopped you from …" I couldn't say "killing yourself."

He ran his fingers down the side of my face, and I leaned into his hand, loving the feeling of his touch. "You say *just* like it was nothing, what you did that day."

"It could have been anyone."

160

"No, it couldn't. You could have walked away while I was on the rocks, but you didn't. You could have driven away afterward without talking to me, but you didn't. I've never known kindness like that. Not in sixty-five years." He leaned in even closer. "You don't know how special you are. You see magic in a blade of grass. You see pain and you don't turn away. You're beautiful and clever and curious and warm." He traced the edge of my ear with his finger. "You see magic everywhere because you *are* magic. It was always going to be you. I never wanted anyone else."

I blushed and looked down at my feet, but he reached out and gently stroked my cheek.

"I love that," he murmured.

I laughed nervously. "You love that I embarrass myself?"

He smiled and held my face so that he could look into my eyes, moving still closer, and I could feel myself trembling. "I love that I can touch something in you. Knowing that I can affect you physically, make you blush—I can't explain it. It's amazing for me."

I carefully took his hand from my cheek and placed it against my chest, so that he could feel my heart thundering inside me. "That's hardly the only effect you have on me." I pressed his hand more firmly against me. "See?"

Now he was blushing as well. "Ah," he sighed, "you're like a hummingbird." He gently took his hand from underneath mine and moved it back to my face, and his own face was so close to mine that I could feel his soft breath. Carefully, slowly, he pulled me closer, closing his eyes as he did. I closed mine and felt his lips softy press against my own. It felt like a wave of electricity was flowing through me. He was so close, so beautiful, so gentle. I reached out for him, and as I slid my arms

161

around him I could feel his free hand slide to the small of my back, pulling me to him so that there was no longer any space between us. He kissed me again, less carefully this time. My heart beat even faster, and I tightened my grip on him, never wanting him to stop. Our lips moved together, and I could feel the raggedness of his breath.

"I love you," he whispered into my lips.

I almost couldn't speak. "I love you," I whispered back.

We clung to each other fiercely, as if the words we'd spoken had confirmed the rightness of what we were doing. His hands tangled in my hair as he kissed me, and I felt dizzy with feelings I didn't know I was capable of, as I lost myself in the taste of his mouth, in the warmth of his arms. I knew he was feeling the same way. He let out a quiet moan, and I felt his body stiffen. Then he gasped.

And then he was gone.

I opened my eyes, hurt, thinking he had pulled away, but he was nowhere to be seen. Then I saw it—saw *him*. In front of me floated what I could only describe as a mist. He was like a fog, except contained by an invisible barrier. He glowed, faintly. Beautifully. I reached out my hand, and was surprised when my fingers slid effortlessly into him. He was warm, and felt soft on my fingertips. I felt him shudder faintly when I touched him.

"Will?" I whispered. "Can you hear me?"

He swirled around my hand, and I took that as a yes. "I'm so sorry, Will."

He flowed around my entire body, and it felt like being caressed by a soft wind, like warm sea foam floating around me. Even this way, I could feel the tenderness in his touch.

"You're so beautiful," I whispered.

The tears were welling up in my eyes, but I didn't want to make this worse for him by falling apart. I cleared my throat before I spoke, hoping he wouldn't hear how close I was to crying.

"I'll write an e-mail to Dr. Kleeman for you," I said, trying to keep my voice even. I opened his laptop and quickly sent her a message from his e-mail account saying that he had the flu and would be out the rest of the week. I hoped that would be enough time.

I didn't know what else to say, and I didn't think I could hold myself together much longer. I had a feeling, somehow, that what Will really wanted was to be alone.

As I closed his apartment door and began my walk back to the bus stop, my tears finally began to fall. I knew it would be a long time before they stopped.

The next few days were mostly a waste. I thought about Will almost every minute, but I knew it would be a while before he could be human again, and I wasn't sure what we would do, now that it was so obvious what we couldn't have. Now that we'd admitted how badly we wanted each other, there would be no going back. We could never be "just friends" again.

I tried not to think about what it had been like to kiss him, but every time my mind wandered, that was exactly where it went, and I was back in his arms. Every time I closed my eyes, I could feel his touch on my lips, like a bruise that couldn't heal. But the ache in my heart was real.

When he still hadn't called after three days, I started to worry. I thought of asking Liv if she'd seen him on campus, but didn't feel like I was up for opening that particular can of worms on top of everything else. I decided to suck it up and call him, telling myself I just wanted to make sure he was okay. He didn't answer.

I couldn't stand it anymore, so I went back to his apartment that evening. I stood in front of his door, listening, but it was completely quiet. My heart sank. What if something had happened, and he wasn't able to make himself human again?

I knocked on the door, and there was silence for at least a minute. I reached out to see if it was locked, but as I extended my hand the door slowly swung open. I inhaled sharply when I saw Will standing in the doorway. He looked terrible—worse even than I'd seen him the first time we met, when he'd decided that life was not worth living anymore. He was pale, unshaven, and had dark circles under his eyes like he hadn't slept in a week. He looked at me, his eyes pained, and he opened his mouth but didn't speak.

"Will?" I said, my voice barely above a whisper. "Are you all right? I was worried, and I ..." my voice broke off, and I could feel the tears coming again. I was torn between wanting to throw myself into his arms and wanting to run away.

"Cara," he said softly, reaching out and gently wiping an escaped tear from my cheek. "I'm so sorry." I could hear the tears in his voice, and realized that he was suffering far more than I was. I felt like an idiot for being so selfish.

He took my hand and led me into the living room, which was a mess. I sat on the couch next to him and was grateful that he never let go of me.

"I'm more sorry than I can tell you, about everything. I didn't mean to worry you; I just didn't know if you would ever want to see me again after what happened before."

"Why?" I asked, "Why would you think that? I knew who you were, I mean, I was surprised, but it wasn't exactly a total shock."

He smiled faintly and squeezed my hand. "Still, though. There's a big difference between knowing something and actually seeing your boyfriend turn into mist in front of your eyes."

I looked away, trying to hide the fact that I couldn't help smiling. "Is that what you are? My boyfriend?'

He grinned back at me. "It seems like a ridiculous label, considering. Calling you my girlfriend is almost an insult."

That stung. "What do you mean?"

He shook his head. "You don't understand what this is like for me. I've been alone for so long, and even before that there was no one, really, no one like you. There was never anyone who came close. You mean more to me than I can tell you, and when I tried to show you ..."

"Poof," I said quietly, letting my hands curl up against his chest.

"Poof," he agreed, but his face was sadder than I'd expected. "Maybe this isn't what you want. What happened before—the 'poofing' as you so eloquently put it—that isn't something I can fix. I can't be with you the way a real man could be."

"You *are* a real man. You're just different," I said, moving closer so that I could lean against him. "It's okay. It's enough for me, just to be with you."

He put his arm around my shoulder, and I leaned farther into him. "I'm not sure it will be enough for me," he said.

I didn't say anything then. The truth was that I knew that ultimately it wouldn't be enough for me, either, but I would

165

rather be with him, in this restricted way, than not be with him at all. I suspected he knew that, but it would just hurt him if I said it out loud. Still, there was one question that I couldn't help asking.

"So was it worth it?" I whispered.

He laughed. "Oh, yes. Yes, yes, yes, a thousand times, yes. I'd kiss you again right now, if I wasn't pretty sure it wouldn't take me six months to re-integrate again so soon."

He did kiss me again. This time was more careful than the last, and I made sure not to press myself too close to him. My heart was still racing, and as I felt his breath coming faster, he pulled away. "This is going to be harder than I thought," he said, and laughed.

I laughed, too, but the pain in his eyes was terrible.

The Journal of Will Mallory

I don't know if anything has ever hurt more than having my humanity torn away at the moment I finally felt most human.

I do feel human now. I have to admit that. I am, for the first time, finally understanding how physical the human experience is, and how exhilarating it is to be aware of your own body and the world around it. I feel like I'm on some sense-enhancing drug, and every smell, every taste, every whispered word, every tentative caress seeps down through my skin and into my blood.

I want all of it now, the entire experience. I long for physical love. For a family. Amazing how Cara has brought that out of me, made me face it. I can't hide it any longer, from her or from myself.

I'm pulled apart by what I want and my own limitations, and I have to accept that those limitations might be permanent. I fantasize a hundred mundane scenarios: making Cara breakfast while she reads in our bed, painting her while she pulls weeds in our garden, teaching our children to swim in the sea. I don't know why I can't stop thinking of these things, if it's just because I can't have them, or something more. Eolians have youth but no childhood; closeness but no love. And on Meris there will be no one waiting for me with hopeful eyes or warm arms.

Adeep and I are progressing in our project; it turns out that what I needed all along was a chemist, even if he remains convinced that we're simply generating some new catalyst for Kleeman's research. As we move on, I've become uneasy about the work we're doing. I fear what it might lead to: a choice I'm not ready to make.

Is it better to live half the life I truly desire, or to live fully the life that's possible—the life I was born to?

Chapter Thirteen

The Elephant in the Bio Department

My mother came back from Virginia not long after that, and the next few weeks were not entirely pleasant. Even when Liv wasn't busy with classes she was making up a string of increasingly convoluted excuses to stay out of the house and I barely saw her. I had no such luxury. I had almost no time for Will beyond our after-school meet-ups, and I wondered if he thought I was deliberately avoiding spending time with him.

We were having a characteristically awful afternoon; Liv was reading, as usual, and I was attempting to make dinner using the crock-pot that my mother bought us after she realized how much pizza we were consuming. Mom was spending the day with some acquaintances in San Francisco, and I'd offered to cook for us that night, so we wouldn't have to go out again. I was worried that my attempt at minestrone would fail to meet with her approval and was making some garlic bread to go with it.

"What are you reading about?" I asked.

Liv didn't bother looking up from her book. "Biological ice nucleators."

"Huh?"

"Cloud bacteria. They make it rain."

"Oh."

"God, it's a mess in here." She slammed her notebook shut and began rifling through her papers. She grabbed a book out of the pile and held it up to me.

"Can you keep your existentialist garbage away from my work?" She asked, holding my copy of *Waiting for Godot* by the corner, as if it might be contaminated with something toxic.

'"Oh, sorry," I said. "I was reading in there last night. I guess it got mixed in with your stuff. Just put it on the table and I'll get it when I'm done."

She flung the book at the kitchen table so hard it slid off the end and almost knocked over one of the chairs.

"Geez!" I exclaimed, slamming my knife down on the cutting board. "Don't take this out on me. None of this is my fault."

"She never visited before you came here," she said, glowering. "Not once."

"I'm sorry my presence is forcing you to be involved in our fabulous family psychodrama," I said. "What exactly would you like me to do about it?"

"Nothing," she muttered. "I'm going to my office. I can't get anything done here."

"You can't go now, she'll be here in an hour!"

"I don't give a damn. I can't put my life on hold for her anymore. Tell her I have work to do and I'll see her tomorrow." She stuffed several books into her backpack and stormed out the front door, leaving me speechless.

Our mother arrived punctually at six o'clock. I greeted her with as much enthusiasm as possible, in the hopes that she might not care Liv was absent. I shouldn't have bothered.

"Where is your sister?" she demanded, after I showed her my watery excuse for soup.

"Um, well, she had a lot to do. She's so busy with school, you know. She went to campus to get some stuff done, so we'll have fun without her. We never have mother-daughter alone time. It'll be great." My smile was so fake it hurt my face.

The look on her face was almost a sneer. "Nonsense. You went to all this trouble; the least she can do is show up. She learned this from your father."

"Really, it's just soup," I said. "It's not a big deal."

"It *is* a big deal. What's the phone number there?" she asked, picking up the phone.

"Mom, please don't bug her, she needs a break—"

"Give me her number, Cara."

I gave it to her, knowing I would pay for it later. No one answered the phone, and my mother slammed it down on the receiver.

"Get your shoes on," she said. "We're going to campus."

"No," I said, shocked that she would take it that far. "Please, Mom. Don't."

But my mother had made up her mind, and there was no stopping her. I briefly considered staying home and out of the huge fight that was about to erupt, but I was worried things might get worse without me there as a referee. We climbed into her rental car and drove the ten minutes to campus in complete silence.

As we walked down the hall to Liv's office, my mother paused briefly, and I hoped that she was changing her mind.

"Is there a drinking fountain here? I'm parched," she said.

"Yeah, just down the hall." No sense starting a screaming match with a dry throat.

I continued down the hall, hoping to give Liv a warning, and automatically opened her door without knocking.

171

There, half lying on her desk, was my sister, locked in what is referred to in polite company as a passionate embrace with Dr. Yarrow. Or Steve, as I guessed I'd better start thinking of him. They didn't hear me open the door, and during the tenth of a second as I stood there, helpless, things were already starting to progress at an alarming pace. I quickly backed out of the room and slammed the door as hard as I could.

"Mom," I called, much too loudly considering that she was now ten feet from me, "I found her!" I hoped my sister had enough sense to pay attention and stop what she was doing. Otherwise, things were about to get very, very ugly. I wished I could transform into someone else and escape.

My mother gave me a withering glare and then opened Liv's door. Liv was sitting at her desk, and Steve was on the other side of the room, holding a strategically-placed stack of books.

"Oh, hi, guys," Liv said perfectly calmly, though she was unable to control the flush that had spread across her face. At least her shirt was on the right way. "Sorry I had to skip out on dinner, but I had tons of work to catch up on. This is Dr. Yarrow, my adviser. Dr. Yarrow, this is my mother, Claudia Gallagher, and you've met my sister."

Steve cradled his books in one arm and reached his hand out to my mother, who shook it coldly. "It's nice to meet you, Ms. Gallagher. Liv is a great student. We really enjoy having her in the department."

"Yes, I'm sure you do," my mother said icily, and Liv's color deepened further. Steve tried to hide it, but the look of mortification on his face was unmistakable.

"Dr. Yarrow, would you mind terribly if I had a minute to speak with my daughter?" my mother asked, and I knew things were coming to a head. I felt sick to my stomach.

"Of course. It was good to see you again, Cara," he said, nodding at me. "I'll see you tomorrow, right Liv?"

"Sure," Liv said.

After he left, my mother shut the door and then turned back to my sister. "What exactly do you think you're doing, Olivia?"

"I beg your pardon?" Liv responded calmly. When she'd lived at home, Liv had always deferred to our mother, though grudgingly. But she'd been on her own for the last five years, out from under Mom's thumb. It suddenly occurred to me that the storm I was watching was a long time in coming.

"Don't patronize me," my mother said. "I'm not an idiot. I thought you were smarter than this, Liv. I thought you had learned from my mistakes."

"You mean, learned from watching you torture Dad for eighteen years?"

"How dare you," Mom said, and her face was red now as well. She was beginning to quiver with rage. "Don't presume to understand my relationship with your father. You have no idea what I went through with him."

"Oh, I think I have a pretty good idea, actually," Liv said, and I could see that her hands were shaking. "You never kept much to yourself over the years. No one made you marry him, Mom! I don't know why you did it in the first place."

"I didn't have a choice." Mom was practically screaming, and I realized that Liv had pushed a button I hadn't known was there. "I was pregnant!"

I was shocked. I knew, of course, that Liv had been born nine months after my parents' anniversary, but I always just assumed she was a honeymoon baby. Liv, on the other hand, did not look all that surprised. Apparently it was just me who had been a fool all this time.

Liv did not respond, but Mom wasn't finished, anyway. "Look at you! Having an affair with your professor? Where do you think this is going to lead?"

"I fail to see how this is any of your business," Liv said impassively. I wondered how she was staying so calm; usually Mom's outbursts set her over the edge. Her hands were now firmly clasped together to keep them from trembling.

"Because I care about you, Liv. I don't want to see you throwing your life away. What if you want to break up with him, but he tries to sabotage you? Or, if you don't, what do you think is going to happen after you finish school? You won't be able to get a job here—you'll have to leave to start your career. Is he going to give up teaching at McNair to go with you? Of course not. Are you going to give everything up to stay with him? You've worked too hard for that."

"You're overreacting, Mom. Don't presume to know what choices I'm going to make. I know what I'm doing with my life."

"Your entire future is at stake!" Mom shouted, slamming her fist down on Liv's desk.

They were now three feet apart, and a contrast in temperaments—my mother red with rage, and Liv still eerily calm.

"You know what?" Liv replied. "I don't have to listen to you anymore. I don't live under your roof. You don't pay my tuition. I don't have to sit here and listen to you have a tantrum

174

because you can't control my life since you screwed yours up. So you can go now."

Mom was speechless, and so was I. I wondered how long Liv had been rehearsing that particular speech.

"Fine," Mom said, finally. "Cara, come with me. We'll go pack your things."

"What?" I said. "What are you talking about? I just started school!"

"Then you can start again in Virginia next week. I've decided that we're moving back."

My shoulders began to shake. "You can't do that, Mom. Please."

"You're going to punish me by taking Cara away?" Liv said, and her voice quavered. "You can't do that."

"I can take her, and I will. She needs an adult to look after her. She never should have come here in the first place. Neither of you is mature enough to have made this work."

I felt like I'd been slapped. Hadn't I always looked out for myself, even when I'd lived at home? My schoolwork, my plants, it had all been me, a hundred percent.

"Mom," I said, "Please, I want to stay. I like it here."

She ignored me. "Let's go, Caroline."

Then I remembered the only thing that would give me a reprieve.

"I'm taking the SATs on Saturday," I said. "It's my last chance to take them and still get my college applications in on time."

"Fine," she said. "You have until Sunday."

My head spun. I needed more time than that—time to do what, I didn't know. Talk her out of it? Find some kind of a loophole that would save me? I just knew I couldn't leave. "I'd—

175

I'd like to get some letters of recommendation. From a few of my teachers."

"Fine!" She shouted. "You have until Tuesday morning. Whatever loose ends you think you need to tie up, they'd better be settled by then."

She opened the door and glared at both of us. "I'll be by to pick you up on Tuesday morning. Make sure you're packed by then.

She walked out the door without another word.

I sank down into a chair and burst into tears. Liv came and crouched next to me, putting her arms around me so that I could bawl on her shoulder.

"I'm sorry, Cara. We'll fix this. I'm so sorry."

"No," I said between sobs. "It's not your fault. It's just—everything's breaking apart!" And it was true: first my parents, and then my mother and Liv. And now she was taking me away from everything I loved most. Away from Liv. And, oh God, away from Will. How could I leave now, just when everything was finally perfect? I felt like I was falling and wondered if it would ever stop.

When we got home, Liv unplugged the crock-pot and ordered a pizza. We ate together in the living room, but neither of us spoke until after dinner, as we lay on opposite sides of the couch with our feet resting on each other's legs.

"You can't imagine how guilty I felt, leaving you alone with her when I left for college," Liv said.

I closed my eyes and tried not to cry again. It was something I didn't like to think about, the time after she'd gone. I'd never understood, until that point, exactly how much she'd been protecting me all those years. The way she would forcibly drag me off to the library, despite my protests, even at eight o'clock at night. Or to the movies, or to Starbucks—anyplace that wasn't home. It wasn't until she'd left that I'd realized that she had a sixth sense for when a fight was brewing, and that she was getting me out of the house before it erupted. That she picked me up from school so I wouldn't have to be alone in the car with my mother, her favorite venue for picking at my faults, since she knew I couldn't escape. That she would scrape my leftover dinner onto her plate every night so that I wouldn't be yelled at for wasting food. I never understood why she did any of it, or the thousands of other little things she did to protect me from our mother's perpetual anger, to try to give me a chance to be happy.

Then one day she was gone.

I'd cried every day for a month after she'd left. My mother would catch me and threaten to drag me to a shrink, or make me take medication, as if that were the most terrible punishment she could think of. My friends seemed to recognize that something was wrong, and they tried to help. The girl across the street invited me for sleepovers every few days. That helped, having friends. I'd had friends back then. It was only later that they were gone, too. Because, of course, two months later we'd moved again. And then I was *really* alone.

That was our move to Sumatra, which my mother despised. My one boon, that I'd begged from my father as soon as our things were moved into the new house, was a small greenhouse in the backyard, which became my sanctuary. That was where I'd grown my first orchid, purple and frilly and perfect. I never showed it to anyone.

I looked up at Liv, who was regarding me quietly. "It wasn't your fault," I said. "You had to go."

"I know." She shifted her weight and laid her cheek against the back of the couch. "What are you thinking?"

"Nothing," I said. "I'm just sad."

"I know. Me too, I guess." Then she looked at me hard. "And what else?"

I knew she was trying to take my mind off the thing with our mother, but I couldn't deny that there was definitely a *what else*. Well, she *had* asked. "Um, I'm a little grossed out about you and … Steve."

She laughed, but her face was tired. "Okay. Get it all out there."

"What is he, like, forty?"

"Thirty-eight, actually."

"Isn't there a rule against this kind of thing?"

"Um, there is, actually," Liv said seriously. "He could get in a lot of trouble."

"Well, I'm not the one you have to worry about spilling the beans."

"Oh," Liv groaned. "Oh, no. Mom. She wouldn't. Yes, she would. Oh, I'm screwed."

"Maybe you should try to be more discreet for a while," I suggested. "You know, avoid doing it on your desk."

"We weren't—wait, how much did you see?" Liv said, horrified.

"Too much," I said with a laugh. "I'm still trying to erase the mental image."

"Maybe you need to learn to knock."

"Okay, but still. That was just stupid."

Liv groaned again and buried her face in her hands.

"Doesn't it bother you at all? The age difference?" I asked.

"No, it doesn't," she said. "He's amazing. He's brilliant and funny and sexy," I grimaced at the last word, and she kicked me. "And he really likes me."

"Of course he does. You're twenty-two."

She kicked me again.

"Do you worry at all about what Mom said? That you'll end up giving up too much for him?" I asked.

"It's way too early for that. I'm going to be in school for three more years at least. After that, who knows? I'm not going to waste time worrying about that. I just want to be happy."

"Are you in love with him?"

"Too early," Liv said. "I'll tell you when I know."

"We'll throw you a party," I said.

"Good. Have ice cream."

I was happy for her, really. Liv hadn't dated in high school, and if there had been anyone special in college, she hadn't told me about it. She was as frightened of the opposite sex as I was. I sincerely hoped that Steve would be good for her, and that he wasn't just using her as some kind of grad-student trophy. But really, how different was this from my relationship with Will? Who, after all, was old enough to be Steve's distant ancestor. And wasn't even human.

This would have been the perfect opportunity to tell her about Will, but I'd had enough drama for one day. I yawned and thought about going to bed.

"Go to sleep," Liv said, smacking my leg lightly. "I'll call Dad in the morning and straighten everything out."

I untangled myself from Liv's legs and struggled to my feet. "Okay. Goodnight."

"Cara, all we need is a letter from Dad telling the school not to dis-enroll you and extending my guardianship until you turn eighteen. She's not going to bother dragging this to court—by the time it gets anywhere, you'll be too old. We just have to tie it up for another month."

I nodded.

"Everything really is going to be okay."

"I believe you," I said. And I did. Mostly.

But when I got up the next morning, nothing was okay.

My father's cell phone was turned off, and his inbox was full. How was that possible? So I tried calling him at the embassy. He wasn't there.

He was on a three-week regional tour.

They wouldn't send me his itinerary.

"This is his *daughter*," I screamed at the man on the other end of the phone. "It's an emergency!"

"I'm sorry, but this is all confidential. If you leave me a message, I'll make sure he gets it as soon as he calls to check in."

"That isn't good enough!"

Liv grabbed the phone from me. "Listen to me, you mindless little bureaucratic automaton …"

Before she could say anything else, there was an audible "click" and Liv set the phone down.

"Well, that went well," she said.

"What am I going to do?"

"We'll keep trying. There has to be somebody we know at Dad's embassy."

Liv spent the next hour on the phone, running off a list of the names of all the people she could remember at State who might be in Latin America.

"Davies? Kendall? Rodriquez?" she said. "Ana Rodriquez? That's perfect. Transfer me to her."

Ana and her husband used to socialize with my parents in Northern Virginia. I listened as Liv explained, without giving away any details, that we had to find my father. She hung up and looked at me triumphantly. "He's in Costa Rica until Monday."

I left him a message at the embassy in San Jose, and then looked up at Liv. "What if he doesn't get it? He might not be at the embassy for a few days, if he's on some kind of a tour. Ugh!" I shouted, throwing my phone across the room. "Why didn't he take his stinking phone?"

"You know he always forgets it," she said, patting my shoulder. "He probably didn't want Mom to be able to call him."

"You're probably right about that," I said. "But Mom's dis-enrolling me next week."

"I'm sure he'll check his messages before that."

I wasn't.

I was almost in tears by the time I got to Will's apartment, and when he opened the door I stood there and sobbed.

"Cara!" he cried, pulling me close. "What happened?" He pulled me inside and shut the door, and stroked my back until I could speak. I told him everything; about the divorce, and about my mother wanting to take me away.

"But you'll be eighteen soon," he said.

"I know, but Murray's a magnet school. Once she dis-enrolls me, I'll lose my spot. I can't change schools three times my senior year—especially not in the first quarter when these grades count for colleges! Once she takes me out, that's it. I'll have to go back with her."

He let out a deep breath. "Why is she doing this?"

"She's mad about something she found out about Liv."

181

"I see." He didn't ask what that meant, and I wondered if he already knew. "What does Liv say?"

"She's hoping Dad will do something, but I can't reach him! He's in Costa Rica. If I wait for him to get back, it'll be too late."

"Could you fly down there? Talk to him face to face?"

I buried my face in my hands. "I'm taking the SATs tomorrow. And even if I weren't, if my mother found out I was gone, I'm not sure what she'd do."

He reached out and put his arms around me.

"I like it here," I said, burying my face in his chest. "This is the first place that's ever been mine. And ..." I couldn't continue. I dug my fingers into his shirt, full of the things I couldn't say.

He leaned away from me, wiping the tears from my face.

"Maybe she doesn't have to know you're gone."

I looked at him in confusion until he pulled a piece of my hair from behind my ear and ran it through his fingers. He smiled at me and raised his eyebrows.

My stomach flipped when I realized what he was suggesting. "Are you sure?"

He nodded.

We leaned toward each other conspiratorially. "How's your algebra?" I asked, sniffing away the last of my tears.

"Excellent."

"My passport says I'm seventeen."

"I can fix that. Do you need money?"

"I have my Dad's credit card."

"And if he flips out?"

"I have money left over from my nursery job last summer."

"You don't speak Spanish."

182

"I'll manage."

He pressed his forehead to mine. "I'll help you pack."

He drove me to the airport less than an hour later. I slid a lock of my hair into his hands, kissed him, and ran all the way to the gate.

Chapter Fourteen

The Feminine Mystique
(Will)

Liv was at work when I arrived at her apartment, so I was able to enter as myself. I reminded myself that Cara would be back Tuesday morning. For four days, I would have to pass myself off as a girl who was still nearly as mysterious to me as humanity itself.

I was terrified.

I walked into Cara's room, closed the door, and stood staring at her dresser.

Transforming is an odd sensation to describe. One second, you know what you are, and then you can feel the changes coursing through you like a giant wave. It's a somewhat uncomfortable experience, though not painful. I held the lock of Cara's soft hair in my hands and felt the wave move through me, and then the strange sensation of body parts where none had been previously.

I had never seen Cara naked before, though God knows I've thought about it. It didn't seem right, seeing her this way for the first time now, when it wasn't really her. I tried to remind myself of that. This was not Cara. It was just me.

That thought didn't help when I lifted my shirt over my head and felt the silk of her skin against my fingers. Was she always this soft, or were my new hands, softer and more delicate than my last ones, just more sensitive? I tried not to think about it. *Not Cara's body. Not Cara's body.*

Right. Oh, hell.

I was completely naked and looking up at the ceiling as much as possible, trying not to stare at the body that made me want to explode into a million pieces. I opened her underwear drawer and picked up the largest pair I could find, which, truth be told, did not seem nearly large enough. Without looking, I put them on, but they didn't seem to cover enough of me, and no matter how much I tugged at them, I still felt completely exposed. Maybe this is what women's underwear were like these days. I tried to remember that day that we had sat together in our underwear at Loch Lomond, the only time I had seen so much of her, but that just conjured up the image of Cara, slipping out of her sopping wet, perfectly clinging dress. Cara, half-naked in the golden sunshine. I shook my head to clear it. This was not helping me.

I slipped on a T-shirt, trying very hard to ignore the sensations this produced, but my underwear were still bothering me. Cara had a mirror on the back of her closet door. Surely, if I took a quick look just to make sure everything was in the right place, it wouldn't hurt. I walked over to it and looked.

It was the first of several mistakes.

The curve between a woman's waist and hips is something that is maddening to all human males of the heterosexual variety. I was no longer a human male, so there was no reason the sight of her slim waist, her perfectly shaped hips, her long legs should have had the effect on me that it did. I gasped and turned away, but it was too late. I could already feel myself losing control. I had to get out of that room—had to distract myself. I ran out into the hallway, vaguely, helplessly aware that I still had no pants on. I slammed my body against the wall. Hell, that hurt. Hurting was good. Pain was good because it was so much better than ... something else. I closed my eyes and smacked my head against the wall a few extra times for good measure.

Losing containment is a bit like realizing your entire body has suddenly gone numb. There is a split second when, if I feel it happening, I can pull myself together. Sometimes. It doesn't always work, especially if I'm feeling particularly overwhelmed. This time, I knew I was okay as soon as I was out in the hall. Still, I found myself getting more and more upset, and I couldn't understand the strange noises that were coming out of me.

Then I realized I was hyperventilating.

The front door slammed and Liv was with me in a second. "What is *wrong* with you?" she said, grabbing me by the shoulders and shaking me like a rag doll.

"I can't do this," I said, gasping for air. "I can't. It's too hard. She's too—I'm too—"

"She?" She said. "You mean Mom? What is it?"

I took a deep breath. Right. Mom. "I'm okay," I said with a hiccup. "I'm just worried about the thing with Mom."

"Yeah, I know. I've been calling Dad, too. We'll figure it out."

Then she looked at me again. "Where are your pants?"

"Uh—"

"Wait, where is your *bra*?"

Damn it.

I went back into Cara's bedroom and managed to stuff myself into a pair of jeans that seemed ridiculously tight on my legs. I remembered thinking Cara looked good in these, but how did she sit? And that wasn't the worst part. That came later, when I had to delve back into Cara's lingerie drawer, and I came up with what looked like a reasonable bra.

I could not hook it.

I found Liv in her room.

"What is it, dingbat?" she said.

"I'm having some trouble," I said. "With my bra."

"What, did you outgrow it? I told you to stop eating all that ice cream. If they get much bigger we're going to have to start using you as a flotation device."

I ran my hand over my face, not sure whether to laugh or cry. "No, I think it still fits. I just can't get it hooked right."

She stopped what she was doing and looked at me. "*What?*"

"I, um, hurt my hand."

She looked at me incredulously. "You're kidding."

I crossed my arms and glared at her. "Could you just help me?"

She rolled her eyes and lifted the back of my shirt and hooked the two sides of the bra together. I cursed the gods of women's clothing and went off in search of something useful to do.

I spent the next hour with one of Cara's old English tests, copying her essays over and over to get the hang of her handwriting. It made me feel closer to her, tracing the words she'd written with her own hand. I wondered where she was. I hoped she didn't do anything stupid. It was killing me to sit there, knowing she was out on her own, maybe in trouble.

But she needed me right where I was, so I copied out a few more lines in her slanted script.

187

Liv defrosted something that was meant to be a frozen lasagna, and I watched her pick at her dinner, trying to copy her mannerisms. I had never really looked at her carefully before; she was pretty, in her way, though not so much as Cara. Of course, no one would ever be as attractive to me as Cara. I knew that, but she had the same eyes, large and dark, that tilted up slightly at the corners. The same mahogany-colored hair. The same full lips. I looked away and cleared my throat, hoping she hadn't noticed me staring.

It took me a long time to go to sleep that night. Cara's bed was filled with her scent, and as I would start to drift off, my hair would brush my cheek or I would hear the sound of my breathing, and I would reach for her, thinking she was with me.

It didn't make sense, the responses I was having. It shouldn't have been possible—I wasn't even male anymore, let alone the man I'd been when I'd fallen in love in the first place. Why should I be turning myself on this way?

It was then that I began to have an uneasy feeling: Had my experiences in my old body, as Will Mallory, permanently altered my mind? That was known to happen—that we could be shaped by the minds we occupied when we mimicked another creature's DNA. Is that what was happening to me? Would my physical need for her follow me into every body I took from now on? Would I want Cara this way for the rest of my life?

Could I endure that?

I put my hands on top of the comforter to keep from accidentally touching myself in my sleep, and eventually I was out.

Chapter Fifteen

The Education of Will Mallory
(Will)

I was a groggy mess the next morning; I'd slept badly, and my midnight trip to the bathroom—during which I'd remembered too late that I could no longer use the toilet standing up—had not helped. I staggered into the bathroom and splashed some water on my face, and while I tried to figure out what that crusty substance was in my eyes (did Cara have this every morning?), Liv walked in wrapped in a towel.

"Uh, good morning," I said. Right. She was my sister. It was only normal for us to be in the bathroom at the same time.

"Unh," she grunted, and started the shower while I reached for my toothbrush.

I should have realized, right then, that this was my cue to leave the bathroom, never to return. Nothing good can ever come from sharing a bathroom with a woman. Even if that woman is, in theory, your sister. Only she isn't.

I was still heavily out of it, so I finished brushing my teeth, and was halfway through figuring out what to do with my hair—what in the hell is mousse? Do you eat it, or apply it to your head to grow antlers?—when Liv turned off the water.

"Oh, damn," she said. "Can you get me a clean towel? This one's all wet."

Could I get her a towel? Where the hell were the towels?

"Uh …" I stammered. "Where are they?"

There was a very long pause before she answered. "In the linen closet, genius. God, I hope you're sharper than this on your SATs."

Linen closet. Where was the linen closet?

"Oh forget it. I'll get it myself."

Before I could even shield the innocence of my eyes, she pulled back the curtain and I was assaulted with Full Frontal Liv.

My face may have melted off in horror.

I did the only thing I could. I fell flat on my ass.

I crabwalked backward out of the bathroom, trying to look anywhere but at Liv's glistening nudity. But She Kept Coming At Me.

"What is *wrong* with you?" she shrieked. "Are you on drugs? *Please* tell me this isn't drugs." I could tell her face was contorted in disgusted shock, since it was the only thing I could look at. "I'm fine!" I protested, scooting down the hall on my butt. "Really!"

She clapped her hand over her face. "Oh my God. People think I'm the weird one." Then she reached out and opened a door—the door, incidentally, directly across from the bathroom—and pulled out a towel. I sank down into the carpet, a puddle of overwrought Eolian, while she wrapped herself up.

"Am I still driving you this morning?"

I blinked. "Driving me?"

"TO TAKE YOUR SATs!"

Oh, right. That. I nodded, and scuttled off to my room to get dressed, grateful that my ordeal with Liv was over.

Or nearly over.

Because I still needed help with my bra.

190

Taking the SATs was not difficult for me. Not that it wasn't a long, tedious process, but the questions themselves were easy enough. I'd had a lot more time to read and study mathematics than the people for whom the test was developed, however. The students around me were uniformly unhappy as they filled in scores of tiny bubbles with number two pencils, like worker bees tending a honeycomb. I wondered why humans were so intent on tormenting their young.

The prospect of attending school, however, was another matter. I had no idea how I was going to pass myself off as Cara in front of her peers. My only hope was to keep my mouth shut as much as humanly possible. I spent the hour before school cowering in Cara's room with a schedule of her classes in one hand and a map of the school in the other.

As I'd taken Cara's suitcase out of my trunk at the airport, it had suddenly dawned on me that she had never spoken to me about her classmates. Not once.

"Wait!" I'd called, as she'd run toward the terminal. "How am I supposed to know what to call these people?"

"Wing it!" she'd shouted back.

I swallowed hard at the memory. How was I going to do this?

Liv drove me to school that morning, looking at me oddly the entire way. I suspected I wasn't entirely fooling her, but the truth was so bizarre there was no way for her to suspect it. Still, I was going to have to do better. I just didn't know how.

I got out of the car, took a deep breath, and went off to face the hordes of adolescent drones.

My early classes were not so bad. People greeted me, and seemed friendly enough. I took copious notes and kept my head down to avoid attracting attention.

Then it was time for lunch.

I'd spent a year and a half at McNair, so I thought I was used to dealing with crowds, but when you are a six-foot-tall man, people give you a much wider birth than when you are a five-and-a-half-foot-tall girl. People bumped into me repeatedly with their shoulders and elbows, hitting parts of my body that I certainly didn't want to be touched, let alone smacked into. I had trouble seeing where I was going, and I began to feel like a salmon swimming upstream to spawn. A salmon that was likely to be scooped out of the water and eaten by a grizzly bear before I got where I was going.

I'd packed myself a sandwich, and at lunchtime I found an out-of-the-way corner outside to eat, near my next class, Calculus. I pulled out my book and tried to review the basics; I am not particularly good at higher-level math, at least by Eolian standards, but I'd had to use it enough at McNair that I was still familiar with it. As I was reading, I became aware that there were people standing over me. I looked up, and there were two boys, one quite tall, the other shorter and broader. They were leering at me in a way that made my insides twitch.

"Um, may I help you?" I asked.

They laughed derisively. "Eating lunch with all your friends, Cara?"

I groaned inwardly. I was not prepared for this.

"I'm just trying to get a leg up on Calculus," I replied.

"Another hot date after school?" The short one said, and the tall one snickered. The short one was doing most of the

192

talking, but it was the tall one who worried me. He seemed menacing, somehow. I wondered how Cara knew him.

"Sorry, what?" I asked.

They both laughed. "Haven't you humiliated yourself enough yet? Really, the imaginary boyfriend thing is getting kind of old."

"The—the *what*?" I said, and I could hear the anger in my voice. What had Cara been enduring with these asses? Why hadn't she told me any of this?

"Please, Cara, it's getting really tired. Just give it a rest." They grinned at me again and left, and as they walked away, I heard them whisper a single word, loudly enough so that I would be sure to hear it:

"*Bitch.*"

Is this why Cara never talked about school? Had she been putting up with this all year? It sickened me to think of these half-wits talking to her this way. Why hadn't she told me?

I packed my books away and headed off to class. As I was walking down one of the corridors, I felt someone snap my bra through my shirt, which would have been bad enough, but it seemed to come unhooked in the process. I spun around, but there were so many people I couldn't tell who had done it.

I ran to the bathroom and hid in one of the stalls, trying desperately to get my bra re-hooked. I couldn't seem to get the sides together; as soon as I'd hook one of the eyes, the other would pop out again. I was nearly three hundred years old. I had lived as dozens of species. And I was being outdone by a woman's undergarment. If I had ever been more humiliated, I couldn't recall it.

This was not a disaster, I told myself. I could always go to class without a bra. Couldn't I? I looked down. No, I couldn't. I

193

would attract way too much attention this way. And I was so miserable that I couldn't even get worked up about how I looked with the damn bra off. I smacked my forehead against the stall door, and before I knew it I was crying.

Was it easier to cry in this body? I wasn't sure. It certainly was harder to stop. I wondered if this was something to do with being a woman, or something to do with Cara in particular. I let the tears come, since I didn't seem to have any choice in the matter, and hoped that it would be over soon.

There was a soft knock on the stall door. "Are you okay?" said a quiet voice.

"I'm fine," I said.

"Are you sure?"

This was likely my only chance to get help, so I opened the door. The girl on the other side had a concerned face and curly black hair.

"Somebody unhooked my bra in the hall," I explained.

"Ugh. There are some real jerks at this school. I'm sorry."

I looked at the floor.

"Was there something else wrong?" she asked.

What was the use? I might as well get it over with. "I can't get it re-hooked," I muttered.

She was incredulous. "Uh, did you try just taking it off and putting it back on?"

I lifted my head and looked at her. "How would that help?"

"Well, you know, you have to put it on backwards and then turn it around."

I was stunned. Did all women know this? I cursed under my breath, but out loud I just said, "Oh."

"Well, how have you been putting it on all this time?" She shook her head. "You know what? Never mind. Turn around and I'll do it for you."

I complied, though it was obvious she thought there was something mentally wrong with me. Hell, maybe there was.

After I got my shirt pulled down I ran to class, but I was still five minutes late.

The teacher gave me a withering look as I sat down. "Books away, Cara," he said. He was a man in his sixties, and did not look kind. "We're having a quiz. You'll have to hurry to catch up."

A quiz. Well, no matter. I was sure it was nothing I couldn't handle. I pulled a pen out of my bag and started to work, trying to be mindful of my handwriting.

"Miss Gallagher," the teacher said rather abrasively, "you may recall that we do not use pens on examinations in this class.

This was really too much. I looked up at him. "Why not?" The students around me laughed uncomfortably, and the teacher—I remembered his name was Mr. Harris—glared at me.

"Because it is the policy of the entire Math Department. I do not want to have to grade through your hatch marks when you have to cross out a mistake."

I was having trouble disguising my anger. "Why would I make a mistake?"

"Are you attempting to be funny?"

"No," I said. "I'm asking an honest question. Why would I make a mistake on your piddling little test?"

The other students gasped and began murmuring to one another, and Mr. Harris brought his fist down on his desk with a loud thud. There was instant silence in the room.

"Get out," he spat.

"What?"

"Get out."

"Where should I go?"

"Go talk to your guidance counselor about your terrible attitude! I don't care. Just get out of my classroom."

I grabbed my bag and left. What else could I do?

I'd known that the crucible of human adolescence was unlike anything I'd experienced on my own world, where the young are carefully steered into adulthood by those who share their experiences, their knowledge, with kindness and patience. I'd had no idea that high school was like this—inane busywork punctuated by incidents of disrespect from other students and faculty members alike. No wonder Cara so often spoke of wanting to graduate and move on to college. I couldn't imagine how anyone could survive four years of this without major psychological trauma.

I hated the idea that she had to live through this every day. I vowed that I would do whatever it took to make this easier for her.

Tomorrow, I told myself, she would be home. I could only hope that she'd managed to get what she needed from her father. I couldn't imagine what her mother had been thinking, trying to force her away from her sister, her school (such as it was), her home. From me, though she obviously hadn't known about that. What had she hoped to gain? Blind obedience, from someone who was far more woman than girl? Was it so hard for her to accept that her daughter was no longer a child?

I slept better that night, knowing that she would be back soon. I'd seen the look in Cara's eyes when I'd taken her to the airport. Deep down, I knew she would come back with what she needed. Nothing was going to stand in her way.

I'd just finished brushing my teeth the next morning when my phone rang. My heart raced when I heard Cara's voice on the other end.

"Is Liv still home?" she asked.

"She just left," I said.

"Good." The phone clicked. A minute later, I heard the key turning in the lock. I threw the door open, and looked into her beautiful, smiling face.

Clutched in her hands was a large manila envelope.

She closed the door behind her and ran her eyes over me, laughing. "Gosh," she said. "I'm a mess."

"I've been avoiding the shower," I admitted, making my way back toward Cara's room, while she followed. "Hang on, I'd like to change back."

After I'd changed and put my own clothes back on, I groaned. "God, that is so much better," I said.

She laughed, shaking her head so that her hair bounced across her shoulders. I wanted to touch her so badly I could taste it. Instead, I tried to concentrate on the envelope in her hands, and the gleam of triumph in her eyes.

"You look happy."

She held up the envelope. "Notarized letter from my father to the Muro Alto School District," she said. "Telling them that, for the next five weeks, I am the object of a custody dispute, and that I am to remain enrolled at Murray. And another re-asserting my sister's guardianship for the same period."

I pulled her into my arms. "Thank God," I said. "So it was worth it."

197

She ran her fingers through my hair, setting the nerves in my scalp on fire. "Thank you," she whispered. "What you did— that was amazing."

I laughed softly. "Hardest three days of my life."

She rolled her eyes. "Come on."

"Really. And that's saying something." I stretched myself out on her bed, and she sat down next to me, her hip resting against mine.

"I got you thrown out of Calculus."

She was horrified. "What did you do?"

"I did math in pen."

She groaned. "Oh, no."

I reached up to stroke her cheek, and I looked into her eyes. "Why didn't you tell me it was so bad there?" I asked softly.

She buried her face in my chest and didn't speak for a while. When she did answer me, she didn't look up. "Sometimes I feel like I'm living some kind of a double life," she said. "When I'm with you, everything's so perfect. I feel so strong. When I'm there, everything's just wrong. When we're together, I like to pretend the other part doesn't exist. Like it's just a bad dream. The parts with you are the only parts that feel real."

That I understood, but it didn't make me feel better. "I hate it," I said. "I hate that you have to endure that. It shouldn't be that way."

"I know," she said. "It's only a few more months. And it isn't so bad, really. You just have to make yourself invisible while you're there."

"You should never have to make yourself invisible."

198

She looked up at me and smirked. "If it makes you feel better, I'm not very good at it. Sometimes I feel like I'm walking around with a giant target in the middle of my chest."

I grimaced. "Yes, I saw that."

She was quiet while she thought about that. "Oh."

There was no point in elaborating; I didn't want to share with her the unpleasantness I'd experienced, which, after all, had been meant for her. It only would have made her feel badly.

"On the other hand," she said, wrapping her arms around my neck. "You did miss out on a lot of the good parts of my life."

I grinned at her, catching her mood. "The good parts?"

"Mmm-hmm."

"I'd hate to have missed out on the good parts." I nuzzled her ear.

"Yes, that would be tragic."

"Dreadful."

"Devastating."

"Hmm. I'm devastated, yes."

"Well, we'll have to do something about that."

She kissed me with her perfect, sweet lips, and I wanted to lose every part of myself in her, to forget everything outside of that one moment. Not even to be an Eolian anymore—just to be a man, kissing a woman, loving her.

She was a thousand miles deep and I wanted to swim in her until my lungs burst.

She slid her fingers up the outsides of my shoulders, slipped her tongue into my mouth, and I lost all the feeling in my arms and legs.

No, I thought, *please, just a little longer—just a little more of this, more of her.*

199

There was no more. I pulled myself away, body aching, and tried to remember how to breathe.

"It's okay," she whispered, and my heart broke.

Because she loved me, and I loved her. And that would never be enough.

I would never be enough.

When I got home that night there was a message for me from Adeep.

"Dude," he said. "I have something you absolutely have to see. This is going to change everything."

Chapter Sixteen

Surprise!
(Cara)

I made up a story about my father's letter arriving via Fed-Ex, and Liv gave it to the school district on Tuesday morning. On Tuesday afternoon, after several hours of screaming and a possible aneurysm, my mother flew home to Virginia. I was safe; I had Will, and Liv, and my new home, and everything was perfect.

Except that my mother was no longer speaking to me.

Not speaking, but I still had an inbox full of e-mails, which ranged in tone from Mostly Angry to Really Angry and back again. I didn't answer them. I didn't know how. There was a part of me, a big part, that wanted my mother. The rest of me wanted my life even more.

Liv told me she'd come around, and Will said the same thing. She was angry, they both said, but not at me. At losing control. I wasn't so sure.

There was nothing I could do about that, so I concentrated on living my life instead. The life I had chosen for myself, for the very first time.

The next couple of weeks were spent in a holding pattern, and I tried to figure out how to balance my schoolwork and my time with Will and Liv. I worked through lunch every day, spent my afternoons with Will, sometimes outdoors, sometimes studying together in his apartment, sometimes just talking. Sometimes kissing until his body couldn't take it anymore, leaving him panting and struggling to hold onto himself. After a while that got better, too, and our kisses lengthened, softened, lingered. And when that invisible hand would reach out and pull him back, reminding us that there would always be limits to how close we could get, we would just hold each other and talk until the feeling passed and he was firmly himself again, whispering countless promises, a thousand secrets, from within the circle we made with our arms.

It was during one of those afternoons, as we were lying on his couch together, when he quietly said my name.

"Mmm?"

"I can age," he said.

"What?"

"If I stay in the same form, I get older."

I leaned up and looked at him.

"I just wanted you to know," he said. His voice was a million miles away.

I didn't know what to say, so I just touched his cheek and kissed him, while he looked at me with eyes full of questions I couldn't answer.

My evenings were spent with my sister, when she was around. She was teaching again, and now that all the undergrads were back on campus, I saw less of her than I had over the summer. But I had homework that needed attention, and my plants to tend, so it never occurred to me to feel lonely. They were thriving on our kitchen windowsill, as if they were as filled with life as I was. I was tired a good bit of the time, but I

202

was happy. My time with Will was the best part of my day, always.

Liv was giving me a hard time about my lack of extracurricular activities, and told me regularly that I was going to have trouble getting into college with nothing to list on my applications. I knew she was right, but the truth was that I couldn't stand the idea of spending a second longer than absolutely necessary at Murray. I decided I would have to make up for it by getting a part-time job, which didn't thrill me since I knew that would mean working retail. Which would involve dealing with customers.

As luck would have it, Vivoli's was hiring, and I managed to talk myself into a position a few days a week.

Then, finally, the day I had been looking forward to since Will and I first became friends arrived—October fifteenth. My eighteenth birthday.

It was absurd that one day should make a difference in a relationship as unconventional as ours. He was, after all, older than the country I lived in. Nevertheless, this one day meant that he could no longer get into trouble for being with me, at least legally. More importantly, it meant that I could tell Liv. I doubted that she would be pleased to hear I was dating a twenty-three-year-old grad student (I didn't plan on telling her the entire truth), but at least now she might be a bit more comfortable with the idea. At the very least, there'd be nothing she could do about it.

My birthday fell on a Friday, and while I had to work after school, I had plans to celebrate with Liv that evening. Will and I were going to wait to get together until Saturday—my birthday present from him was a pair of tickets to see the opera that evening in San Francisco.

The store was empty as five o'clock approached. It was usually a quiet time of day; most people were getting ready to eat dinner, and the dessert rush was still hours away. I would not be working then, however; I was set to leave in fifteen minutes. Just as I was thinking about hanging up my apron and taking off a few minutes early, I heard the bells on the front door jingle and I looked up to see Morgan, Molly, Adam, and the rest of their group coming into the store.

My heart sank. In the weeks that I had been working there, my classmates rarely came in, since the shop was on the other side of town. I tried to look like I was happy to see them.

"Hey!" Molly said, beaming. "I was just telling everyone that you worked here, and since it's your birthday, we decided to come down and surprise you. So, happy birthday!" She looked extremely pleased with herself, and I could tell she thought she was doing me a huge favor.

"Thanks," I said. "Did you guys want anything?"

"Can you hook us up with some free ice cream?" Morgan asked, looking over the list of flavors next to the cash register.

"Um, well, no," I said, glancing over my shoulder to the back room, where Meghan, the assistant manager, was filing some paperwork. "I could get into a lot of trouble for that. I'm sorry."

Adam scoffed and rolled his eyes, and Morgan gave me a treacly smile and said, "That's okay. I really shouldn't be eating this stuff anyway. I'm sure if I worked here, I would just turn into a complete cow."

I fought the urge to moo.

I was getting ready to tell her that I was on my way out when she spotted the bouquet of yellow roses sitting on top of the gelato case. Will had sent them earlier that afternoon, and I'd left them out so that I could look at them while I worked. I kicked myself for doing it now, even more so since I had left the card attached.

"Ooh!" she said. "Did these come for you?"

"Yeah," I said, reaching for the vase. "I didn't realize they were in the way, I'll just move them. I was actually getting ready to leave anyway—" Before I could get them away from her, she deftly reached up and snatched the card out of the arrangement. At least she didn't read it out loud.

"Who's Will?' she asked with a smirk.

"He's my boyfriend," I said, reaching for the card, which she reluctantly handed back. It made me sick to think of her reading his words to me. *For my beautiful angel. Yours, Will*

"Aren't yellow roses for friendship?" she asked.

"They're my favorites," I explained. "But I really do need to go."

"Oh, but that's why we're here!" she said. "Molly told us it was your birthday, and my parents are out for the whole night so we decided that, since you're still new and don't have any friends, we'd throw you a little impromptu party." She smiled at me serenely, as if she were the queen bestowing a great favor on some poor peasant.

"That's really nice of you," I said, "but I already have plans with my sister tonight. I'm sorry."

"You aren't going out with your boyfriend?" she asked with a tight smile. She obviously still thought I was making him up. She must have thought I'd sent the flowers to myself.

"Not tonight, no," I answered.

205

"Can't you just come out for an hour?" Molly asked, her face pleading. "I can give you a ride home afterward." I was pretty sure that if I didn't go, Molly, whose idea this obviously was, would be tormented about it later. I knew she was trying to be nice by including me in her group.

"Okay," I said, trying not to sound as reluctant as I felt. "I'll just call her and tell her I'll be a little late." I grabbed the phone on the back wall and dialed quickly, while Morgan whispered something to Adam.

Liv sounded surprised that I wanted to spend time with my classmates, but at least she wasn't angry. I promised her I'd be home by seven so that we could still get Chinese takeout and watch a movie.

Morgan's house was in a neighborhood full of large, multilevel houses, which stood out in a place where most people lived in ranch-style single-stories on small lots. These houses were clearly designed for show. The front lawns were impeccably manicured, and as we drove up Morgan's driveway, I could see a small fountain bubbling amid some rosebushes. The house was just like Morgan, really: beautiful, but verging on tacky.

"Home sweet home," Morgan said, opening the front door. "The parentals won't be back until at least twelve or one, so we have lots of time to relax."

She led the group into her formal living room and turned up the stereo; it was so loud I could barely hear the conversations going on around me. I looked for Molly, but she was talking to Allison. I couldn't hear what they were saying, but they were leaning so close that I didn't feel like interrupting. Adam was standing behind them, talking to Ethan. He looked up when he saw that I was looking at him, and sneered at me. I looked away immediately.

I was trying to decide if anyone would notice if I wandered out into the back yard, when I saw Morgan open what I had taken to be a small closet. It was, in fact, a liquor cabinet, and people began lining up with glasses in hand as she poured shots of tequila. I recognized it as the same expensive stuff I'd seen in the houses of my parents' friends—the kind with the worm in the bottle. This appeared to be standard operating procedure for their get-togethers; no one looked the least bit surprised. I wondered how often Morgan served two-hundred-dollar bottles of liquor to her friends without her parents noticing. Or maybe they did notice.

I remembered what Will had said about being an actor, and realized I was doing the same thing. Watch as Cara Gallagher plays the role of Social High School Student. See how she flips her hair? How she smiles like she means it?

I wondered if we were all doing the same thing, playing parts for each other. Or if it was just me.

"Come have one," Morgan said, holding a glass out in my direction. "It's your birthday!"

"I can't, thanks," I said. "I'm meeting my sister after this. If I come home smelling like booze, she'll kill me."

"Oh, sorry, sweetie," she said, handing the shot to someone else. "Why don't I make up a batch of smoothies?"

"That sounds great, thank you," I said. I hadn't eaten since lunch, and I was starving. At least I would have something to tide me over until I got home.

Morgan disappeared across the foyer into the kitchen, and came back a few minutes later with an enormous pink tumbler full of something orange, complete with a straw. "Here you go," she said, handing it back to me with a smile.

"There's no alcohol in this?" I asked, examining the contents.

"Nope. It's completely virgin." She looked at me pointedly, her eyebrows raised. Like me, she meant. The girl standing behind her snickered. I smiled back at her as if I had no idea what she was getting at.

"Thanks," I said, taking the drink from her, and sipping it carefully. It tasted pretty much like an Orange Julius. I drank about half of it right away, not realizing that I'd been so thirsty as well as hungry.

Morgan went back to pouring the tequila—some people were already lining up for refills—and I wandered around the room looking for a conversation to join. Jonah and Alex were talking about the English paper we had due next week, and that seemed like something I might be able to participate in, so I sat down in the armchair next to them.

Jonah, who played baseball and swam on the varsity team, smiled when I sat down. "Did you finish *A Farewell to Arms* yet? It's killing me."

"No," I said, and I held up my purse. "I've got it with me, actually. It's ridiculous, right?"

I sipped my drink and tuned out as he and Alex discussed the lameness of Hemingway in general, and Catherine Barklay in particular. I'm not exactly sure how long I sat there ... ten minutes turned to fifteen, and then I seemed to lose track. I didn't realize how far out of it I was when Alex gave me a disturbed look. "Did you hear me at all? Are you okay?"

"Oh, sorry. I think I'm coming down with a migraine," I said.

The truth was that I had gone from feeling perfectly fine to completely wretched in less than five minutes, and I knew immediately that Morgan had lied to me about my drink. The room lurched, and I felt sick to my stomach. Molly was still talking to Allison, but her voice seemed too loud to me. I walked over to her, trying not to stumble, and leaned over her chair.

"I really need to go home now," I whispered. I had to hold myself up on the arm of her chair to keep from toppling over.

"I can't leave now," she protested. "We're talking about the prom theme. It's important."

"But I have to go," I said. "I'm supposed to be having dinner with my sister."

"I'll take you in half an hour, okay? Why don't you find some guys to talk to. I think Adam's here somewhere."

"But—"

She gave me an annoyed look.

"Please, Molly ..."

She shooed me away and turned back to Allison. It was probably just as well—I suspected that she was only slightly more sober than I was.

I wasn't sure what to do next. If I called Liv to pick me up, I had no doubt she would freak out. She might even call the police. I hadn't seen Alex or Jonah drinking, but I didn't think either of them was driving. I decided that Will was my best bet, even though I was horrified at the thought of him seeing me like this. I didn't see a lot of other choices. I certainly couldn't walk back—I wasn't even totally sure where I was. I hated myself for getting into this mess.

I staggered out the opened back door, where two people I didn't know were groping each other next to the pool, and continued through the deck chairs until I found a private spot

209

on the lawn behind the shrubs. I opened my purse, looking desperately for my phone, but there was so much debris in there I couldn't find it. I finally gave up and dumped the entire contents out on the grass. My hardback copy of *A Farewell to Arms* landed on my toe, and I yelped.

I was trying hard not to cry; my head hurt and my stomach was churning. I finally dug my phone out of the pile of crap on the ground and picked it up.

My hands were shaking, and before I could get the phone turned on, someone came up behind me and lifted it out of my hands. I turned, and through my slightly blurred vision, saw Adam, holding my phone up and out of my reach.

"What's the matter, Cara? Aren't you having a good time?" he asked.

"Give me my phone," I said, feeling the anger welling up inside me. I no longer felt like crying—I felt like hitting someone. This was my birthday, and it had been ruined. Worse, I had allowed it to happen, and I wasn't even sure why. "Now," I insisted.

Adam laughed at my slurred speech. "Are you drunk, princess? I think this is the saddest thing I've ever seen."

"Give me my phone," I repeated, standing up slowly, so I wouldn't lose my balance.

"Who are you going to call? Your imaginary boyfriend?"

"What is it that you want, exactly?" I said. I was trembling now. I thought I was only experiencing anger, but a second emotion was also building in me, and I recognized that it was fear. My view of the house was entirely blocked by the shrubs in front of me.

"Me?" he said, looking at me and shaking his head. "What the hell would I want with you? You're just a stuck-up little girl who thinks she's better than everyone else. Well, you're not. You're nothing."

"I don't think I'm better than anyone," I said. "I just want to go home. If I'm such a waste of space, why are you out here talking to me? Don't you have friends in there you could be bothering?" I doubled over slightly, putting one hand down on my knee to support myself.

"I think it's time you learned your lesson," he said, and slid my phone into his pocket. He took two steps toward me.

"What are you doing?" I yelled. I searched the ground for anything I could use as a weapon, but there was nothing. The pepper spray Liv had given me was still on my dresser.

"Shut up," he said, and kept moving toward me. He reached out to grab my arm, and I felt panic shoot through me. I had no idea what he had in mind. Maybe he was just going to knock me down, or throw me in the pool. Or maybe it was something worse.

His jaw was set so hard the tendons in his neck stood out, and I could practically feel the testosterone coming off him in waves. He smelled like alcohol and something acrid I couldn't identify, a smell that woke up some ancient, reptilian part of my brain and told me to fight or get the hell out of there.

I was drunk, but so was he, and I was not nearly as impaired as I looked. I grabbed my book off the ground and, with as much force as I could muster, swung it into his face. The corner of the book rammed into the side of his nose, next to his eye, and he swore and stumbled back, with his hand over his face. Then, before he could come at me again, I kicked him in the crotch, tripping myself and falling on my hands and knees in the process.

211

He fell to the ground, groaning and cursing. "You'll pay for this," he said through gritted teeth. "Every day, I will make you pay."

I reached into his pocket and grabbed my phone; he didn't try to stop me. "Go ahead," I said. "Tell everyone."

He didn't respond, and I quickly gathered my things and headed in the direction of the gate which led to the front yard, not wanting to go back in the house. I lurched over the weedless expanse of grass until I got to the bottom of the driveway, where I collapsed onto the ground, clutching my phone so hard my knuckles turned white.

I was relieved that Will answered right away when I called. "What's wrong?" he asked, his tone urgent.

"I'm in trouble," I said, and a sob escaped my mouth before I could stop it. "I'm at a party, and I've had too much to drink—"

"Just tell me where you are," he said firmly. "I'm coming to get you."

"I'm not sure exactly. The street was Villa Lobos, but I don't know the house number. I'm out front, anyway."

"I'll find you," he said. "Don't go anywhere."

I hung up the phone and threw up on Morgan's driveway.

I wasn't sure how long I waited for Will, but I do know he came quickly. I was feeling less sick now that my stomach was empty, but I was so tired. I saw Will's navy-blue car pull to a quiet stop in front of me, and then he got out and carefully helped me inside.

"Do I need to take you to the hospital?" he asked, touching my forehead gently to gauge my temperature. He took a small towel out of the glovebox and used it to wipe the tears and sweat from my face.

"No, I'll be okay," I said. "I feel a little better now." I leaned my head against the back of my seat and moaned.

"Well, I can't take you home like this," he said, shaking his head. "Liv will lose it."

"You have to. She's waiting for me already."

He shook his head and turned the car in the direction of my apartment. "What happened to you back there?" he asked. "You don't drink."

"I know. I didn't know there was alcohol in my drink. It just tasted sweet. This girl, Morgan, she lied to me"

"She got you drunk on purpose? Why?"

"'Cause she doesn't like me."

"Why wouldn't she like you?" he asked. I was glad that he cared about me, but I didn't particularly want to continue this conversation. I just wanted to close my eyes and rest. And get the taste of vomit and orange juice out of my mouth.

"I don't know why," I said at last.

"Okay. We can talk about it when you feel better, but you're going to have to tell Liv something."

I groaned again.

The car came to a stop, and I was startled when I opened my eyes and saw that he had parked in the lot in front of my building, rather than pulling up in front of the stairs to drop me off.

"What are you doing?" I protested. "Just drop me off. I'll tell her I got a ride from someone at school."

"I can't do that," he said. "You're too far gone to go up all those stairs by yourself."

213

"Fine. Then dump me in front of the door and go. She can't see you with me right now. You know what she'll think?"

"No, Cara," he said, unbuckling his seat belt. "I can't do this anymore. It isn't right."

"Please," I begged. "We'll tell her everything. Just not tonight."

"I can't," he said, opening his door. "I can't lie anymore. It isn't good for either of us. It makes me feel like we're doing something wrong."

He came around to my side of the car and helped me out of my seat, and I could see that there was no use in arguing. I was eighteen now, anyway. I had promised him that I would tell her after my birthday, and time was up. If I wanted Liv to treat me like an adult, I would have to act like one. No more sneaking around. I walked slowly to maintain my balance as we climbed the steps, but he held his arm around me the entire way to make sure I didn't fall.

I paused in front of the door, looking at Will. "Are you sure about this?" I asked.

He nodded. I knew he was right. I just wished I wasn't worried I'd puke on Liv before I got all the words out.

I turned my key in the lock and walked into the apartment, to see Liv standing in the kitchen, phone in hand, looking like she was about to murder someone.

Chapter Seventeen

Honesty, Part Two

She hung up the phone as soon as she saw me, and her eyes were wild. "What happened to you?" she cried, and I hoped I didn't look as bad as I felt. I tried not to stagger too much as I made my way into the living room. "I've been calling all over town trying to figure out where you were. You weren't answering your phone."

I remembered that I had turned the ringer off while I was at work, but before I could apologize, she turned to Will, which is exactly what I'd been afraid of. She looked from him to me and back again, and then her face went red.

"You got her drunk?" she said, stepping toward him. She was so angry I was worried that she might actually punch him. "You got her *drunk*? How could you? She's a child! And I knew, I knew the whole time that she was sneaking around with you. And I never did a thing about it, because I thought she was old enough to figure things out on her own. Look at her! Look what you've done to her!"

She grabbed me by the arms and forcibly sat me on the couch. "She's gray," she said to Will, her voice shaking with rage. "How much did you give her?"

"Liv!" I said, with the limited force I could manage. "It wasn't Will. He didn't give me anything. I told you, I was at a party—"

She held up her hands. "Don't do this, Cara. Don't lie to me anymore."

"I'm not lying, Liv. They spiked my drink. I called Will to pick me up, since I was afraid you would do this."

"You should give her some water," Will interjected. "I think she threw up before I got to her."

Liv sniffed me. "Ugh," she grunted. "She smells like someone got sick in a distillery." She sniffed again. "In an orange grove."

Not waiting anymore, Will went into the kitchen and got me a glass of water, along with a package of crackers. I sipped the water slowly. I thought of going to look for my toothbrush, but one look at Liv told me I had better wait. She sat down on the couch next to me and crossed her arms.

"Start talking."

"Well," I said. "These kids from school came to Vivoli's while I was working, and they asked me to come out with them for a while, to a party. I didn't really want to go, but I couldn't think of a good way out of it."

Liv folded her arms. "Did you try saying *no*?"

"No," I admitted. I closed my eyes and rubbed my forehead. "I'm so tired, Liv, can we do this later?"

"We'll do it now," she snapped. "Mean kids got you drunk. I think I've got the idea. That's not what I'm asking you about."

I glanced at Will, who was now sitting in the armchair kitty-corner from the couch. I wanted very badly to reach out and take his hand, but I knew I shouldn't.

216

"He didn't know I was seventeen when we met," I explained.

"Clearly," she said. "But you must have told him at some point."

"Well, yeah—" I said.

She turned to Will. "Why didn't you end it, once you found out how old she was?"

"Listen, Liv," I said angrily. "You can't really get on your high horse about this. How is this any different from you and Dr. Yarrow?"

She looked at me with horror, and then glanced at Will, who lifted his hands as if to placate her. "Don't worry," he said to her. "I don't have any intention of telling anybody."

She glared at me. "You told him?" she said, her voice growing shrill. "How could you do that? Don't you understand what could happen if this got out?"

"No," Will said, reaching his hand out to Liv. "No, she didn't tell me. I'm just observant."

"Just not observant enough to realize you were dating a high-school kid," she retorted.

"Liv!" I cried. "Please!"

Liv was silent, waiting for Will's response. He looked at me for a long time before turning his attention back to Liv.

"I understand why you would think that," he said quietly. "I understand why you're angry. You just want to protect your sister, and that's how you should feel. But this," he said, reaching out for my hand, "this isn't what you're thinking."

"Really? Because I'm thinking you've been sneaking around with my teenage sister since August," she said.

"Liv," he said, "I love her. Honestly."

217

She rolled her eyes and threw her hands up in the air. "You've got to be kidding me. If that were true, then you're old enough to know how bad this is for her."

"Why?" I asked. The feelings of sleepiness were receding; I guessed a boost of adrenaline was countering the effects of the alcohol. "In what way is it bad for me to be with someone I love? Will is a good man, Liv. You aren't giving him a chance. Anyway, I'm eighteen now. I don't need your permission to be with someone."

"Don't, Cara," Will said. "I don't want it to be like this. I don't want to come between you and your sister."

"You haven't done anything wrong," I protested.

"Yes, I have," he said. "I should have insisted on telling her, from the beginning." He looked into my eyes. "She has to know everything, Cara. It's the only way she'll understand. Without the truth, everything she's saying is absolutely right."

His meaning took a minute to sink in. "No," I whispered. "Don't."

"What is he talking about?" Liv said, and she gripped my free arm so tightly I could almost feel her fear flowing into me. "What is going on?"

"Will," I began, but he cut me off.

"Liv, Cara and I didn't start off being involved. I was at a very low point last summer. Cara befriended me when I was completely, hopelessly alone."

Liv groaned and shook her head.

"I'm telling you this because I need to tell you the whole truth about myself. I'm not what you think I am."

"Oh," Liv growled. "You definitely are."

"No. I'm not—I'm not human."

218

I looked nervously over at Liv, who had let go of my arm and was laughing. "This just gets worse and worse," she said, rubbing her eyes. "Please spare me and get the hell out of here." She looked over at me. "He's not hot enough to make up for this much crazy, Cara."

"Really, Liv," he said. "I wish there were an easier way for me to explain this to you, but I'm not human. I'll show you, since I think it's the only way you'll believe me. Please don't be afraid."

I felt him squeeze my hand, and felt the familiar sensation of his large, masculine hand slipping into one that was small and feminine. I didn't need to look at him to know that he had taken my form.

Liv screamed and jumped to her feet, letting out a string of curses a mile long as she ran into the kitchen, and stood on the other side of the counter, brandishing the bread knife. Which could have done some serious damage to someone who was willing to hold still for a few minutes while you sawed at them. I let go of Will and got up, putting myself between him and Liv.

"Liv," I said, trying to sound calm. "It's okay. He isn't dangerous. He's from another world, and he can change his form. He came here to study Earth. He won't hurt anyone. I told you, he's a good man."

"What do you want with my sister?" she said, not lowering the knife.

Will reached into his oilcloth pouch and returned to his regular form. He breathed heavily for a minute, and I knew that he was as exhausted as I was. "I'm nothing bad," he said softly. "Everything we've told you tonight is true."

Liv glared at him over her knife. "Are you trying to impregnate her with your alien spawn?"

219

"Liv!" I gasped in horror, but Will laughed.

"No. No alien spawn. I couldn't, even if I wanted to." He smiled, but his eyes were sad.

"Are you the vanguard of an invasion?" she asked.

"No."

"Would you tell me if you were?"

"Um, probably not," he said. "But there's no invasion. My people aren't even armed. It's not our way."

"And you don't eat people? You aren't planning on using human blood as fertilizer?"

I snorted.

Will shook his head. "No, none of that. We're just curious. That's all."

"You aren't dangerous, not at all?" Liv sounded dubious, but she lowered the knife. The muscles in her arms, tense before, now appeared to relax.

"Not at all," he said.

"Why should I believe you?"

"Because," I said, approaching Liv and holding my hand out for the knife. "He's never hurt me. Or anyone else, either."

"She's a child," she whispered, looking at Will.

"I know you see her that way," he said. "But she doesn't, and neither do I."

She watched me carefully as she handed me the knife, which I returned to the drawer. "You're asking an awful lot of me here."

"I know," I agreed. "It's my fault that we didn't tell you sooner about us, and I'm sorry. Please, you have to trust me, Liv."

Liv held out her arms and gave me a long hug. "I do. I do trust you, Cara," she said, and then added in a whisper, "I'm not so sure about him, though."

"Just give him a chance," I whispered back.

"I will, for you," she said. "For you. But if he tries to dissect you …"

Will left soon after that, partly so that Liv and I could talk alone, and partly because Liv was now looking at him like the creature from the Black Lagoon. I didn't blame her, really. I did hope she'd warm up to him quickly. I hated the idea of the two people I loved most not getting along.

After Will was gone, I changed out of my reeking clothes and into my pajamas. I was exhausted, but I didn't want to go to bed before I cleared the air with Liv who was, oddly enough, cleaning the kitchen. I guessed it was a response to the extreme stress.

"Do you still want to watch a movie, or do you hate me now?" I asked, worming my way under her arm. I had no interest in watching a movie, but I hoped that sitting on the couch together might help us mend our relationship, like we'd become friends again through osmosis. She gave my shoulder a quick squeeze and then went back to cleaning.

"You know that isn't going to work this time," she said, slamming a drawer. "No, I don't hate you. Are you up for eating something yet? It might make you feel better."

I looked over and saw a bunch of Chinese takeout boxes on the counter. I hadn't noticed them before. "You already got dinner?" I asked.

She shrugged. "I picked it up after you called, so we could eat when you got home."

I felt like crying. "I'm sorry, Liv. I feel awful." What was wrong with me? I'd chosen to spend the evening with a bunch of people I didn't even like, instead of my sister, whom I adored. Why hadn't I just said no to them? I had no problems saying no to Liv, shoot, I didn't even have problems saying no to Will. Why did I want to please a bunch of jerks I didn't even care about?

"It's okay," she said, not looking up. "Do you want the Ma Po? It isn't too spicy." I nodded and she made me a plate, with lots of rice and extra soy sauce, the way I'd eaten Chinese food since I was a kid. I found it hard to swallow the food with the enormous lump in my throat.

She didn't look at me until after she'd finished eating and put her plate down. She rested her feet on the coffee table, crossed her arms, and shook her head. "Well, I don't know where to start," she said at last. "Do we talk about the mess you're in at school, or the mess you're in with Mr. Spock?"

I put my own plate down and turned sideways so that I could look at her more easily. "The situation with Will and me is not a mess," I said.

"Okay, then, let's start with school," she said. "I've been out of the loop for a while, but unless you've changed a lot more than I thought, drunken parties aren't really your thing."

"They still aren't," I said. "I just made a mistake. I fell into this group sort of randomly. I really don't like any of them."

"So you blew me off to get drunk with people you don't like?" she asked, and I cringed. I was hoping she wouldn't think of it like that.

"I didn't mean to blow you off. I didn't even mean to get drunk. I just—I don't know. I guess I was afraid to say no to them. It won't happen again, ever. I promise."

222

"You know," she said, "there are like fifteen hundred kids at that school. Have you even tried to make friends with anyone *nice*?"

"No," I admitted. "I haven't really tried to make friends with anyone. What's the point? I'll never see them again after graduation, anyway."

She shook her head. "I hate that you're like me," she said sadly.

"I'm sorry."

"I'm going to trust that you aren't going to do something like this again," she warned me.

"I won't, I promise," I said, and I reached out and took her hand.

She squeezed my hand back and then cocked her eye at me. "You know we're going to have to talk about your non-messy interspecies relationship."

I rolled my eyes. "Please don't say that. You really will like him."

"I'm sure," she said. "Intergalactic Casanova who runs around the universe seducing young females. Sounds *very* charming."

"He's not like that," I said, slugging Liv in the shoulder. "And for the record, he hasn't seduced me." I was embarrassed admitting this, but I wanted Liv to understand that Will wasn't just using me. I wanted her to see how wrong she was about him.

"No?" She sounded surprised, which bothered me even more.

"No. He ... can't, actually," I said. I wondered if this wasn't my tale to tell, but I felt like she needed to know.

223

"Oh!" She beamed at me, which made me want to kick her. "He can't—"

"No," I said curtly.

"Oh, well that's something, at least," she said with way too much enthusiasm. I punched her in the shoulder, and when she started howling with laughter, I shoved her sideways into the arm of the couch for good measure.

I told her everything that night, except for the most private details, like how I felt like every cell in my body was on fire every time Will touched me, or how he seemed to understand me better than I understood myself. How he saw all the parts of me I had spent my entire life trying to hide. How he truly understood how damaged I was, and yet loved me anyway.

I focused instead on his qualities: his kindness, his compassion, his insight. I wanted her to see the kind of person he was, and more than that, that he actually *was* a person. She listened as well as I could have expected, and she did seem to make an effort to keep the snarky comments to a minimum.

Finally, at the end, the night's exhaustion caught up with me, and my eyes started to close. Liv laughed as my head began to nod forward onto my chest.

"Go to bed," she said.

"Are we okay?" I asked. My feet were numb from sitting too long, and I struggled to get up.

She stood and pulled me up after her. "We're okay, but no more lies."

"No more lies," I agreed, and then hesitated before I added, "Liv, I really need you to try with him."

"I'll try."

"You know how important it is that this stays a secret?" I added.

"Listen," she said. "I'm a biologist. I have a pretty good idea what would happen to him if he got caught."

I shuddered. "Right." I stretched my stiff arms and turned to go, but Liv stopped me before I could leave the room.

"There's one other thing I'd like you to keep in mind," she said. She was not looking at me, and I knew she was getting ready to say something I wouldn't like. "If he loves you so much, then why is he trying so hard to leave?"

I couldn't look at her. It was a question that tormented me frequently, even though I felt guilty for even thinking it. I gave Liv the same answer I kept giving myself. "I would never ask him to give up everything to be with me," I said.

"I know you wouldn't. That isn't really the point."

I didn't know how else to answer. Could you really love someone and *not* want to give things up to be with them? Was it really love if you didn't? Or maybe it was just pragmatism not to give into those feelings. I was sure my mother had loved my father, once. Perhaps if she'd had the foresight to realize the extent of what she was giving up to be with him, she'd have let him go all those years ago. Then she'd have been left with some happy memories of the time they'd spent together, instead of a lifetime of bitterness. That was why I would never ask Will to stay. No matter how much I wanted him to.

I pushed my hair out of my face and rubbed my eyes. "I just—I don't know," I said. "I need to go to sleep, Liv."

"All right. I'm sorry. I just don't want you to get blindsided by anything that might be coming." I looked at her, finally, and her face was full of remorse.

"I understand, really. I do. I'm just tired," I said, and I started down the hall toward my bedroom.

225

"Oh, and Cara?" she called after me. I poked my head back through the doorway to see what she needed.

"Happy birthday."

Chapter Eighteen

Butterfly

When I woke up the next morning, I felt like I'd been kicked in the head. Why did people do this to themselves on purpose? Get drunk, make a fool of yourself, puke your guts out, and then wake up the next morning feeling like the living dead. Was this supposed to be fun?

I put my pillow over my head and groaned, wishing I could go back to sleep until the pounding stopped. It was no use; my head just hurt too much to sleep, so I decided to drag myself out of bed and go in search of some Advil. I removed the pillow from my eyes, swore at the bright light, and looked at my clock. It was past eleven. I wondered if Liv was still home.

She was, and as I stomped my way into the kitchen, she handed me a bottle of pills and a glass of water. "Here," she said. "You need to drink this. You're dehydrated."

"Thanks," I muttered. The cool water was a relief, and once I was done she refilled my glass for me and poured me a bowl of cornflakes. I felt like I was about eight years old.

I shoveled my cereal into my mouth in silence, annoyed by the sound of the crunching. "Are you going out today?" I asked Liv, after I'd finished.

"Yeah, I have to go to the library. I was just waiting until you got up before I left."

227

"Sorry," I said, ducking my head. "That's two days I've screwed up for you."

"It's okay. Anyway, I remembered that I forgot to give you your birthday presents last night. Are you up for them now, or do you want to wait until you're over your hangover?"

"I'm okay now," I said, trying to smile. "It's just a little headache. Let's see the loot."

She laughed. "Okay. Let me go get them." She disappeared into her room and came out with two small packages. "This one is from me," she said.

I tore off the paper carefully; it was a field guide to the plants of northern California. "Thanks!" I said. "I don't have this."

"I thought you could use it. Especially if you end up at McNair in the fall."

"Assuming I get in," I pointed out. "This is great," I said, leafing through the pages. "Thank you so much, Liv."

She shrugged, "Well, it's not much, but I thought you might like it. This one is from Dad." She handed me the second package, a smaller box that rattled as I took it from her. I peeled off the paper, and inside found … a box of tampons. I looked at her incredulously.

"Ignore the box. It's all I could find."

I opened the box and emptied the contents into my hand. A set of car keys. My eyes widened. "Is this real?"

"Yep," she said with a triumphant smile. "Dad mailed me a check and asked me to pick out something safe for you. He didn't want you having to depend on me to get around all the time."

"You know I don't really mind taking the bus," I said, feeling a little guilty.

"I know. Do you want me to take it back?"

"No!" I shouted, grabbing the keys in my fist. "Can I see it now?"

"Sure, if you really want to go out looking like that."

I knew I looked awful, but I really didn't care. The neighbors would just have to suffer. I stuffed my feet into my shoes and ran to the front door. "Well?" I said, as she hesitated.

"Oh, all right."

The car was parked in the lot out front, next to Liv's; it was a silver model that looked like a cross between an SUV and a station wagon. It was, as I'd expected, not new, but I didn't care. It was mine.

"It's great!" I said, throwing my arms around Liv.

"It has about a hundred thousand miles on it, but I took it to a mechanic and he said it's in good shape. It's got all-wheel drive, in case you need to take it off road."

"It looks amazing. Wow."

"I'll leave you two alone," she said, and started back up the stairs.

I stayed for a while longer, wanting to acquaint myself with the means of my liberation, even though I knew I shouldn't drive it until my hangover was gone. I got in and sat in the driver's seat. The car smelled very faintly of wet dog, but it would air out eventually, or so I hoped. I imagined all the places I could now go by myself. Two months ago, this would have been a dream. The problem was that I no longer wanted to travel alone. It was strange; my dreams hadn't changed, but I no longer wanted to live them by myself. I wanted Will to be with me. At least, for as long as he was still around.

I trudged back upstairs slowly. My headache was mostly gone, but I still had a wooly-headed feeling from sleeping too late. I wanted to go back to bed, but I was pretty sure that would just make it worse. Liv had her backpack on and was about to leave as I opened the front door to go inside.

"Your cell phone was ringing," she said. "I'll be home late. Call me if you decide to go out."

"I will, thanks."

I wondered briefly if it had been my mother calling, but when I looked at the number I saw that it was Will, probably trying to confirm our plans. As glad as I was to hear from him, I was still sad that my mother hadn't called. I hadn't spoken a word to her since she'd left California. I'd been hoping she would call on my birthday, even just to say hello. I wondered if she'd forgotten about it.

I called Will back, and he sounded strange.

"What's wrong?" I asked. "Are you mad about last night?' I was terrified that seeing me act like an irresponsible teenager might have been enough to scare him off. And I was feeling more insecure with him than usual. Liv's words to me had been echoing in my mind since she'd first spoken them: *If he loves you so much, why is he trying so hard to leave?* Even though it was a question I had asked myself and dismissed plenty of times, hearing it out loud, and knowing that Liv was wondering the same thing, haunted me.

"No, I'm not angry at all. I've just been really busy at the lab lately. I guess my mind is still there," he said in a distant voice that made me uneasy.

"Is there something you aren't telling me?"

"No, nothing. Are we still on for tonight?" He tried to sound enthusiastic.

"Of course, I've been looking forward to it all week." I had never been to the opera before, but my father listened to it in his office when he was at home. *Madame Butterfly* was one of my favorites, and I was looking forward to seeing it. I tried to forget about Liv's warning and concentrate on how excited I was instead.

It took me longer to get ready than I'd thought—I wasn't used to dressing up and I forgot how long it took to arrange everything. I decided against makeup, but I did pin my hair up into a French twist, something I had helped my mother do when she'd had important embassy events to attend. I thought of her as I tied up some escaped strands, and wondered if she had ever worn her hair this way for my father before they were married. Did she ever think about me and Liv? Or were we just the forgotten byproducts of her mistake?

I had just finished getting ready when I heard a knock at the door, and I was relieved to hear Liv sounding polite when she let Will in. I smoothed my hair one last time and hoped that my emerald-green dress was formal enough; it was simple and tied at the back of my neck in a halter, and reminded me of a conservative version of something Marilyn Monroe might have worn in the '50s. It was unseasonably warm, so I knew I wouldn't need the wrap that went with the dress. I was more than a little conscious of how bare my shoulders and back were.

I expected that Will would look handsome, but I didn't expect him to look quite so much like a movie star in his tuxedo. I wished for a minute that I had gone with the makeup. At least my hair was presentable.

He smiled when he saw me, and held out what I guessed was my other birthday present— a small pot of white orchids.

231

"You remembered," I said, softly touching their petals with my fingertip. "Thank you." I put the pot on the kitchen counter, and Will offered me his hand, which I took eagerly.

"Be careful tonight," Liv said. I wasn't sure which of us she was talking to.

"It's just the opera, Liv," I replied. "We'll be fine."

"We'll be home by one," Will said, smiling. "The traffic out of San Francisco can be heavy on weekend nights."

"I won't wait up."

As we got into his car, he gave me an appraising look. "You really do look beautiful tonight. Like a Greek goddess."

I flushed and he reached out and touched the edge of my face with his fingertips. "Ah, there it is," he said, sighing. He smiled but his eyes were troubled.

"What is it?" I asked.

"Nothing," he said, letting his hand fall from my cheek, one finger trailing along my bare neck. "You're just devastating." He turned back to the road and pulled out onto Camino Real.

It was nearly an hour drive to the San Francisco opera house, and I had been looking forward to having the time alone with Will to talk, but he was so reserved that I didn't know where to begin. I didn't want to call him out and ruin our evening with a fight, and, frankly, I was afraid of what he might say. Was he angry I'd been so stupid last night? Did he regret telling Liv the truth? I kneaded my hands and tried to focus on the scenery as we drove up the Bay.

After a while I got up the courage to reach for his hand, and he looked at me and smiled, as though he had just remembered that I was there. I was grateful, at least, that he took my hand in his and didn't let go. Maybe I was overreacting;

maybe he was just preoccupied with school. I tried to forget it and told myself to enjoy the evening.

When we arrived at the opera house, Will pulled into a nearby lot and handed the keys to the valet. The opera house was gorgeous, the front was graced with Greek columns and looked like something out of the Renaissance. Inside, the marble entryway was capped with a magnificent vaulted ceiling. I felt like I was inside a French palace, and with Will there, I didn't even feel out of place, even though we seemed to be the youngest people there by a good twenty or thirty years. Many of the other operagoers were enjoying a glass of champagne before the start of the first act, but we went and took our seats in the balcony.

"Are you excited?" Will asked, leaning over to speak in my ear.

"Oh, yes," I said. "It's wonderful." And it was; it was magical being there with him, and I felt like a princess who had woken from an enchanted sleep and was just beginning to discover how wondrous the world really was. I reached up to kiss his cheek, but he turned his face and I met his lips instead. His lips lingered on mine for longer than I expected, and when I pulled away, we both giggled like children.

"Stop that," I commanded in a quiet voice. "You're going to give these old fogeys a heart attack."

"It's not their hearts I'm worried about," he whispered, and he kissed me again. The old woman sitting behind us cleared her throat loudly, and we pulled apart. I was embarrassed, but I could tell Will was enjoying himself, so I leaned over and kissed the edge of his jaw again. Then the lights dimmed and we both turned toward the stage, our hands clasped with our fingers intertwined.

I knew the story of *Madame Butterfly* well, having listened to the recordings of it so often. Still, I felt a pang of sadness when Butterfly appeared on the stage, singing about her great love for her fiancé, Lieutenant Pinkerton. The audience knows he is only marrying her as a temporary diversion while he's stationed in Japan, until he can go home and find a "real" wife.

Butterfly, however, has no idea that Pinkerton's vows are only temporary, and she sings to him on their wedding night, telling her how much she loves him.

> *Beloved, you are the world, more than the world to me.*
> *Indeed I liked you the very first moment*
> *That I saw you.*
> *You're so strong,*
> *so handsome! Your laugh*
> *is so open and so hearty!*
> *The things you say are so fascinating.*
> *Now I am happy.*

I felt myself stiffen at her words: *Now I am happy.* She had no idea what was coming, that she would be abandoned in only a few months. I thought of myself, and my own newfound happiness, and again of Liv's warning. Was I a fool as well? Could I really be more to Will than just a distraction?

And what would happen to me after he left me alone with my shattered heart?

By the third act, when Butterfly finally realizes that she's been deserted, my heart broke with hers. I didn't even know I was crying until Will reached over and wiped a tear from my cheek. I couldn't watch the final scene, in which she kills herself so that she won't have to live with her dishonor. When the lights came up and the audience began applauding wildly, I was stunned; I had simply forgotten they were there.

We were both silent as we left the opera house and walked back to Will's car, though I wondered if he actually understood the real reason I was unable to speak. Maybe he thought I was just trying not to break the spell of the opera by talking about it, the way some people are quiet after watching a movie. We were halfway to San Mateo before he spoke to me.

"That really moved you, didn't it?" he said warmly, taking my hand.

I pulled away, and he looked over to me, surprised. "Did I say something wrong?" he asked.

"No," I said, and I couldn't keep my voice from quavering. "It's just I'm—am I making a fool of myself?"

"Making a … I don't understand. How?"

I couldn't look at him when I answered. "I just hope that if you felt … like Pinkerton … that you would tell me."

He looked outraged. "What do you mean, *if I felt like Pinkerton*? Is that what you're thinking now? That I'm using you?"

"I don't know," I said, feeling wretched. "Not using me, but not really in love with me, either."

He groaned. "I can't do this while I'm driving." He took the next exit onto an overlook next to the Bay. The stars were out now, and the lights of San Francisco were still visible to the north. It would have been beautiful, if I hadn't been so utterly miserable.

He got out of the car and came around to my side and opened my door, and we walked to the edge of the overlook, where a low stone wall marked the crest of the hill; beyond, it sloped down to the Bay. He sat on the wall, and as I did the

235

same he took off his jacket and slipped it over my bare shoulders. The night had grown chilly, and I was grateful for the warmth.

"What have I ever done," he asked, as I tucked my arms into his sleeves, "that made you feel like I don't love you? Tell me, so I can make things right. Because I do love you. I've loved you from the very beginning. Would I have told you the truth about myself otherwise?"

I didn't want to tell him; I'd promised myself that I wouldn't. But Liv's words had been pressing on me, and were weighing even more heavily on me that night.

He was looking at me expectantly, and I knew I would have to say something, even though I was sure I would regret it later.

"Tell me," he repeated.

"You're leaving," I said quietly, averting my eyes from him.

Nothing could have prepared me for his response.

He stood up, walked a few feet back toward the car, and then turned and came back, his face pale with shock.

"How did you know?"

"Oh," I said, as my breathing grew heavy. I felt like I had a lead weight on my chest. "I thought—I just meant, someday. You're leaving *now*?"

I barely understood what he told me after that; something about a collaboration with Adeep, and the development of some new crystalline compound that he could use to power his ship. I must have been staring at him completely glassy-eyed, because he was halfway through a sentence when he suddenly stopped speaking and sat down next to me.

"I'm sorry, Cara," he said, rubbing his temple. "This isn't how I wanted to tell you. I didn't want to tell you at all tonight. I wanted this to be special for you. For both of us."

"Special," I echoed. I was cold despite his jacket, and my entire body was shaking. I wondered if I would ever feel warm again. "How long have you known?"

"I wasn't sure until this morning," he croaked, and then cleared his throat.

"Oh," I said. "Oh. Oh, God."

"Cara," he said, his face a mask of pain, "what choice do I have? I love you. I know you think you've been some sort of diversion to me, but it isn't true. You are part of me now, part of my soul, and when I leave I will no longer be whole. But you're so young, and I can't stand the thought of you having any regrets. You say that you can live a celibate life with me. I know you believe it, but how will you feel in ten years? Or twenty? And when all your youth is gone and you can never get it back, will you regret that you wasted it on me? We both know that, in the end, you will stay with me because you'll feel obligated, and because you won't be able to bear the thought of hurting me. It's who you are. You will never push me away, no matter how much you might resent me, and then your entire life will have been wasted. How can I live with that?"

I didn't know what to say. I knew, in every fiber of my being, that he was wrong. I wanted him, had always wanted him, and would always want him. Before him, I had been like an empty shell. No, like a carcass, dragging my way through my miserable life, and then he came and made everything beautiful. Made *me* beautiful. And everything that had ever happened to me in my life, even the bad things, made sense because they made me who I was, made me the person that he loved. But

237

now none of that mattered because he was leaving, and I would just go back to being a half-dead thing wandering aimlessly through my non-life.

I didn't say any of that. What was the use? He wanted to leave—he *needed* to leave. I wouldn't make him feel guilty for that. I looked down at my hands, and a single, silent sob escaped my lips.

We sat in complete silence for what felt like several minutes, and I stared at the ground, trying to make sense of the turn my life had taken. I shook my head from side to side, not wanting to believe it. Finally, he reached out and took my face in his hands, tilting it up so that he could look directly into my eyes. His luminous gray eyes were so sad, and at the same time so achingly beautiful, that it was painful to look into them.

"If you ask me to stay, I'll stay," he murmured quietly as he looked at me with pleading eyes. I suddenly understood that this was what he wanted—for me to beg him to stay with me. He did love me. That part of him really did want to stay.

He wanted me to make the choice for him.

I wanted to, more than anything in the universe. I wanted to cry and beg and plead with him to stay with me forever, to tell him that I didn't care about making love or having children or any of it; that I just wanted *him*, and I knew that he would stay. Then, for a while, we would be happy together.

But what then? What if he gave up his only chance to go home, and then, one day, he realized that I was not worth it? What if the frustration of not being able to be physically intimate was too much for him to bear? What if one day I looked into his eyes, and instead of the love that was there now I saw only hate? Because he would hate me, eventually. He would be miserable—wanting a home he'd never see again, living a

238

human life he'd never fully experience—and it would be my fault. I wouldn't be responsible for making him unhappy. I couldn't. I loved him too much for that.

I'd seen that before, what happens if you ask too much of the person you love. Seen it in my mother's hate-filled eyes, in my father's back as he walked out the door every morning, fleeing from his own guilt.

So while the words threatened to rip themselves directly out of my throat: *Yes, I need you; I want you; don't leave me*, I was silent, biting my lip so hard I was sure it would bleed. I didn't want him to see me cry, so I pressed myself into his arms before the tears came. I tried to keep my breathing even so that he wouldn't be able to feel my sobs, but I couldn't stop the trembling.

He tightened his arms around me. "It's all right. I understand," he said quietly. I could hear the ache in his voice, and I knew that he didn't understand at all. Then he added, in the faintest whisper, "Remember me, when I'm gone."

I felt my heart shatter until I was sure there was nothing left.

There was only one question left to ask, though even forming the words was almost more painful than I could bear. "How long?" I whispered.

"About a week," he said softly. "Dr. Kleeman has some experiments planned with this sample, so it has to be before that."

A week. Could I live my whole life in a week? I decided I would have to try. I told myself that I would not waste any time falling apart now. There would be plenty of time for that after he was gone.

Chapter Nineteen

Betrayal

I didn't want to go to school that week. It seemed like even more of a joke than usual; who cared about recursive algorithms when my heart was being ripped out and sent forty-four light years away? I knew there would be fallout from skipping, especially after my disaster last Friday. Morgan and her cohorts would think they had gotten to me. I didn't care. I would deal with them later. I wanted to spend every last second with Will, though I wasn't sure why. I could store up as much of him as I wanted, like a camel drinking in the desert, but I would still be just as empty once he was gone.

I remembered with a mixture of pleasure and agony the way he had kissed me goodnight after he had told me he was leaving, holding me so tightly that I'd been unable to breathe. I wasn't sure how I'd had the strength then, to keep from asking him to stay. I had to remind myself over and over that it was wrong to ask, but I wasn't sure that when the time came for the real goodbye, the final moment, that I would be able to do it. Part of me hoped that I wouldn't be strong enough, and that part grew larger every second. I tried to remember the way my mother looked at my father during an argument—a picture of disgust and resentment—and imagined Will looking at me that way. It helped ease the urge to beg. I knew I was doing the right thing. I would rather die than have Will look at me like that.

Sunday passed, and I didn't hear from him. I wondered if he was trying to give me time to come to terms with everything, or maybe he was just trying to make the final repairs on his ship. I resisted the impulse to call him. I didn't want him to remember me as a pest.

That sentiment was gone by Monday morning, when I still hadn't heard from him. I waited until Liv was gone, called the school and told them I had mono, and called Will, who didn't answer. This sent my anxiety into overdrive, and I decided to go to campus to find him. The problem was that I had no idea where to look. For all I knew, he could be off at some other lab for the day, or at his ship. I decided to try the Physics Department first. It seemed like the logical place to start, and I didn't know where else to go.

I was just turning the corner in front of the building when I saw a flash of blue hair.

"Adeep!" I called. He turned toward me and smiled.

"Pretty, pretty, pretty Cara," he said. "Are you here to see me? Say that you are."

I could barely look at him. "I'm actually looking for Will."

"Ah, stupid wanker. He doesn't deserve you. Kudos for getting him to switch teams, though."

"Have you seen him today?"

"Not today. If you find him, let him know our sample's ready to go, okay?" He grinned and shook his head. "This is totally going to land me that post-doc at MIT."

My mouth was dry. "That's great."

He held up the notebook he was carrying. "I have to photocopy some papers for Dr. Singh. Will's office is up on the third floor, all right?"

"Thanks."

There were a lot of offices on the third floor, and though I looked, I couldn't find names marked on them anywhere. I peered through the cracks in the doors to see which ones had lights on, and when I found one, I knocked. A woman's voice ordered me in. I hoped that she would be able to help me find Will, and my heart raced in my chest.

I entered slowly, and stopped two feet in. I simply couldn't go any further; the entire floor was covered in boxes, and each box was topped with stacks of paper. The bookcases that lined every wall were overflowing, and books were stuffed sideways on top of each other. The office's occupant was a woman who appeared to be about seventy, with long white hair pulled back into a severe-looking bun. She changed from one set of eyeglasses to another when I came in, and pushed herself back from her desk, which was also piled high with papers.

"I don't give extensions," she said. "It says so right on the course syllabus. So you can save us both the trouble of asking."

"Oh, um, I'm actually not one of your students," I explained. "I'm looking for Will Mallory."

"Ah," she said as she closed her laptop. She gave me an appraising look. "You're the girl." When I didn't respond, she laughed. "I'm sorry," she said. "I forget that the names are not outside right now. They painted last week, you see, and they haven't put them back up yet. I'm Shelby Kleeman."

"Oh," I said, "It's nice to meet you." I wondered what Will had told her about me. I was surprised he had mentioned me at all.

242

"Sit, please," she said, pointing to the chair on the opposite side of her desk. It was piled with books, which I carefully placed in a stack on the floor.

"You must excuse my housekeeping abilities," she said. "You know, perfectionism is the enemy of the creative mind."

I fought a smile. It was the kind of thing Liv might have said.

"You are looking for Mr. Mallory."

"I couldn't find his office. Is he here today?" I asked.

She leaned back in her chair. "No," she said. "He's not here."

I could feel my face fall. Was this it, then? Was he gone? Without even a goodbye?

"Will he be back tomorrow?" I asked. I wondered if she knew that I was begging her for some tiny scrap of hope.

"I don't think he'll be back tomorrow, no."

I felt like all the air had been sucked out of the room. She was regarding me calmly with her large, pale eyes. She looked sad, I thought. Would she miss him, too? But she couldn't have known the truth about him. He wouldn't have told her.

"Oh," I muttered, and I slowly got up to leave. "Thank you."

"Wait," she said, motioning for me to sit back down. "There are some things I want you to understand first. About why I did what I did."

"Why you ..." I repeated. "I don't understand."

She slid the wedding band off her thin finger and twisted it between her fingertips, and I wondered if she was as crazy as Liv had said, or if she even remembered that I was in the room. Then, finally, she seemed to make up her mind, and she palmed her ring into her fist and looked up at me again.

243

"You know Will is a special boy," she said.

"Well, yes, of course."

She shook her head. "No. You know how I mean *special*, yes?" she said, and looked at me pointedly.

Did she know? Had he decided to tell her? Maybe this had to do with the crystalline compound he was telling me about. Maybe he had told her, at the end, so that she would give it to him. Still, I didn't want to give away anything he hadn't already divulged. So I just nodded. "Yes," I said.

"I always had a feeling about him," she said. "I wasn't sure at first, what it was. He's a bright boy, but he lacks a mathematical mind, you know. I thought at first he had just faked his transcripts, so I called the Physics Department at Delaware to check. Of course, they had never heard of him. But then, he knows too much about other things, things a graduate student shouldn't know, about cosmology, and about physical problems we haven't yet addressed. And he's so strange, but not in the normal way that physicists are strange."

There was a long pause before she continued. "Did Will tell you I have a son?" she asked.

"No. He didn't."

"I have. I have not seen him for eight years. My only son. He is in Federal Prison, you see. He is a physicist, too. He lost his position, and the Russians offered to let him come work for them—we have contacts there, through my husband's family. First he had to give them his research, but it was classified, his work, and you don't give classified nuclear information to the Russians, even if it is based on your own research. It was a stupid, stupid thing he did. Now they will never let him out."

"Oh," I said, "I'm sorry." I didn't understand any of this, but I was growing more and more uneasy by the second.

244

"A mother would do anything for her child," she said. "Anything, you know. Anything. I had a chance to help him. I knew I had to do it. It was the only chance I would ever have. You understand, I had no choice."

I struggled to breathe. "What did you do?" I asked. "What did you do to Will?"

"I waited," she explained. "I knew what he was doing, that he needed the fuel for his ship. I waited until it was ready, and made sure he had access to it, so that he could take it. Now I have fulfilled my side of the bargain, and he can go home, and I haven't really harmed him. He is free now. So you see, it was not really so bad, what I did."

"What did you do?" I shouted as I rose to my feet. I looked down at her and saw how old and frail she was. "Tell me!"

She looked away from me, and I could tell she was tired. "There was a man, a federal agent, who had been looking for someone like Will. He knew that he was nearby, but he didn't know who he was. So I made a bargain. Now my son is free, and Will can go home."

I felt my stomach seize as I understood her words. She had given Will up. The only question remaining was, was he already gone? Had he left without even a word to me?

"I have to find him," I said, overturning my chair on the way to the door. As I ran from her office I heard her reply.

"You can't. He's already gone."

I ran then, faster and harder than I had ever run before, though I knew in my heart what I would find. I ran to the other side of campus, to Will's building, and by the time I had climbed the stairs to his apartment I was so winded I thought I might pass out. I stood in front of his door, panting, and I knew that as long as I stood out there, I could maintain the illusion that he

245

might be inside. As long as I stayed there, he was still with me. I still had the chance to tell him not to go. I knew, then, that I would. I didn't care if it was the wrong thing to do anymore. My moment had come and I was weak, and it didn't matter what the consequences might be. I wanted him, and that one thought was completely consuming. Nothing else mattered. I closed my eyes and envisioned it: I would knock, and he would come to the door, and I would tell him how wrong I had been about everything, and that I loved him, and that he had to stay with me, and he would tell me it was what he had wanted all along and he would kiss me and everything would be wonderful and we would be together and I could breathe again.

I saw it then—I saw all of it. He would stay in his form, and we would grow old together. Maybe we would even adopt children someday; I knew he would be a wonderful father. We would go kayaking, and he would show me the kelp forest I had always wanted to see, we would see the world together, and every second I would be touching him, smelling him, feeling him, and I would never forget how close I came to letting him go, and I would get down on my knees and thank God every day for letting Will stay with me, for letting me keep him, for giving me another chance. Please, God, I prayed, though I had never been religious before, please let me keep him and I will do anything. Anything. Just let me keep him. The words echoed in my mind over and over: *please, please, please.*

Then there was nothing left for me to do but knock.

No one answered.

Maybe he was in the bathroom. Maybe he was getting himself ready to leave and hadn't heard me. Maybe he was asleep. I reached out and turned the knob. It was unlocked, the door opened under my hand, and I stepped into the apartment.

246

It was empty.

All the furniture was still there, of course—that belonged to the university. But his books, his paintings, his computer, even his sheets, all of them were gone. I was alone, standing in the living room where Will and I had eaten ice cream, where Will had kissed me for the first time and felt it so deeply that he had literally fallen apart. I fell to my knees then, but I didn't cry. There were no tears for something like this. To cry requires the presence of a person in pain. There was no person, no *me* anymore. There was only the pain. I didn't feel the void. I *was* the void.

It was all the worse because I knew it had been my fault. With a single word, everything might have been different. He still would have had to run, I couldn't have changed that, but we could have run together. I wouldn't have been left behind, wishing that just once I had told him that I needed him.

I knew it was too late, but it was all I had left, so as I knelt on his bare floor, I whispered, "*Stay*."

Chapter Twenty

Held

How do you gauge the passage of time when time no longer matters to you? Nothing mattered to me anymore. I was alone. The most pathetic thing was that I realized that nothing had really changed, I was just back to where I started before Will had come into my life and woken me up. I would just go back to being asleep. Anesthetized. The version of *Sleeping Beauty* that no one remembers, where the princess tells Prince Charming, "Thanks, but I don't really need you," rolls over, and goes back to bed.

I finally understood that I really had been asleep before. How do you go back to "normal" once you've realized that "normal" is worthless? For my entire life, I'd had one great hope: I would leave home, go to college, and finally be able to take charge of my own destiny. I wouldn't be dragged from country to country like an oversized carry-on bag. I wouldn't be treated like a miscreant by unhappy, child-hating teachers. I would be a scientist, like Liv, and I would immerse myself in the lives of other species, and not have to worry about the difficulties I had with my own. Now that hope was gone, and I saw how empty that dream had been.

What use is a dream, alone in the dark?

I would have been in control, but I would still have been just as alone as ever, hiding in my little cave, never wanting to let anyone touch me. Will was the only one who had ever made me want to change that. Who had ever made me want to come out in the sun, who made me see what I was capable of becoming.

Still, there was Liv. My best friend. It was not the same, no matter how much I loved her; there was too much of a wall between us, and that was never going to change. But I would go home, and muddle through, and we would eat pizza and fight about the laundry. It was not much, really, compared to what I'd lost, but it was something. Enough to get me off the floor. It's as much as I could have hoped for, enough to be able to find the strength in my body to go home.

So I went home. I would tell Liv, and she would say she was sorry and try not to act like she had known all along how this would turn out. She would feed me ice cream, and I would pretend to feel better, and I would go on with my sorry existence, just as I had always done.

I dragged myself up the steps to my apartment, feeling the exhaustion in every muscle. I unlocked the door and walked inside.

And fell over the contents of the coat closet, which were strewn across the entryway.

The apartment had been completely ransacked. All of Liv's books and papers were scattered over the floor, and even the kitchen cabinets had been emptied. The refrigerator stood open, and all the containers inside were either overturned on the shelves or flung onto the ground, leaking puddles of milk and leftover Chinese food onto the tile.

249

That wasn't the worst part.

All my plants, everything in the window garden I'd so carefully tended, had been uprooted and torn to bits. Dirt covered the floor under the window, mixed with pieces of broken pottery. They were all dead. I picked up a piece of my maidenhair fern and held it in my hand. "Oh," I whispered, "I'm sorry."

I couldn't save them.

Bob's terrarium was also in pieces on the floor; the soil I'd piled into the bottom to give him a place to burrow was gone. There was no sign of the pupa that Bob had become. Had they smashed him, too?

I ran down the hall and into Liv's room, and it was the same, and her computer was gone. I already knew what my room would look like when I got there.

Like Liv's, my computer had been taken, and everything else I owned was on the floor. I saw with dismay that my opera dress, which I had left hanging over my chair, was missing. Had they been spying on us last night? I wondered how long they had been watching us, and how they knew to tie Will to me. And to Liv.

It suddenly occurred to me that I should run, but I didn't know where to go. Where was Liv? Was she still on campus? I pulled out my phone and tried calling her, but there was no answer. Damn. I would have to go back to campus and find her, though I had no idea what we would do. Maybe I should just tell them the truth. What did it matter, now that Will was gone? No, I decided, I wouldn't run. It didn't matter if they caught me. I was only human. I couldn't possibly be of any interest to them.

That thought didn't bring me any comfort when I looked up to see a strange man walking into my bedroom. Only I quickly realized that he wasn't a stranger. He was the man who'd grabbed my arm, all those months ago. The one who was supposed to be from Cal Tech. Of course. Why was I surprised?

The look on his face frightened me—triumph, as if he knew he had already won. I jumped to my feet as he approached, and he held out his hands as if to calm me.

"Easy there, Caroline," he said with a smile, "Or do you prefer that I call you Cara?"

"I prefer Ms. Gallagher, actually," I shot back. "Who are you, and what have you done with my apartment?"

He smiled and flashed a badge—inscribed with the FBI insignia—from inside his jacket. "I think you know quite well who I represent, Ms. Gallagher. My name is Charles Dalier. I have been observing you for some time, and I know all about your relationship with the alien known as Will Mallory."

"What are you talking about?" I said. The less he thought I knew, the better.

"Please, let's not waste time on this. I am well aware of how much you know. Do you recognize this?" he reached into his jacket pocket and pulled out a small glass container, but it appeared to be empty.

"There's nothing in there."

"Look closer." He stepped toward me and I took the container from him and held it a few inches from my eyes. I tried not to gasp; there was, in fact, nothing solid inside the container, but I recognized the dense, slightly bio-luminescent gas immediately. "What is that?" I asked, and I didn't have to feign my surprise. I wondered how he had gotten it. Did he have Will already, then? My heart sank.

"If you don't stop this, I am going to become angry, Cara. Tell me where he is."

251

"He's gone," I said, simply.

"Gone?"

"He went home," I explained. "He's not coming back." I could hear the despair in my voice, but as I looked up at Agent Dalier, I could tell he was not convinced.

"For both our sakes, I hope that isn't true," he said, taking the glass container from me and putting it back in his pocket.

"What do you mean by that?"

"I'm disappointed, Cara, that you've been harboring this dangerous creature for so long, when you knew that you had an obligation to report him to the proper authorities."

"*What*?"

"Oh, indeed. Unfortunately, you are not the only one in your family to make that mistake. I notice that you haven't asked me even once about the whereabouts of your sister."

"Liv?" I said, feeling the horror rise in my stomach. "Liv's at school," I protested.

"That's where she should be, yes," he replied with an acid smile. "When she learned that her younger sister had skipped school with a fake illness, she came home to find her. We have her in custody now."

"What for?" I demanded.

"For harboring an enemy of the state, of course. The charge that you also face."

"I don't—I don't understand. Liv didn't know anything. We didn't do anything wrong. Will never did anything wrong. He wasn't dangerous—"

"That wasn't your call to make, my dear. My colleagues and I are going to get answers about Mr. Mallory. If we can't get them from him, we will have to get them from you and your sister. However, we would obviously prefer to have these

252

conversations with Mr. Mallory himself. If we had him in hand, we wouldn't have a need for you or Liv."

"I told you, he's gone," I said, my voice rising sharply. At least they didn't have Will. But they did have Liv. I thought briefly of calling the police, but calling the police on the FBI seemed ridiculous. Who else would I call? Maybe my father knew someone, he had a top-secret clearance, but I doubted that was high enough.

He ignored my statement. "If you bring Mr. Mallory to me in the next twenty-four hours, I will see to it that your sister is released," he said, backing toward the door. "Otherwise, I will keep her, and we will come for you as well. Consider carefully where your loyalties lie, Ms. Gallagher. Mr. Mallory is not human. He is not your blood. And you do not understand his motivations. He's lied to you, Cara. Used you. And now left you alone to clean up his mess. Think about that."

He opened my door, but before he went out he turned to me one last time. "Twenty-four hours, Cara," he said, and then he was gone. I listened until I heard the front door of the apartment open and close, and I ran to my bedroom door to make sure he had really gone. I was alone. I fell into a heap on my bare bed and tried not to break into a million pieces.

Will was gone. Liv was gone. I thought I could never be in a lower place than I had been that morning in Will's empty apartment, but this was a thousand times worse. Had Liv been hurt? No, I told myself. They wouldn't hurt her unless they knew they couldn't get to Will. Which wouldn't be for another day, when they realized that he really was gone. I would call my father, but I knew, deep down, that he would be unable to help, even in the unlikely event that he did believe me. There was nothing left to do but wait for them to come back and take me.

Maybe I could persuade them to let Liv go once they had me. She knew less than I did, after all. I breathed deeply, trying to calm myself down. There was nothing left to be upset about. It was over now, and I was out of choices.

I looked down at the floor under my window; on top of a pile of books was my orchid, the one Will had given me only a few days before. I'd set it on my windowsill that night, wanting to have that little piece of him close to me. It had been pulled out of the pot, the roots pulled to bits, and the pot itself lay sideways on the floor, as empty as I felt. I gathered the wilting petals and held them cupped in my hand, still able to smell their lingering fragrance. I balled them into my fist, feeling my nails bite into their soft flesh and fell forward with my head against my knees. The numbness was starting to wear off, and I wanted to cry. No, I wanted to scream. I picked up the pot and flung it against the wall, where it shattered into nothing. It gave me no comfort.

I had nothing. No Will. No Liv. Not even my plants. I was alone.

Then, without warning, there was a loud knock at the window, and I was so startled I threw my hands over my head, half expecting a blow. I looked up warily, but I couldn't see anyone, and, anyway, we were on the third floor and there was no balcony, so how could someone be knocking? I must have imagined it.

Then I heard it again, and my heart stopped. Throwing itself against my window, in a kind of frenzy, was a blackbird. In his beak was a small oilcloth pouch.

I couldn't have opened the window any faster if there had been a fire in the room, but the screen was still in the way, and I couldn't budge it. I sobbed as I tried to pry it loose. Finally I

254

gave up and stood up on the desk and kicked it, again and again, until it finally bent in half and I pushed it out the window. I could hear it fall to the ground below with a crash. The blackbird flew inside, and I collapsed on top of the desk.

The next thing I felt was the pressure of Will's arms around me, and I cried out and buried my face in his naked chest.

"What did that screen ever do to you?" he muttered.

I was laughing and crying at the same time as he stroked my hair. "You left," I sobbed.

"Did you think so? Did you really think I would leave without saying goodbye to you?" he said tenderly.

"I saw Dr. Kleeman," I explained.

"Ah, so you know. They did come for me, but I'm not so easy to catch."

"I guess not, but they were here,"

"Yes, I see that," he said, looking around the room. "They're still here, actually. They were watching your apartment from a truck across the street when I got here. So we might not have much time, depending on whether they noticed you beating the hell out of the window just now."

"No, you don't understand," I said. "Liv. They took Liv." I could barely get the words out. My relief at seeing Will again was gone, and in its place was the despair at the realization that my sister had been captured.

"Liv?" he repeated, and I felt his body freeze inside my arms. "Why did they want Liv?"

"They know everything. They knew that I knew, and that Liv knew, and the man—Agent Dalier—he said that if I didn't turn you over to him, he would keep Liv, and arrest me, too."

"What did you tell him?" he asked, and his voice was both calm and sad, which only frightened me more.

255

"I told him you were gone."

He sighed deeply. "I'm so sorry, Cara. I'm sorry for all of this. Please don't be afraid, I won't let you or Liv suffer on my account. It'll be all right."

I pulled myself back so I could look at his face. "What do you mean?" I asked. "You aren't seriously thinking of turning yourself in."

He stroked my face with his finger. "What else can I do? I can't let them take you. They would never let you go. How could I live with that?"

"Don't you know what they'll do to you?" I countered. "It's a million times worse than what they would do to us."

He flashed a mischievous grin. "Don't worry about me. Like I said, I'm not easy to hold onto."

"You don't know that. They know exactly what you are. For all you know, they've come up with a way to keep you from escaping. I didn't tell you—they have a sample of you."

"A sample?" he said, looking troubled.

"Yes, in a little glass vial. How did he manage to get that?"

He frowned. "I'm not sure. He knows more about me than I thought he did, but it doesn't matter. I still have to turn myself over to him, I can't do anything else. I won't run off and leave you and Liv to rot for my sake. I'll just have to take my chances."

"But if you can't escape—"

"If I can't, then I can't. And you will go on, and you will live your life, and be happy. You are my angel. As long as I know you are safe, what happens to me doesn't matter."

"It matters to me," I said. I took a deep breath as I prepared to say the words I'd longed to say to him for the past two days. "I know it's wrong for me to ask, but it's what I

256

want—for you to stay." I was crying hard, but I forced myself to continue. I didn't know if I would ever get another chance to tell him. "I love you, I love you so much, and when I thought you were gone, I felt like something inside of me died." I choked and barely managed to speak the words I'd longed to say: "*I need you.*"

He had tears in his own eyes. "Cara, if you knew how much I wanted to hear you say that, how much I hoped you would … but I didn't want you to think I was forcing you to keep me." He pulled me close again. "It's not wrong for you to ask, if it's what you really want. What was wrong was for me not to tell you it was what I really wanted in the first place." He coughed, and I could tell he was trying to keep himself from crying as hard as I was. "But now, I don't think I can stay. If Dalier even suspects I'm still here, he'll never stop watching you."

He held me tightly until I was able to stop myself from sobbing. "We could run away together," I said into his shoulder.

"We could," he said, "but even if we got you away, what about Liv? It's the only way. I have to leave, and he has to see me go."

"Assuming he isn't dissecting you instead," I said bitterly.

"Yes, assuming that."

I knew he was right, but that didn't ease the pain. I thought I had gotten Will back, and now that hope had been dashed again. It was almost too much to bear. I wanted to curl up in a ball and just be one with my misery. But I couldn't; I still had to think of Liv.

He rested his cheek on top of my head, and through my hair I could feel that his face was wet. "Do you feel it too, then?" he murmured. "The emptiness?"

257

"Yes," I whispered. "It feels like a black hole inside me, spreading out everywhere."

"I know." He pressed his lips against my hair. "I know."

He leaned down and kissed me, and I reached up and pulled his face closer to me, wanting the moment to last. But there was no pleasure, only the anguish of knowing that this would be the last time. When he finally pulled away, I had no choice but to let him go.

"I'm sorry," he said, catching his breath. "This is so much harder for me than I would have thought. My people don't have such intense emotions. Grief isn't so powerful for us. Or regret."

"Regret? Do you regret being with me?"

"Oh, no, never. Not for an instant. I regret how much this has hurt you. I regret that I couldn't find a way for us to be together."

"Well, I don't have any regrets," I said. "Even knowing that I would have to lose you, I wouldn't have changed anything. These last few months have been the most wonderful time in my life."

"For me, as well," he said. "I wish there were some way for me to tell you how much, how deeply, I love you."

"Don't worry," I said. "I already know."

We held each other in silence, trying to wring out the last few seconds of our time together.

Chapter Twenty-One

Exchange

It took every bit of resolve I had left to pull away. "Liv," I reminded him.

"Yes," he agreed. "Liv. We don't want to leave her with them any longer than we need to. There is one other thing." He flipped through the former contents of my desk, and it wasn't until then that I realized that he was completely naked. Of course, I thought. He flew in as a bird. He finally came up with a scrap of paper and a pen, and wrote down a ten-digit number. "This is the number of my account at the United Bank of Switzerland. It's not a lot, but there should be enough there to take care of you and Liv for the rest of your lives. It's a numbered account, so if you lose this number, you won't be able to access it. Do you understand?"

I nodded. He slid the paper into his oilcloth pouch, and then slipped that around my neck. "It isn't much," he said. "But it's all I have left to give you."

"It's all right. You've given me enough already."

He smiled wistfully and kissed me quickly. "I don't suppose you have anything I could wear? I hate to turn myself in like this."

There was no hope of any of my clothes fitting him, but one of Liv's oversized shirts might work. It would be better than nothing, anyway, so I sifted through the mass of debris the FBI had left on her floor. I shouldn't have been surprised when I came up with a man's shirt and pair of pants. Steve's, probably. They would be too big for Will, but at least he would be able to walk out of the apartment with his dignity intact.

He dressed himself quickly, and then took my hand. "You should stay here," he said. "There's no reason for you to watch this."

"No," I replied. "I'll go with you. I want to be with you until the very end."

"All right, then," he conceded. "Off we go. To the very end."

I could see the box truck on the other side of the parking lot as soon as we started walking down the stairs, and I was surprised that I hadn't noticed it before. We walked toward it slowly, hand in hand, and I could feel my heart accelerating with every step. Two black-suited agents, one of whom was Dalier, got out of the truck. I had the sudden impulse to run. Something about Dalier was off, but I couldn't put my finger on it. I squeezed Will's hand, and he squeezed mine back. His eyes never left Dalier.

"Mr. Mallory," Dalier said smoothly. "It's good to finally meet face to face."

Will nodded, but was silent. The second agent quickly slipped a pair of handcuffs over Will's wrists, and walked him to the back of the truck. Then, with alarming speed, he pulled something out of his coat—a Taser, I thought—and shoved it into the small of Will's back. Will cried out in pain, and I screamed.

"Stop!" I begged. "He's already going with you, please!"

The second agent opened the back of the truck and thrust Will inside.

"Don't hurt him," I pleaded.

"Oh, don't worry," Dalier said, with a smile, and I suddenly understood why I was afraid. "You'll be able to look after him yourself, more or less." He grabbed my arm so hard I gasped in pain, and clapped his other hand over my mouth. Before I could even think of fighting him off, the second agent was there again. Together the two men cuffed my hands and threw me inside the back of the truck. I landed on the hard metal floor with a crash. The door slammed shut behind me.

"No!" I heard Will shout. "This was not our arrangement! I will not cooperate with you as long as you are holding them."

Them? I lifted my head and looked around— there, at the far end up the truck, was Liv, handcuffed and gagged. Her left eye was swollen, and she had a scrape across the side of her face, but she was conscious. Will was next to her. As I tried to get up he struggled to get to me—which was when I realized that the three of us were not alone. A third agent, a behemoth of a man dressed entirely in black, stood between me and the door to the truck, and in his hands he held an automatic rifle. When Will moved toward me, the man jerked his gun toward him. "Stay back," he ordered.

Then I heard Agent Dalier's voice through the back of the truck. "You see, Mr. Mallory, I understand the situation perfectly. I know that under normal circumstances, I would be unable to hold you. I need her to control you, and I need the sister to control her." I could hear his footsteps receding, and both doors to the cab opened and shut. Then we began moving.

261

I crawled to the back of the truck and pressed myself against Will, and I leaned over to whisper to Liv, "Are you all right?"

She glared at me and said a few garbled words into her gag. It sounded vaguely like "I knew this would happen."

I looked at Will. "What did they do to you? Was that a Taser?"

"No," he said quietly. "I don't know what it was. There was pain, but I think a Taser would have made me revert. That was something else."

"Quiet!" the man with the gun snapped.

I glanced over at Will. His eyes were fixed on the oilcloth pouch, which was still around my neck, then moved up to meet mine. I understood. He needed it. But the man with the gun was staring at us intently, and there was no way for me to give it to him. I would have to wait for the right moment, but I wasn't sure how long we had. I pressed myself against Will's side and tried to stay calm.

My moment came sooner than I expected when we hit a pothole and the truck bounced a good foot into the air. I threw myself down on my side as though I had fallen, and quickly grabbed the oilcloth pouch in my teeth and pushed it into Will's hands. He slid the cord over my head in one swift movement.

"Get up!" shouted the man, and I heard the gun cock. "Now!"

I did as I was told, moving slightly in front of Will to block the agent's view of his hands. He didn't seem to notice that the pouch was no longer around my neck. From my peripheral vision, I could see Will's fingers fumbling inside the pouch. Then he glanced over at me and leaned toward Liv. "Keep down," he whispered. Will jabbed something between his teeth, and as the

262

man cried out and raised his gun, Will became a bird and flew directly toward him. His handcuffs clattered to the floor beside me.

The man tried to fire, but Will was too fast, and before he could adjust his aim, Will was human again and only inches away. He gasped, as if he had not understood before what Will was capable of, and Will spun and smashed his elbow directly into his face. As the agent staggered back, Will wrestled his gun away and brought the butt of the weapon hard down on the back of his head. He fell to the floor, unconscious.

Will felt the man's pockets, coming up with a cell phone, a pocketknife, and a set of keys which he used to unlock Liv and me. I untied Liv's gag, and she rubbed the side of her head as she glanced at Will. She gave me a bemused look. "Is he naked a lot?"

Will looked slightly embarrassed as he pushed experimentally on the back of the truck. "It's locked from the outside," he explained.

"Wait," Liv said. "Wait a minute—"

"We have to get out of here," I said. "I think we're out of town by now. We haven't stopped for a while."

Liv's frown deepened. "Those days when you couldn't work your bra?"

"I think it's just a regular padlock." Will said, jiggling the doors. Pointedly ignoring Liv.

"What are you talking about?" I asked Liv.

Liv glared at me. "That wasn't you."

Oops.

Liv's mouth fell open. "Son of a bitch saw me naked!"

"*What*?" I asked.

"I didn't enjoy it!" Will protested.

263

"What??" I cried.

"Son of a bitch!" Liv shouted.

Will waved at us to be quiet. "Can we talk about this later?"

"WHAT??"

Will held up his hand and picked his oilcloth pouch off the floor, putting his dark hair and black feather back inside. He pondered its contents for a few seconds before he finally found what he was looking for. "Don't ask where I got this," he said. He handed me the phone and the knife he had taken from the unconscious agent. "Hang onto these, just in case."

He backed away from us, all the way to the far end of the truck. Then he smiled and looked dead into my eyes. "Trust me," he said.

Suddenly, taking up most of the truck was a gigantic grizzly bear.

Liv opened her mouth to scream, and I smacked her on the shoulder. "It's just Will!" I said. "Be quiet!"

I shouldn't have worried about them hearing. Will let out a roar and slammed his shoulder into the truck's door. The entire truck shuddered, and I could hear the agents in the front shouting as we came to a screeching stop. Will rammed his body into the back of the truck again, and the door flew open. I grabbed the oilcloth pouch and Will's clothes, Liv grabbed the gun, and we followed Will out of the back of the truck.

Agent Dalier and his associate were already there, waiting with guns drawn. They fell back as Will reared up and let out another deafening roar. The second agent raised his gun, and, as Dalier shouted at him to stop, he fired. Blood spurted from Will's shoulder, and he charged the man with the gun, knocking him to the ground with a single swipe of his huge paw. I pulled

264

Liv back with me, careful to keep the two of us on the other side of Will. I knew he could only fight as long as he knew we were safe. If Dalier got a clear shot at us, it was over.

Will paused and glared at Dalier, who stared back. I looked from man to bear, not sure who would be the first to back down. Eventually, Dalier lowered his gun. Will looked over his shoulder at me and nodded his great head at the back of the truck, and I knew what he wanted. "Come on," I said to Liv, and we climbed back in and, together, shoved the unconscious body of the third agent out of the truck and onto the ground, and I untied his shoes and took them with me. I ran to the front of the truck, but when I turned, Liv hadn't followed me.

She was behind the truck again, and as I ran toward her, she raised the rifle and aimed at Agent Dalier. "You hit me."

"It was necessary."

"You kidnapped my sister."

"Again, necessary."

She took the safety off the rifle. "Give me one reason why I should not shoot you."

Dalier's face remained calm, but I could see his hand twitch. "Because," he said. "I'm a federal agent. No one would ever stop looking for you. As it stands now, no one is dead."

"So you're saying that if I let you live, you aren't going to continue chasing us?" she asked.

He glanced at Will. "Of course."

"How stupid do you think I am, exactly? I will ask you again, why shouldn't I shoot you?"

Before he could answer, I saw a car coming down the road.

"Liv," I said. "There's no time for this. Shoot him or don't, but we have to go."

265

Liv hesitated for a second before lowering the gun with a grunt of disgust. Then she followed me into the cab, and Will, now human again, was close behind her. I tossed him his clothes and the agent's shoes and he pulled on his pants as I swerved the truck back onto the highway.

"There was something wrong with that," I said, stomping on the accelerator.

"Really?" Liv said. "I thought it was delightful."

"No, I mean, they made it too easy for us. Why would they cuff Will's hands in front of him? Why would they leave the pouch with me? They must have had some idea what it was."

"You're right," Will said as he pulled his shirt over his head. "They must be hoping to track us. We need another car."

"What is the plan now, exactly?" Liv asked, checking the mirror on her side of the truck. "No one's following us, as far as I can tell."

"I need to get back to my ship," Will said.

"You can't really believe they're going to leave us alone after you're gone," I said. "I think we need a new plan."

"I have a better idea," said Liv. "Give me the phone you took off the big goon in the back." I handed it to her and she dialed quickly.

I heard a male voice pick up. "Steve?" she said. "This is Liv. I know, a long story. Listen, I need you to do something really important for me, and I need you not to ask any questions. Okay, first thing, Cara and I are being chased by a *hideously* crazy FBI agent."

At this point she had to pause while there was a lot of noise on the other end of the line. "No, really. I need you to listen. He thinks we're harboring an extraterrestrial." More noise. "Shut it, Steve! Look, if you haven't heard from me in two

266

hours, I need you to call your friend Bill at the *Chronicle*, and my father at the embassy in Montevideo. No, this is real. I need you to promise. Okay."

She hung up the phone. "Do you really think that will work?" Will asked.

"It will if you're gone. Bill writes front-page stuff all the time, and he'd be all over this. I don't think Cara and I are worth enough to them to risk a big public embarrassment."

Will smiled at me. "She has a plan."

I rolled my eyes. "You always have to be the smart one, don't you?"

"Always," she said. "Now we need to split up and get you to another car before Agent Mulder catches up with us. You don't know how to hot-wire a car, do you?" she asked Will.

"As a matter of fact, I do."

I looked at him in surprise, but he shrugged. "After sixty-five years, you pick these things up."

"Really?" I asked. "Can you crack a safe, too?"

He smiled. "What kind of safe?"

Liv laughed. "You know, you aren't quite as awful as I thought you were."

"Glad I have your approval."

She snorted. "I wouldn't go that far." She shot him a dirty look. "*You didn't enjoy it?*"

"I—"

"Just forget it."

There was a gas station ahead, and she pointed at it. "Pull over there. You're going to have to be fast. Oh, which way will you be going?" she asked.

"West and south," he said. "Down the coast."

"We'll go north, then. We'll lead them away for as long as we can."

"Wait! Liv," I said, "What if your plan doesn't work? What if they don't care about the newspaper and the State Department?"

"I have twenty-two years of repressed anger and an automatic weapon," she said with a grin. "I'll figure something out."

"Don't even joke about that."

"It won't come to that. I promise." She looked over at Will. "Now get out."

I pulled over beside the gas station and opened my door. "Wait," shouted Liv, grabbing my arm. "Where are you going?"

"I'm going with Will," I explained.

"No, Cara, stay with Liv," Will said. "It's safer this way."

"No," I said firmly. "I'm going with you. To the very end. I told you."

He hesitated, but he could see the resolve in my face. "All right," he said. "Going with me is safer than sitting here arguing. Let's go."

"How are you planning on getting back, exactly?" Liv said, still hanging onto my arm.

"I'll find a way. I'll have a car, after all."

Liv let go, reluctantly. "Go, then," she said. "Be careful."

I kissed her cheek and slid out of the cab, and she moved over to take my place behind the wheel. Will got out on his side and as we backed away from the highway, she sped off. She must have been going ninety miles an hour by the time she was out of sight.

We made our way quickly to the gas station, where there were about half a dozen cars parked outside. One belonged to

268

the owner, and the others must have belonged to people shopping at the mini-mart or using the bathrooms. "Which one?" I asked.

"That one," he said, pointing at an old gray sedan near the edge of the lot. "They've left the window down. And it looks too old to have an anti-theft system."

Will reached in and unlocked the doors, and we slid inside as quietly as we could. He then kicked off the access panel below the steering wheel and began fumbling with the wires. He took the pocketknife, stripped away some of the insulation, and twisted some of the wires together. I was surprised by how fast he was. "Have you done this often?" I asked.

"Not often," he said. "Let's just say it's come up before."

"You've had an exciting time here on Earth," I said, fastening my seatbelt.

"Actually, it was fairly dull before you came along."

The engine came to life and we sped off.

Chapter Twenty-Two

Past Imperfect

Will drove fast, looking frequently in the rearview mirror, but no one seemed to be following us. "We're heading down the coast," he said, pointing ahead. It won't be long now."

"Where is it, exactly?"

"In the reserve at Pomponio."

"Really? How come no one's seen it?"

"It's hidden," he explained. "You would say it's cloaked."

"Got it," I said. "Fancy alien technology. Too bad you don't have a phaser."

"That would have been handy."

We drove for another half-hour, and as the adrenaline wore off, it sank in that this was really the end. I would watch Will get on his ship, he would fly off home to the stars, and I would be left to go home, alone. If I was lucky and didn't end up in a jail cell somewhere.

I stared at him, trying to memorize every line in his face, every fleck of color in his gray eyes. He caught me staring, and smiled. "What is it?" he asked.

"Nothing," he said. "I'm just trying to fix you in my mind. So I can remember that you were real."

He looked abashed. "Cara, if there were any way I could stay with you—"

"I know," I said, cutting him off. "I know you would."

He reached out and put his arm around me, and his hand was tight on my shoulder as he pulled me closer. I rested my head against him, trying to feel his warmth in every part of me. "Will you still remember me," I asked, "in a thousand years?"

He swallowed hard and winced. "I don't like to think about that."

"We won't talk about it, then," I said, reaching up to smooth the hair out of his eyes.

We arrived at the entrance to the wildlife refuge, and left the car running in the lot. I took Will's hand as we jogged down the trail. After about ten minutes, we veered off onto the dunes.

It was not an easy walk, but after another few minutes we came to a clear, flat area. The ground was more dirt than sand, and it was easier to walk on. "It's here," he said. He reached out his hand as if to touch something.

His hand made contact, and the air shimmered briefly. Then, materializing in front of us, there was a ship. It was not as large as I had thought it would be, but then, I remembered it was only designed to carry one person. It was shaped like a wing, about thirty feet long. Its silver shell glimmered as the sun broke through the clouds. I reached out to touch it, and was surprised to find the hull warm under my hand.

Will turned to me and laughed bitterly. "How many times have I had to say goodbye to you now?"

"Does it make it easier for you, saying it over and over?" I asked, slipping my arms around him.

"No, it doesn't. In fact, the more times I say it, the more ridiculous it seems. That I would actually be able to get on this ship and leave, with you standing here."

I wanted to make it easier for him. I knew we were out of options. "Maybe we're just torturing each other," I said. "Maybe you should just kiss me one more time, and then go."

He leaned down and pressed his cheek against mine. "I will love you until I'm nothing more than a few fragments scattered on the wind."

"I will love you until I'm nothing but dust." I thought of the old myth of Gaia and Uranus—the love between the Earth and Sky, which is how life began. Dust and wind. But like them, our love was not meant to be.

He carefully placed his hand over my heart. I could see the tears in his eyes, the tension in his jaw. His breath caught as he whispered, "Goodbye, hummingbird," and he bent his head to kiss me with soft lips.

Then I felt something else. Something hard against the back of my head. Metal. I gasped and Will pulled back.

"If you move, even one inch, I will kill her."

I didn't have to turn around to know who it was. Agent Dalier was standing directly behind me, with one hand on my shoulder. The other hand held a gun that was pressed into the back of my skull.

"Back away, now," he commanded. Will's eyes were horrified—hollow—and he complied.

"Now," he said, "you're going to take us onto your ship."

"How did you find us?" I asked.

"You're friend Mr. Mallory isn't as untrackable as he thinks," he said, pushing me ahead of him as we walked toward the ship. "We've found that if you bombard his tissues with a low dose of a specific type of radiation, it makes him light up like a Christmas tree for the next six hours. Then, all we have to do is watch the satellite telemetry come in. You see, Mr. Mallory,

272

even if you decide to sacrifice your little pet here, we would still be able to find you. You can't escape."

"I have no intention of escaping," Will said flatly, and he touched a sequence of touchpads on the side of the ship. A hatch opened with a hiss, and a ramp slowly lowered to the ground. He turned and looked at Dalier. "What do you have in mind to do now?"

"Go up," Dalier said. "We will follow you."

Will walked up the ramp, and we followed. "If you hurt her," he said, "I will never do anything you ask."

"Aren't you noble."

We walked down a short corridor, and then we were in what I guessed was the control room. Across the front was a large viewscreen, which was shut off. In the middle of the room was what appeared to be a control station, consisting of a large panel about four feet across and illuminated with various small lights of different colors. In the center was a sphere, half set into the panel.

Agent Dalier took his hand from my shoulder and pulled something out of his jacket pocket. I looked over my shoulder and saw that it was a camera. He handed it to me. "I want you to take pictures of everything in this room."

I looked at Will, and he nodded, so I photographed the viewscreen, the control panel, and the corridors behind us, the beep of the shutter the only sound apart from my pounding heart and my breathing.

"Do you have an engine room?"

"Yes."

"Show me that."

We went back out into the corridor and down a flight of steep steps, into the bowels of the ship. There was a single room

273

at the bottom; it was small and the air was stale. The walls were lined with controls and flashing lights, and labeled with words in a language I couldn't read.

"I want you to show me this ship's power source," he said to Will.

Will hesitated. "The power source I'm using now isn't very stable. It would be better if it wasn't handled more than necessary."

Dalier chuckled. "Very well," he said. "We'll have a team out here by the end of the day to collect your ship for study. I'm sure it will prove very interesting to our scientists. We've learned so much about you already, thanks to the sample we obtained of your biological material."

"How did you get that?" I asked. It was a question that had bothered me since I first saw the glass vial containing part of Will. It didn't seem like the kind of thing he would leave behind without noticing.

"I'm sure Mr. Mallory knows how we came by it," he said. I looked to Will, who didn't react to this statement at all.

"I do have some idea where it came from," he said. "I'm not sure how *you* got it."

"Is young Cara aware of your past?" Dalier said. "Does she know that she was not your first human plaything?"

Will winced. "She knows," he said, resigned. I, on the other hand, was shocked. Will had told me about the woman he had been with before, but how could Dalier know?

"I will tell her, nevertheless. She should know exactly the kind of creature you are. It's only fair, after all. It was a luxury you didn't give Annabelle."

Annabelle. He had never told me her name. Will looked haggard. "Go ahead," he said. "I doubt you have any information I haven't already told her."

"Sixty years ago, Mr. Mallory was masquerading as an artist in New Orleans, although he went by the name of William DeTroix at the time. He was quite successful, actually. Not without talent. At any rate, he met a young woman named Annabelle Lewis, a college student, and she fell hopelessly in love with our friend here. Despite the mores of the times, she allowed him to seduce her. But, during this seduction he tired of her. He transformed into his true form and fled, leaving her alone."

He paused to gauge my reaction, and then continued. "She was, of course, terrified. After he was gone, she discovered that he had left some part of himself behind in his rush to leave. She collected it in an empty jar, and, though she went quite mad afterward, she never told anyone about the sample."

He turned me slightly so that he could get a better look at my face. "She did go mad. Science being what it was at the time, she was convinced he was a demon, but that wasn't the worst part. She loved him anyway, even believing him to be evil. Which, of course, he was. What other kind of creature could so thoroughly seduce, and then abandon, an innocent young girl? She appeared to recover, eventually. After a time, she even married and had a child, but she never got over him, or over the madness. All her life, she would wake in the dead of night, crying out for her demon lover to return to her. Of course, he never came back. She was completely broken, ruined, but he had moved on."

Will's face was contorted in agony, and I knew it was the first time he had heard the end of this story. "How," he said, "how do you know this?"

"She told me," Dalier said impassively, "before she died. She gave me the sample, which she had kept all her life, hoping he would come back for it. In the end, she told me everything." He took his eyes from me, and looked coldly at Will. "I was her son."

I felt a shock of pain as all the pieces fell into place, and I suddenly realized how dangerous Dalier actually was. He was not, as I'd thought, just an overzealous FBI agent. He was a son out for vengeance against the creature that had hurt his mother. He would never let either of us go. He would use me, for the rest of my life, to make Will suffer.

Will shook his head, "No," he said. "No. It wasn't like that. I didn't use her. I cared about Annabelle. You have to understand, when I reverted, it was because I'd lost control of myself, not because ... and after that, I was too afraid to come back. She would have despised me."

"Shut up!" Dalier barked. "She worshiped you, and you destroyed her! She died calling your name!"

Will sank to his knees. His eyes were glazed, and he whispered, "I'm so sorry. Oh, Annabelle, I'm sorry."

"You understand now," Dalier said into my ear. "You see what he is? You still think he's this poor, lost soul? He's a monster."

"No," I said, and my voice quavered. I thought of Annabelle. How could she not have loved Will? Of course she had. Her pain had been real. "But it wasn't his fault. He didn't mean for it to happen that way—"

"Still, you defend him," Dalier scoffed. "Well, it's what I expected. My mother defended him, too. Right until she died. She always said he would come back for her."

He jerked the gun back to my head. "I've seen enough here for now. Let's go."

Will rose slowly to his feet, and I could see that the light was gone from his eyes. He was completely defeated.

But I wasn't.

Despite everything, I knew that Will was not guilty of the crime Dalier accused him of. He had made a mistake. A terrible one, but that was all. He was no monster. I would not live out my life as the instrument of his torture. I would rather die than live that life.

I knew in that instant that death was a reasonable alternative, but I was still going to fight for my life. For Will's life. I tried to remember the self-defense classes Liv had dragged me to a few summers ago, and I took a deep breath to center myself.

Dalier had the gun pressed to the side of my head, but I knew he would hesitate to shoot me. Once I was dead, he would have no more hold over Will. I could feel his breath against the back of my neck, and I knew he was close.

Will slowly got to his feet, and I could tell that he had seen the change in my eyes, because now he looked horrified. "No," he said, and I knew he was talking to me.

Dalier jerked the gun back against me. "Now!" he barked. His attention, his anger was focused on Will, and I knew this was my chance. I quickly brought my head forward and slammed it back into his face. I felt pain and a snap as I flattened his nose. He swore and let go of me and I spun with my hands up, ready to go for his eyes. As my nails bit into his eyelids, he threw my body against the floor, pinning me under him. The gun was pointed at my face.

His face was the picture of madness, as blood streamed from his broken nose, and I knew I had miscalculated. He'd wanted his revenge to be slow and painful, but now that he knew he couldn't control me, that option was gone. He'd realized that he would have to either have his revenge right then or not at all.

"You stupid, stupid, little girl," he said, and he cocked the gun. He glanced at me and grinned. "This one means more to you than my mother did, obviously. And now you get to watch her die. It will be fast, though. Merciful, compared to what you did to my mother."

Will's roar was inhuman, pure agony and rage. I struggled under Dalier's grip, struggled harder than I thought was possible, and managed to jerk my head to one side. I heard the gun go off and felt something hot and wet graze the side of my ear.

Then Will's body slammed into Dalier knocking him off me. I tried to get up, but my head was spinning from the blow I'd taken when I'd hit the floor, so I just slid my body against the far wall.

Dalier and Will grappled for the gun, a tangle of fists and kicking legs, but Dalier's grip on the gun was iron. Will's body was younger and fitter than Dalier's, but Will was not a trained fighter, and I watched with terror as Dalier punched Will repeatedly in the face. I knew that if things went too far, Will would revert, and I would be done for. The smart thing would be for me to run, but I didn't. I was frozen.

Then Will made a mistake. He looked for me. And that instant of distraction was all it took.

Dalier threw him into the wall.

The gun was pointed directly at Will's head.

I felt myself shaking. "Dalier," Will said quietly. "The power cell for this ship is located behind this wall. If you shoot, it will detonate the entire ship. We'll all die."

Dalier scoffed and cocked his gun. "So you're not invincible after all," he said. "What happens to you if you're shot? Will you die, or merely suffer? Let's find out."

I heard the gunshot in the same instant as my own scream.

A scream that was quickly met by Will's cry of agony, as the bullet pierced his left shoulder. His hand covered the wound, trying to keep his blood from pouring out of him and onto the floor, as he panted hard, trying to keep himself together. I could tell it wasn't a mortal wound, but his body was rebelling, and he was struggling to hold on. I saw his fingers twitch, and knew that he wanted the samples around his neck, which were tantalizingly out of his reach. We both knew that before he could touch them, there would be a bullet going through his brain. It wouldn't kill him. It couldn't. But I would have no hope of escape.

"Suffering it is." He raised the gun again, aiming for Will's other shoulder.

Before Dalier could fire, I threw myself on top of him.

Dalier wasn't expecting my attack, and went down to his knees as my arms reached around him for the gun. He twisted his torso, and leaned sideways, bringing me down into the floor, but I got my knee underneath me and kicked him in the face so hard he fell forward and dropped the gun. He lunged for it, but I kicked it away from his hands and it skittered across the metal floor. Dalier turned and backhanded me across the face. As I struggled to get up, Dalier raised his fist to strike me again.

"Dalier!"

I looked up to see Will on his feet, gun in hand. He fired. He missed.

Before I could do anything else, Dalier grabbed me and spun me in front of him, his arm tight around my neck in a headlock. I struggled, but he tightened his grip until I was gasping for air. "Not this time, lovely," he muttered into my ear.

He looked back to Will. "Go ahead. You are free to kill me, of course, but you'll have to shoot her first. The two of us are all that's standing between you and your escape. Shoot us and leave. Go on. Show her what you really are."

Dalier tightened the arm across my throat, and I continued to struggle against him as I could feel myself getting dizzy, getting weak. Will looked from me to the gun in his hand. There was nothing he could do.

"How interesting," Dalier said, as I clawed at his arm with my weakening hands. "Shall we go now? Slide the gun back to me, and we'll forget this entire unpleasant episode."

I felt myself getting blurry in Dalier's grip, and saw the terror, the conflict, in Will's eyes. Dalier had left him with two choices: my death, or our mutual imprisonment. There was no third way. For one instant, those eyes softened, then turned to steel.

He raised the gun and pointed it at me.

"I'm sorry, Cara."

I was not afraid.

Chapter Twenty-Three

No Escape

Dalier let go of me in confusion, and as I crumpled to the floor, Will turned back and fired into the ship's power cell.

He'd chosen a third way.

The entire ship lurched, and there was a rumble from inside the wall as the room filled almost instantly with smoke. Within seconds I could barely see the other side of the room.

I screamed for Will. "Where are you!" I cried. "I can't get to you!"

"Cara, get out of here! You can't help me!"

I heard the sound of a blow, and through the smoke I could see Will throwing his body onto Dalier, pinning him to the floor. "Go!" he roared.

I was halfway up the stairs when the explosion rocked the ship.

The floor pitched and I lost my balance and fell, sliding facedown against the metal steps until I was able to catch myself. I knew no human in the engine room could have survived.

I didn't know what that would mean for Will.

I crawled down the steps. I had to go back.

Another explosion came from somewhere else in the ship, and the smoke in the engine room was so thick it was nearly opaque, the air so hot it forced me back. My eyes burned with smoke and tears.

I ran.

The explosions were coming faster, part of a chain reaction that seemed to be leading up to something huge, and as I ran through the ship, I heard the sounds of metal fracturing. The ship began to shake so hard I was sure it was coming apart. I ran down the ramp and made it to the edge of the clearing before I threw myself down on the ground.

What I saw next shocked me—it was Will, human, with Dalier slung over his shoulder, running toward me. As he neared the edge of the clearing, the rumbling started to build. He flung Dalier down and threw himself over me. "Don't look," he ordered.

The explosion was enormous, like a sonic boom, and I trembled under Will's body. There was a bright flash, and from under Will's arm I could see the orange color of flames. My ears rang and I could feel the heat, like a blast from a furnace. I pressed my face into Will and prayed for it to end.

It ended quickly, and the echoes of the final explosion reverberated in my entire body. Will pulled himself off of me, both of us struggling to breathe the hot, acrid air. He touched the side of my face. "You're hurt," he said, and I felt my cheek; it was wet and sticky. I realized that the side of my face and neck were covered with blood.

"It's not serious," I said. "It just grazed my ear." I carefully felt the edge of my ear, and there was a small piece of skin missing. I had been lucky. The bullet was meant to go into my brain. I wondered if my struggling had been successful, or if, at the last minute, Dalier had missed on purpose. I guessed I would never really know.

The ship was gone, and I was surprised by how little debris remained. A few large pieces of metal still smoldered, and a large crater had opened in the earth where the ship had been sitting. "I should have run farther," I muttered. I looked up at Will. "How did you do that? How did you not revert?"

"I did revert," he said, rubbing smoke out of his eyes.

"But—I thought—"

"I know. I don't know how I re-integrated so fast. It's never happened before." He coughed, and I did the same. "Maybe it was just instinct."

I looked at him, spattered with Dalier's blood, and saw that he was rigid with tension. His right hand was balled into a tight fist, as if he were holding something.

"What's in your hand?" I asked.

"Oh," he said, uncurling his fingers. "I forgot about that." He held his hand out to me, and I took what appeared to be a black grain of rice.

"What is that?" I asked.

"It fell out of me when I reverted," he said. "My guess is that it's a tracking device of some kind."

"Ah," I said. "So that thing about the radiation?"

"A lie. He wanted me to think he could still track me even if I went out of my solid form. I think the Taser was a distraction, so I wouldn't notice him implanting this in my back." He took the tracking device and put it on a rock. Then he took a second rock and smashed it.

I looked at Dalier, who was lying on the scrub grass about five feet from me, and walked over to him. His face was bloody and badly burned, but what shocked me was that his pale-blue eyes were staring directly ahead. He was clearly dead. There

283

was no need even to feel for a pulse. Will was watching me, but when I turned to him, he stood up and walked away.

I went and stood next to him. "In sixty-five years," he said, "I've never killed anyone. Never."

"He killed himself," I countered. "You didn't kill him."

"I did kill him, Cara. And, really, didn't I kill Annabelle, too?"

"No. You didn't. You made a mistake. A big one. But you couldn't have expected what happened. It wasn't your fault."

"I should have seen it," he said. "She was always a little touched, I think. I don't think I understood until later. She was such a kind girl. You would have liked her." He swallowed. "I liked her. Oh, I should have known. I never should have gotten involved."

"You were young." I put my arm around his shoulders. "It wasn't your fault."

"Wasn't it, though? And now her son is dead, too. Because of me."

"He's dead because of his anger. Because of his hate. Not because of you." I put my other arm around him, and he rested his forehead against my bloody face. "You have to let it go, Will. Or it will eat you up, just like it ate him up."

We sat in silence, listening to the remnants of the ship crackling and settling as they burned.

"It looks like you're stuck with me," he said at last, looking up at the ship. "I'm here for good. But if that's not what you want, I won't stay with you. After everything you heard today, I won't blame you for wanting me gone. Not at all."

I tightened my grip on him. "I've never wanted you gone. All I've ever wanted is to be with you." I took a deep breath. "You blew up your ship. To save me."

He nodded.

"Oh, God, Will, I'm so sorry." I closed my eyes tightly, trying not to cry.

"No," he said, kissing my forehead. "I don't have any regrets."

"Maybe not now—"

"Not ever," he said. "Never, do you understand? Being human, with you, has been the very best part of my life."

There was such conviction in his voice that I had to believe him. I turned and kissed him gently, drawing a shaky breath. "What will we do now? Do we run?"

He glanced at Dalier. "We may not have to, actually."

I stared at Dalier's glassy eyes, and then looked back to Will. "Oh. *Oh.* That's why you saved him, even though he was already dead?"

"It's disgusting, I know," he said, lifting his face from mine. "If I'm going to infiltrate his group, if I'm going to undo what he's done to us, I'll need to be able to match his form, and I'm going to need his ID and whatever else he's carrying around."

I nodded. "It's okay. I understand."

"If I do this, if I can take his place and discredit him so thoroughly that no one will pay any attention to anything he's ever said, it will mean that we can be together without running. I will be able to be with you the way I am now. In this body."

The thought was like a miracle to me: we would be together. Still, so much risk. "Wouldn't it be easier for you to just take another form? Then you wouldn't have to leave now. Now that he's gone, they probably won't watch me as closely anyway."

285

He shook his head. "If Dalier's friends at the FBI find out he's dead, they'll want to know why. There will be an investigation, and that's the last thing we need. Anyway," he reached for my hand, "I want to be with you in this body. Don't misunderstand, in another form, I would still love you completely. But not everything would be the same. For either of us."

I blushed and he laughed. "That, for instance," he said, touching my scarlet face.

"How long, do you think?" I asked. "How long will you have to be gone?"

"I can't really say. Maybe only a few months. I won't lie to you, it might be longer. I just won't know until I'm inside."

Longer than a few months. My heart sank. "Are you sure about this, Will? Maybe we would be okay. I mean, if you took another form, maybe things would still work. Maybe the way you feel about me would be even better."

"No," he said firmly, and grinned. "It would not be better."

I smiled back, but the tears were coming now, and I couldn't stop them. His own smile vanished as he saw the pain in my eyes.

"I will come back to you," he said, his face serious, his eyes sad. "I swear I will."

"What if you can't?" I said, struggling to get the words out. My voice was little more than a whisper.

"I'll find a way," he said. "We'll be together again. You have to trust me."

"I do trust you," I said. "I'm just afraid."

"Don't. Don't be afraid. I'm doing this so that we can be together. So that no one will ever come and disturb us again. I'll come back the instant I can."

"What will you do then?" I asked, tucking my face into the side of his neck. "You can't go back to Dr. Kleeman."

"No, and there's no reason for me to, anyway. I don't know what I'll do next, but it will be with you. You are all that I have left in the universe now. You are everything."

I felt hot tears running down my face, and it was a long time before I could speak. I concentrated on the feeling of his warm body holding me. Right now, he was here with me. I tried to focus on that, on the time I had left with him.

I pulled him closer, surprised that that was even possible. "You've turned my life into a fairy tale," I murmured. I felt silly saying it out loud, but he had to know the truth. "I was hidden in a tiny room in a tower, and then you came and climbed up to me and I wasn't alone anymore."

He brushed his lips against my forehead. "I don't want you to feel alone, ever, but it isn't enough for me to be in the tower with you. You need to get rid of the wall."

"I'll try," I said softly. "Until I met you, I never even wanted to. I never even wanted to be free."

"Be free," he whispered, and he bent down and pressed his lips to mine. And there in his arms, my wall crumbled into dust and I was free.

Chapter Twenty-Four

Know Thy Enemy

I didn't watch Will as he carefully put on Agent Dalier's clothes, and took the various items in his pockets. I didn't watch as he buried him. I didn't want to look as he took Dalier's form. I was still looking away when Will came and put his hand, now older and rougher, on my shoulder. "It's time," he said simply. "There's still the matter of the two agents who saw me transform. So I should be getting back."

I nodded, and together we got into Dalier's black sedan, after Will cut the engine of our stolen car. "I'll call the police once I've taken you home," he explained. "They'll come and pick it up."

"What will you do about the other two agents?" I asked.

"They've already had some pretty nasty head injuries," he said. "But I might need to perform some pharmaceutical intervention."

I put my seatbelt on and wiped some of the blood from my face onto my sleeve. "I hope Liv's okay," I said.

"I think Liv can take care of herself." He laughed. "But if she's run into any trouble, I'm in a position to help her. Don't worry. You should be careful, though, about what you say in your apartment. I'm sure the place is bugged, and I may not always be the only one listening."

"What about you? What are we going to say happened to Will Mallory?"

"I withdrew from McNair when I thought I was going home," he said. "That part's taken care of. I told them I was taking a backpacking trip to Europe to find myself."

I laughed then, despite myself. "You didn't think that was a little clichéd?"

"Sometimes clichés exist for a reason." He winked.

"Okay," I said. "I'll stick to that. You're in Europe, having your overprivileged American breakdown."

"I see you've got it down."

"Will I hear from you at all?"

"I'll try," he said. "I may not be able to contact you. If anyone suspects, even for a minute, this will have all been for nothing."

"What should I do?" I said forlornly. "What do I do with myself, while I'm waiting for you to come home?"

He reached out and took my hand. "You'll get up in the morning. You'll go to school, and you'll do your homework, and you'll drive Liv crazy. You'll apply for colleges, and if I'm not back yet when the time comes, you'll go. Someday—soon, I hope—I will come back, and you will tell me everything that I missed. And you will tell me how you pined for me every moment, and how you cried yourself to sleep in your pillow every night. But you won't really pine for me, or cry; you'll be happy. Because I want you to be happy. And if you ever find yourself wanting to pine, or cry, you'll tell yourself *Will loves me, he's coming back to me, and we will be together.* Then you'll smile because you'll know that it's true."

We were in front of my apartment building then, and I knew this was it. He took his oilcloth pouch and hung it back

289

around my neck. "I need you to keep that safe for me while I'm gone," he said. "I can't take it with me where I'm going, and I'll need what's inside so that I can be me again."

"I will keep it safe," I said. "I promise." I reached for him and held him close to me, trying to ignore the smell of stale cigarettes clinging to Dalier's clothes and the strange, foreign feeling of his arms. "I love you," I said. "I'll be waiting for you. You *will* come back."

"I will come back," he repeated. "I'm leaving my heart with you. Don't forget."

He kissed my cheek, whispering, "Go now, love."

I got out of the car and watched until he was gone.

My front door was unlocked, and when I went inside, Liv was already there, trying to clean up our wrecked home.

She gasped when she saw me, and I remembered the blood. "What happened to you?" she said, running over to examine my face. "Come on, I'm taking you to the hospital."

"No," I said, waving her off. "I'm fine. I just cut my ear. Will you help me clean it up?"

We went into the bathroom, and I took off my bloody shirt and Liv carefully wiped up my face and neck with some damp paper towels. "This looks awful," she said.

"I can't even feel it now," I lied. It still burned, but there was no point in making her worry. "You don't look so great yourself," I added, pointing out her swollen, scraped face.

"Yep, we're quite the pair today. Maybe we should go troll some bars later." She paused then. "Oh, my God," she said. "What's all this blood on the back of your head?"

I'd forgotten about that. "Oh, that's not mine."

"Nice."

I washed my hair after that, and she smeared my ear with antibiotic ointment and bandaged it for me.

"Are you going to tell me what happened?" she asked finally while I pulled on a clean shirt. "Is he gone?"

I looked around, remembering Will's warning not to talk in the apartment. "Will you take a walk with me?"

I waited until we had walked quite a way from the building before I started talking. "Tell me what happened to you first," I said.

"Well, I was pulled over by an unmarked police car, but the guys driving it were obviously not cops. Dressed way too nicely. I told them that if they didn't let me go, I would have my friend run a story in the *Chronicle* about FBI agents going off half-cocked and harassing young women, and that my father was the deputy ambassador to Uruguay. The one guy rolls his eyes at the other guy, and says something about Dalier being a lunatic. Then he tells me that Dalier isn't representative of the Department, and apologizes for the inconvenience, blah, blah, blah, and then I called Steve and he picked me up and brought me home."

My jaw was hanging open. "What did you tell Steve?"

"Practical joke," she said. "I just hope I don't have to do it again, because he's not going to believe me a second time."

"Wow, Liv. You're a total badass."

"Not really," she said. "I never did get to shoot the big gun. So tell me, did Will make it home?"

"No. He didn't." I explained everything to her, about being followed by Dalier, how I got hurt, how Will blew up his only way home to save me. And about how Will was now infiltrating the FBI, trying to discredit Dalier, so that he could eventually come back again.

291

"You really love him, then?" she said, once I was finished. We had turned back and were making our way home.

"I do. Really, Liv, I do."

"What is that like?"

I looked down and my feet. "It's wonderful," I said. Then I smiled at my sister, who was struggling to keep a straight face. "It's like eating a never-ending chocolate bar that doesn't make you fat."

"Sounds nice," she said with a laugh. "Are you hungry?"

"Starving," I admitted.

"Pizza?"

"Please."

The look on the pizza guy's face when he came to the door was priceless, as he looked from Liv's now-black eye and scratched face to my bandaged ear, to the foot-deep pile of debris on the floor. He backed out of the door so quickly that we couldn't even give him his tip. "Guess he thinks we're running a Fight Club in the living room," Liv said with a laugh, and started eating the pizza right out of the box. All our dishes were in broken bits on the kitchen floor.

"I guess that means I won. You look worse than I do."

"Yes," she agreed. "But I don't have to go to high school tomorrow."

I groaned. "I was almost shot in the head today. Doesn't that justify a day off?"

"You already had a day off today," she reminded me. "You were out with fake mono, remember? I've been meaning to talk to you about that."

I got up from the table, taking my pizza with me. "Sorry," I said. "Remember, the first rule of Fight Club is that you don't talk about Fight Club. I'm going to bed."

I lay in bed that night, and wondered where Will was. Had he gone to D.C., or was he still nearby? I wondered if he was missing me, too. I tried to comfort myself with the fact that he wasn't really leaving, not permanently, anyway. I would see him again. I didn't cry, not that first night. I fell asleep clutching his oilcloth pouch in my hand. He was coming back, I told myself. He was coming back.

Chapter Twenty-Five

Alone

The full blow of Will's departure didn't hit me until the next morning, when I woke up and realized that I had to go to school. Worse, I had nothing to look forward to afterward. Will wouldn't be waiting for me to call. I wouldn't sit on the bench in front of the library, waiting to see his dark head bobbing among the sea of students coming down the walkway. We wouldn't sit in his apartment, studying together, facing away from each other with only our backs touching. We wouldn't trace secret messages on each other's arms while sitting in the dark at the movie theater. I wouldn't hear his stories of the people he had been before he met me, and we wouldn't laugh together about the insanity of the universe. He wouldn't kiss me, and I wouldn't feel alive. I would go to school, and I would go to work, and I would come home. The end.

I would do all those things, because I had told Will I would, and because I had no choice. College still loomed on the horizon, and I still clung to the hope that I would be spending that time with Will. He was coming back. He'd promised.

I dragged myself out of bed, put clothes on my aching body, and drove myself to school.

I was not pleased to encounter Molly on my way into first period.

294

"Cara!" she called. "Hey! I thought you had mono."

"False alarm," I said. "It was something else."

"Oh, well, okay. You look awful, anyway. What happened to your ear?"

"I got in a fight," I said, and she gave me a look.

"Okay, whatever. What happened to you on Friday? You missed all the excitement. Adam stepped on a rake in the backyard and gave himself a black eye."

"Really," I deadpanned. "He stepped on a rake."

"Yeah. He's been getting a really hard time about it, too, poor guy. I think he must have been pretty drunk."

"Must have been."

"So, where did you go? I tried looking for you, but no one knew where you were."

"Morgan spiked my drink. A lot. I got sick and went home."

Molly shook her head at me. "No, Morgan wouldn't do that. It must have been somebody else."

"She handed me the drink herself."

"Well, then, maybe you had food poisoning or something. Morgan wouldn't lie about that. She's a little high on herself, but she's a good person. Anyway, she doesn't hate you that much."

"What do you mean, *that much*?" I demanded.

"I mean, she was kind of jealous of you and all, but I kind of thought that was over once that thing with your boyfriend came out—"

"What?" I said, and I stopped walking. Molly stopped, too, and I turned so that I was facing her. "What do you mean? Why would she be jealous? What thing with my boyfriend?"

"I don't know. Maybe you weren't paying attention, but some people were noticing you at the beginning of school.

295

You've lived all over the world, and you live with your sister, which is cool, and then you start telling people you have a college boyfriend. Maybe she got a little jealous, I don't know. Then the thing about your boyfriend being fake came out, and I thought she was over it. Still, she wouldn't get you drunk like that on purpose."

"Look, Molly," I said. "I'm going to spell it out for you. Morgan is not a nice person, and she *did* get me drunk on purpose. Whether you think I deserve it or not, because I may have done something that made her jealous, is beside the point. I'm done with that group, and I'm done with Morgan. So, please don't ask me to hang out with them anymore, and don't bring them by Vivoli's to bug me while I'm at work."

Molly looked hurt at first, and then angry. "Wow. You really are stuck up. I guess everything Adam says about you is true."

"What Adam says about me?"

"Well, yeah, you were a total bitch to him."

I gaped at her. "If you knew Morgan and Adam hated me, then why did you invite me to that party? Was it your idea, or Morgan's?"

She didn't answer.

"Fine" I said. "If it makes me a bitch to have a backbone, I'll take it."

"Whatever," she said. "I hope you and your backbone have a wonderful life together." She turned her back on me and stormed off. I was not sad to see her go. She was just using me as a stepping stone to climb the Murray social ladder, with Morgan reigning supreme at its summit. In any case, Molly had thrown me to the lions one too many times. I was done trying to be nice to people who treated me like crap. I didn't care what they thought of me anymore.

I somehow made it through my morning, though my teachers were all giving me dirty looks and asking me about my fake mono diagnosis. After second period, I started telling people I'd had a bad reaction to a new medication, and that seemed to satisfy everyone.

I didn't see Adam until I was coming back from lunch, and that was the single thing I'd been dreading most.

I saw him from down the hall, and I admit that I felt some satisfaction at the bruise next to his nose, which had spread under his eye like a blot of blue-black ink. I tried not to smile as he came toward me. Maybe if I stood against the wall, he would walk by without seeing me.

My run of good luck was over. As he walked by me, he deliberately body-checked me, ramming his shoulder against mine, causing me to drop the books I'd been carrying.

"Today," he whispered, his mouth an inch from my ear, "is the day you start paying." He rubbed his shoulder against mine so hard it hurt and kept walking.

My instinct was to pick up my books, but as I started to bend down, I felt something inside me snap, and I was suddenly flooded with anger. What was I doing? In the previous twenty-four hours, I'd been handcuffed, thrown in the back of an unmarked truck, and almost shot. Not to mention that the love of my life was now gone indefinitely. After all that, was I really going to be intimidated by this *nothing*?

I spun around to face him. "Oh, really?" I called, and he turned back around, looking surprised. The ten or so people closest to us stopped in their tracks and looked at me. I was not known as someone who shouted in the halls. Or made a scene. I was making one now.

"Really?" I repeated, and my voice rose further. The hallway was suddenly very quiet. "Do you need me to hit you in the face and kick you in the nuts again? 'Cause I can do that. So if you'd prefer to pass on that, you're going to leave me alone now. You're not going to talk to me, you're not going to put your hands on me, hell, you're not even going to *look* at me. Ever. And since I'm pretty sure I'm not the only girl in this school you're bothering with your pseudo-machismo crap, you should start leaving all the others alone, too. Because once it gets out that all it takes to knock you down is a three-hundred-page book to the face, I'm guessing you aren't going to have a free pass to mess with people anymore."

He sneered at me as if I were beneath his contempt, but he backed away and walked faster than necessary to his next class to the sounds of wolf whistles and laughter.

Half a dozen girls, some whom I recognized and some of whom I didn't, smiled at me and nodded approvingly on my way to class. Adam didn't so much as glance at me for the rest of the day.

There was a pep rally scheduled for that afternoon, so I went to the nurse's office faking a headache and signed myself out for the day—one of the perks of being eighteen. I decided I would spend the time trying to get the apartment in order. There was no reason for Liv to have to clean up the mess. It wasn't her fault, after all.

When I got home, I discovered that it had already been cleaned. Even my room was picked up. Everything was back where it belonged, except for my computer, which I knew I would never get back, and my opera dress. And my poor plants.

Liv wasn't at home—I was alone, in my clean apartment, and my thoughts seemed to echo off the walls at me.

I sat on my bed and stared at the blank walls. Maybe Liv was right. Maybe I needed some posters.

I was contemplating curling up in a ball to wait for Liv when there was a knock at the door, which I found deeply annoying. Liv must have locked herself out again. Or maybe the FBI was coming back for me. Either way, I got up to open the door.

Standing on the other side was my father.

"Daddy?" I said, my voice quiet. I suddenly felt like crying.

"Oh, Carrie," he said, and he hugged me, and it felt like hugging the teddy bear I'd loved and lost when I was a little girl.

"What are you doing here?" I asked sniffling. I did not want to cry in front of my father, no matter how much I felt like I needed to.

"I haven't heard from you in a month," he said. "Shoot, I even sent you a car, and not even an e-mail. I was worried about you. So I have a friend who got me a standby seat on a flight to San Francisco yesterday."

"I'm sorry," I said. "I've been meaning to call you. Things have just been so crazy lately."

"I know," he said. "Things are always crazy, aren't they?"

"Yeah," I agreed. "They are."

We sat in the living room, drinking tea from the only two cups that hadn't been smashed in yesterday's raid. I was glad Liv had cleaned up. I couldn't imagine how I would have explained the mess to him. He told me about Uruguay, and I told him a whitewashed version of what was going on at school.

It was nice, talking to my dad. Especially without the worry that a screaming fight might erupt any minute.

Ah, the screaming. That reminded me. "Have you heard from Mom at all?" I asked, after we were done catching up on the major events of the past month.

"Only from her lawyer," he said. "It's done this time, Cara. It's probably for the best. She's back in Virginia again, and she's getting a teaching license."

"Oh." I said. "I'm sorry, Dad."

"No. I really think this is better for everyone." He looked at me intently. "I'm sure she told you when she was out here how I ruined her life."

"Well, maybe," I said awkwardly. "She was pretty mad when she was here."

He nodded. "I know. She's not entirely wrong, you know. I was selfish. She's right about that part."

"What do you mean?"

"She didn't tell you?" He shifted in his chair and rubbed his eyes. "Maybe I shouldn't be telling you this. You shouldn't have to worry about all the sordid details of your parents' marriage."

I was silent. I wanted to say, *No, maybe you shouldn't be telling me this; in fact, maybe you and Mom shouldn't have been having death matches in front of Liv and me our whole lives,* but I didn't. I was curious. I couldn't help it.

He took my silence as an invitation to continue. "When your mother and I got married, it was right after we had graduated from college, and I was sent directly on my first assignment overseas. We made a deal then, that I would take a position in D.C. after that assignment was over, and she would go to graduate school. So when my term was coming to an end, she got herself a spot in the Chemistry program at Johns Hopkins. Then I got a call. Somebody was backing out of an assignment in Nairobi, and they offered me the chance to take his place. You have to understand, it was a big opportunity. I would be promoted, and it was a chance to really jump-start my career."

"So you took it," I said. I felt a pain in the pit of my stomach, as I remembered my mother telling Liv and me that we didn't understand what she'd been through with my father. As it turned out, she was right. We didn't understand. I had no idea she had even applied to grad school.

"I took it," he said. "And she had the choice, she could go home without me, and go to grad school by herself, or she could go with me to Nairobi."

"Why didn't she go?"

"We had Livvy then, and she was two. She was afraid of taking care of her by herself for two years while she was in school, and she said she didn't want Liv to grow up not knowing her father. We argued a lot about that, and I can see now that that's where everything started to go south. I should have listened to her. I thought she'd get over it."

"She should have gone," I said. "She would have been happier, I think. We all would have been better off."

"Maybe," he said, "but then, we never would have had you. That's the problem with life: sometimes you don't realize you've made a mistake until it's too late. And sometimes you do something that redeems the mistake, that makes it right again, and you're still so angry that you can't even see it."

I didn't know how to answer that, so we sat and drank our tea until Liv came home from school.

301

He stayed for dinner, and took Liv and me out to our favorite Chinese place. He told us he was leaving again first thing in the morning.

"Really?" Liv said. "That's an awfully long trip to make just to be here for one day."

"It is," he said, "but they're expecting me back. It was worth it, to see you two again, even if it was just for a little while."

He asked if we would come and visit him at Christmastime, and we agreed. At the end of the evening, he gave me a piece of paper. "This is your mother's address and phone number in Virginia," he said. "I think you should call her. Let our mistakes—your mother's and mine—be just between us. All right?"

"I'll call her," I said. "I promise."

I lay in bed that night and thought about my parents, and about all the wrong assumptions I'd been making my entire life. Did anybody ever know what really went on between two people? Maybe that was just a mystery that no outsider could possibly understand. I thought about that for a long time. Certainly, I didn't believe anyone would ever be able to understand what Will and I shared. I missed him, that night. I knew he would have been able to help me make sense of everything. It's what he did—he took chaos and molded it into something beautiful. I couldn't believe it was only the second night since he'd been gone. I felt like I'd been missing him for months.

That second night, I cried.

Chapter Twenty-Six

Undercover
(Will)

It was a full week between the time I took Charles Dalier's form and the first time I heard Cara's voice again.

I hadn't started working yet on destroying Dalier's credibility. I needed to get the lay of the land, to figure out what made Charles Dalier tick. Who the man was.

Turns out Charles Dalier was a man who was shtupping his secretary.

I'm not sure why this surprised me so much.

The Special Projects Division is exiled to a far corner of the J. Edgar Hoover Building, far from the more prominent—and more useful—offices on violent crime, crises management, and other departments dealing with more than the things that go bump in the night.

I was the only person in my division with an actual office. My subordinates, of whom there were perhaps half a dozen, were herded into tiny beige cubicles. The badly dressed minions of Civil Service crept around their desks like rats searching for food in a maze; pale, tired, and unhappy—the Special Projects Division appeared to be something of a gulag for the soul. I wondered how much of that had to do with Dalier.

Over his desk hung a plaque with a single quotation from Hannibal: *"I will either find a way, or make one."*

The words hung over my head as I worked, as if Dalier was working to damn me from beyond the grave.

I didn't dare take it down.

I was sitting at my desk on a Friday afternoon, drinking coffee—black, by the way, with one sugar—when one of the lower-level clerks came into my office waving a CD.

"I've got this week's phone logs for the Gallagher apartment," he said, "in case you want to check them."

He nodded at me uncomfortably as he handed them over. He was afraid of me. They all were, there. Charles Dalier was very thorough, very strict, and very much disliked.

I put the CD into my computer and plugged in my headphones.

This was Cara's landline, and there weren't many conversations. I wondered when he'd be bringing me the tapes from her cell phone. Not that I particularly wanted to listen to those, either. I hated invading her privacy that way, but I had no choice. Anyway, it was better me than the real Dalier.

I just wanted to hear her voice. Just once.

I fast-forwarded through a lot of pizza-delivery calls before I got what I was looking for. A boy, calling for Cara. My insides seized up, but he only seemed to want help with a French assignment.

Then I heard her sweet voice, and everything inside of me melted completely away.

That was why I was there, I reminded myself. For her. For us. I didn't know how long it would be before I touched her again, but I knew that I would.

Then my secretary came into my office and sat on the edge of my desk. Asked me if I wanted to go outside for a cigarette.

I did not. But I went anyway.

Heidi Fuller was a beautiful woman, perhaps forty, once divorced, no children. Entirely too good for Charles Dalier, but then, when it comes to men in positions of power, that's usually how it goes. We went outside and smoked a cigarette together, and I was reminded again of how much Dalier's body liked nicotine. Still, even in Dalier's body, I hated the taste.

She leaned in to whisper to me, surreptitiously running her finger up my arm. "Will I see you tonight?"

I tried not to panic. I did not do a good job.

She kissed the side of my neck and I jerked away.

"What's wrong?" she asked.

"I—tonight's not good. I just can't."

"Oh! Did you forget your pills again?"

My pills? "My pills?"

"You know, the little blue ones." When I still looked confused she got annoyed. "Your Viagra."

There was more panicking. Then I had a new thought. A perfect thought. This could be just what I needed.

"Yes," I said. "I forgot to pick them up. Could you swing by the pharmacy for me on your way home?"

"Of course."

I ducked out of work early that afternoon, at the risk of alarming my coworkers—Dalier never left early.

I had a prescription pad to steal. Charles Dalier was about to start some new medication.

It was many hours later when Heidi met me at my apartment, where I sat at my kitchen table nursing a scotch.

305

Turns out that in addition to shtupping his secretary, Dalier was also a raging alcoholic.

Heidi deposited my prescription on the counter and then climbed onto my lap.

No no no no no.

She began kissing the side of my neck and unbuttoning my shirt.

I shoved her onto the floor.

"Hey!" she shouted.

"I'm so sorry," I said. "I think it was a muscle spasm."

She reached over the edge of the table and finished my scotch with a single swig. "That's okay, Charles. It's more fun down here, anyway," she said with a simpering giggle.

The next thing I knew my pants were around my ankles.

It is very hard to flee with one's pants around one's ankles.

I wondered what Cara was doing at that moment. Had to have been something better than fending off a middle-aged nymphomaniac with a bad perm. I reminded myself again why I was doing this.

Who says romance is dead?

Some men buy flowers to show their love. For my love, I endured the death grip of Heidi Fuller, who may have a second career hand-squeezing orange juice or wringing chicken necks. Wrestling crocodiles. Crushing rocks with her bare hands.

I may be in need of some therapy now.

At any rate, I did my best to shield myself from her groping meat hooks and her persistent attempts to gnaw my face off. "Would you mind grabbing a pill for me?" I asked.

She smiled rather brazenly and opened the pharmacy bag. I have to admit that I felt very, very sorry for her.

"What is this?" she asked. "*Thorazine*?"

306

"Oh," I said, trying to look embarrassed. "They must have given you the wrong one."

"Isn't that an antipsychotic?"

I looked away. Coy. Uncomfortable. "Is that how they market it?"

"Charles ..."

"I'd really appreciate it if you wouldn't mention this at work. Now, why don't you come here and kiss me, Amy."

"Heidi."

"Right. Of course."

She did not kiss me before she left with a headache.

So began my campaign to discredit Charles Dalier.

Chapter Twenty-Seven

Waiting
(Cara)

Whoever said that April is the cruelest month never spent a December in the Bay area. The cold, damp air permeated my bones, and I spent most of my time indoors. I was sick a lot. My asthma hadn't bothered me since I was a little kid, but now I wheezed all the time, and I had one cold after another. I'd spent most of November curled up in a ball. I couldn't remember Thanksgiving; it was lost in a haze of cough syrup and television reruns. Liv took to leaving bottles of hand sanitizer all over the apartment and referred to me as Typhoid Mary.

I didn't bother replacing my dead plants. I told myself I was waiting for spring, but I knew deep down it wasn't the real reason. I didn't want a connection to some green thing with roots. I wanted something real; someone I could hold and touch and laugh with.

"You've never been sick this much before," Liv said to me one afternoon as she graded papers at the kitchen table and I lay on the couch with a box of Kleenex.

"I know. It's the weather."

"That's crap. This is barely a real winter. We've lived tons of places colder than this."

"Not damper, though," I said, and I blew my nose so hard I was sure I was losing brain cells.

"It's not the weather, Cara. You know that. It's him."

"Him?" I asked. We were still not saying his name inside the apartment, just in case. "How could he be making me sick?"

"No, you're pining for him, and you're making yourself sick. Look at you, you're a mess. I don't get it. Didn't he promise to come back?"

"Yes, but—"

"But nothing. What do you think he'll say if he comes back and sees you like this? That is, if he can even find your wasted little body in the middle of the piles of used tissues."

I lay back and closed my eyes. "I know. I'm trying, Liv. I am. It's so hard, the not knowing. It's not like I'm getting sick on purpose."

"I know," she said. "I'll pick you up some Echinacea later, okay? You have to try to get some more sleep, though. You know I can hear you at night."

I didn't know that. It was true that I wasn't sleeping, but I did try to keep the crying to a minimum. It was just that as soon as I got into bed, the questions started running through my mind—*Where is he? Is he safe? Has he been caught? What if he never comes back?* I knew that the instant I lay down that the voice in my head would start in on me, and wouldn't let up until the anxiety had peaked and turned me into a quivering mass of nerves and misery. I envisioned Will in a lab somewhere, being taken apart molecule by molecule. I envisioned myself as a little old lady, crying out his name with my dying breath. And still the voice wouldn't shut up. *Where is he? Where is he?*

I avoided going to bed as long as I could. I read, or watched TV, or even did extra homework to keep my mind focused on other things, and eventually I would fall asleep with my face in my book, or on the couch in the living room. The next night I would do it all over again. Anything to shut up that damned voice. It crept into my mind like some kind of burrowing insect anytime things were too quiet. So I had to keep the quiet away.

I blew my nose again. "I'm sorry, Liv," I said. "I didn't realize I was keeping you up."

"Don't apologize, but don't forget that you aren't the only one worried about somebody here."

I wanted to tell her I appreciated it, but I coughed up a bunch of phlegm instead.

I got over my cold eventually, and my health started to improve thanks to the giant horse pills of herbal remedies and vats of chicken soup that were pushed on me by my well-meaning sister. My sleeping was not improving, but I hoped that Liv didn't notice. It had been barely under three months since Will left, and I knew it wasn't long enough for me to be worried. For all I knew, he might not make it back for another year. Or longer. Still, the voice in my head lingered, waiting for any quiet moment to start in on me. *Where is he? Is he safe?*

Liv came home from the Safeway with a sad-looking philodendron one day, and stuck it in the kitchen window while I was sitting at the table doing my homework.

"What's that?" I asked.

"What does it look like? It's a plant, and I'm not taking care of it, so if you don't water it, it'll die."

I stood in the kitchen and looked at the pathetic thing in the plastic pot. "Hey," I said, patting its yellow-tinged leaves. "You got a story?"

It didn't answer.

I poured a glass of water over it. I would go pick up some fertilizer later. Looked like it needed some nitrogen; the potting soil they use for grocery store plants is always crap. "Don't worry," I said. "I'll fix you."

I made Liv pancakes for dinner. On her napkin, I wrote "I love you." It made her smile.

A week later I'd just collapsed onto the couch with a box of doughnuts when there was a loud knock at the door.

It was Adeep.

"Oh, hi," I stammered. "Are—are you looking for Liv?"

His face lit up. "Is she here?" He shook his head. "No, no that's not why I'm here. I came to see you, about those boxes."

"Boxes?"

"Yeah, the ones Will left with me right before he took off for Europe. I still can't believe he did that. Anyway, he was supposed to come back for them, but he must've flaked because I'm still stuck with them, and, you know, my apartment's an efficiency ..."

I stared at him blankly.

"So could you take them?"

"Me?"

"Well, he said if something went wrong, I should give them to you."

"Yeah, yeah, of course I'll take them. Where are they?" I said.

"Downstairs, in my car. I'll bring them up."

I helped him carry the four big cardboard boxes upstairs. "What's in them?" I asked.

"Damn, these are heavy," he said, dropping the last box on my kitchen floor. "Books, I think. So, are you and Will—are you still—"

"It's complicated."

"Right. Okay, well, thanks for taking these off my hands."

"Sure. Thanks for bringing them by. Did you find out about your post-doc yet?"

"It's still too early." He shifted his weight from one foot to the other. "Do you think he's coming back?"

I swallowed hard. "I don't know."

He nodded. He looked a little sad, actually. "Yeah, well, okay. I'm still pissed at him for running that last experiment without me, anyway. Bastard. Okay. I'll see you around?"

"I'll see you."

He let himself out and I tore open one of the boxes.

It was full of books. I pulled one out and opened the cover.

They were Will's journals. All of them. Sixty-five years' worth of his thoughts about humanity. He must have given them to Adeep when he realized Dalier was coming for him. I flipped through them; some were in English, most weren't.

The Journal of Will O'Brien, Eastport, Maine

The Journal of Wiremu Atta. Auckland, New Zealand

El Jornal de Guillermo de la Vega, Havana, Cuba

There were several others that were written in Russian and Arabic and Chinese and Hindi and twenty or thirty other languages that I couldn't make out at all.

I went through all the boxes until I came to the last one, the only one I'd ever seen before. Will Mallory's journal. My Will. I flipped to the last page. There were two entries there, one dated the day after we'd seen *Butterfly* together, and one dated the day Dalier had finally descended on us. Giving these to Adeep must

312

have been the last thing Will did before Dalier raided his apartment.

October 17
Year 64, Day 220
Forms: Five

I don't want to leave, either Earth or Cara. I realize how much I've come to love my new home, the place that's brought me so many sweet memories in such a short time. I will think of them always, of Cara's outstretched hand at Half Moon Bay, of her climbing a tree in her bare feet. Of what it has meant to me, to love her. What it will always mean to me, as I love her still.

For two hundred years I'd never heard of love, living as we do without that kind of specific partnership. Now that I've known it, I don't know how I can be without it.

The thought of leaving breaks me.

I had to wipe my eyes before I read the last entry, which had been scribbled hurriedly in pencil.

I understand, finally, the nature of love and what that condition does to the spirit. Love, simply put, is the marriage of intimacy and need. Because of love, I am more myself than I have ever been.

Earth or Meris makes no difference. Because of love, I am eternally home.

313

Later that night Liv dropped a pile of papers onto my dinner plate.

"What's this?" I asked.

"The mail came late," she said with an enormous smile. "That's my cell phone bill."

"Why are you giving me your cell phone bill? I never use it."

She smacked me in the back of the head. "Just read it, would you?"

She sat down on the couch, but her eyes were twinkling and she never stopped watching me.

"Wow, you sure call the Panda Express a lot," I said.

I turned the first page over and my heart stopped.

Scrawled across the page, over the top of the printing that was already there, was the messy handwriting that I knew as well as I knew my own. Will's handwriting. I flipped through the bill and realized it went on for several pages. He'd written me a letter.

He was safe. Or had been, when this was written. The date printed on it was a month ago. There must have been some delay in sending it out. I glanced up at Liv, who smiled at me, and then I read it. It was hard to make out some of the sentences which had been written so hastily over the top of Liv's call logs, but I savored every word anyway.

Cara,

I hope beyond all things that you are well. I miss you endlessly, and think of the day when I will return. I don't know yet when it will be, but I am making progress.

314

You've probably guessed that all your mail is being routed here, so I've taken the liberty of using Liv's phone bill as my personal stationery. I've sealed it myself to avoid detection at my end, but you should destroy this letter after you've read it. Burn it, or have Liv obliterate it with the laser beams she shoots out of her eyes.

I don't know when this will end, Cara, but I know that it will. Know that I am thinking of you always, and that I am longing for you.

There is one other thing I've been wanting to tell you. I know you worry about me, about what you believe I've given up to be with you, but a choice made with an open heart is never a sacrifice. I hope that one day you will come to believe this, and believe in the choice I've made.

I love you. I miss you. I'll be with you soon.

Yours,
Will

I put the letter down and cried into my soup. Liv got up and hugged me.

"What's wrong?" she asked. "Isn't he okay?"

"He's safe," I said, choking with relief. "He's safe."

And he was coming home.

That night I burned his letter on the stove, and as I went to throw the ashes into the trash I knocked the can over and its contents spilled into the space between the trash and the dishwasher. I reached out to clean up the mess, and discovered there were a number of things that had gotten stuck in that space, things that must've been kicked back there during the raid. There was my missing copy of *Hamlet*, a pile of Liv's journal articles, and a couple of forks. I pulled everything out, and saw that there was something else stuck between the edge of the cabinet and the floor. I leaned over farther and felt something hard and smooth, about two inches long. I picked it up.

It was Bob.

I held him cupped in my hands and laughed. He must have been kicked out of the way once the contents of his terrarium had been dumped out, but he was in one piece, a hard-shelled pupa waiting for summer to come again. I wondered if he had any idea that he'd almost been killed.

I rocked back on my heels, and Liv peered over my shoulder. "What is that?" she asked.

"It's Bob," I said. "He's okay."

"Huh. Bob looks pretty much like a giant cat turd, doesn't he?"

I tucked him into a hand towel and put him on the windowsill; I would find some more soil for him in the morning. He was okay. I knew, then, that I would be, too.

Chapter Twenty-Eight

Dreams and Dreamers

Winter break approached, and I was hoping to get my college applications done before it started. Liv and I were headed to Uruguay, and I didn't want to have to work on my essays while we were gone.

I spent the Saturday before our trip at the McNair library working on my college essays on my new laptop, holed up in Liv's tiny study carrel. I was happy with how productive I was, but eventually I got sick of writing about how plants were my life, or about how reading Faulkner had helped me understand the human condition. None of it was true. But there's no way to write an essay about how your alien boyfriend taught you that a life lived in hiding is no life at all, that it takes more strength just to be yourself out in the world, risking all the pain that can cause, than to try to shut the world out, hoping to keep yourself safe. That, in the end, what it takes for your soul to be brave enough to crawl out of its shell isn't ambition. It's love—the kind of love that reaches inside you and pulls you out, warts and all, to live a life without fear. That lets you live every day as yourself. That lets you be real.

Some people are lucky and get that kind of love from their parents, right from the very beginning. Some live their entire lives and go to their graves never getting it at all, never knowing

317

what it feels like to be someone else's miracle. That isn't the kind of stuff people want to read on an admissions essay. So I wrote about Faulkner instead.

I decided I could stand some fresh air, even if it was cold, and went outside to eat my lunch on one of the benches out front.

I sat down and looked up at the clear blue sky, and tried to warm my face and hands with the sunshine. It didn't work; I was still chilly, and I chafed my hands together before pulling my backpack onto my lap to get my lunch. As I did so, a middle-aged man, balding and potbellied, sat down on the bench next to me. I glanced up at him as he sat down; I knew a lot of the faculty members by sight now, and he didn't look familiar. Maybe he was the father of a student? He didn't look at me, so I ignored him.

My lunch was not in my bag. I pulled out my books twice, checking to make sure that it hadn't been shoved to the bottom, and I realized that I must have left it in the kitchen. I shoved my backpack down on the ground with a grunt of annoyance.

"Did you forget something?"

I glanced up and saw that the paunchy man was looking at me. "My lunch," I explained. "I guess I'll have to go buy something. Not the end of the world, right?"

He laughed. "No, not the end of the world."

He was looking at me again, and I was confused. There was something, something in the way he looked at me …

"Would you like to share my sandwich?" he said tenderly. I looked up at his face, and there were tears in his eyes.

My mouth fell open, and the sound that came out of it was halfway between a gasp and a sob.

"Peanut butter?" I said, and I wasn't sure if I was laughing or crying.

"You're not allergic, are you?" He reached out to take my hand, but I was beyond that and threw myself into his arms.

"You," I whispered. "You're safe. You're here. Oh, *you*." And then I was crying into his neck.

"I'm here," he said. He fingered the cord around my neck. "I'd like very much to kiss you right now, but I think you've suffered enough. Can we go someplace—?"

He didn't need to finish the sentence before I was dragging him back into the library and up into the stacks, where I shoved him into the study carrel I'd been using earlier. It wasn't much bigger than a closet, and the two of us had to mash ourselves together to fit inside. Which was fine with me.

I slid the oilcloth pouch over my head and put it around Will's neck. "I think you can take this back now."

"Thank you for keeping it safe for me." He reached inside, and while my heart did somersaults in my chest, his fingers found what he was looking for. As he smiled at me, he shimmered, and I was looking into the gray eyes of the man I loved.

I reached up and traced my fingers over his face, reacquainting myself with the contours of his jaw, his lips, his nose. "Does that feel better?" I asked. He didn't answer.

He kissed me so hard and so fast that it took my breath away. My arms wound around him, wanting him closer, so close that we wouldn't even be two people anymore, and his fingers knotted in my hair. I reached between us to unbutton the shirt that now hung from his younger, leaner body, and felt the warm skin of his chest under my hands.

I should not have been surprised when he pulled back, gasping for air.

"I'm sorry," he said. "I could feel myself going—"

"It's okay," I said, putting my hands on either side of his face and looking into his eyes. "Just breathe. Stay. Stay with me."

His breathing slowed. "I'm all right," he said. "I guess it's been a long time. I'd forgotten how you felt."

I blushed and he laughed as he pulled me back into his arms. "That, I didn't forget. I spent the last three months thinking of everything I could possibly do to make you blush."

"And?" I said into his bare chest.

"I came up with quite a list. Do you want to hear it?"

I tried not to laugh. "Surprise me. You'll have a long time to work through it now." I leaned away from him to look at his face. "Won't you? It is over now, isn't it?"

"Yes, it's over. I think you would have been impressed with my performance. By the time I was done, I was surprised no one had tried to lock me up in a mental institution. I don't think they'll give much credence to anything Dalier ever said about either of us. They turned off the tap on your phone a month ago."

"A month!" I said accusingly. "Then why did you stay away so long?"

"I had to be sure. Then last week, I was finally fired. They think I've moved to Ireland to write a book about UFOs. Well, they think Dalier's moved to Ireland to write about UFOs." He shook his head. "I need to stop doing that."

I leaned closer to him, running my lips back and forth against his collarbone, making him shiver. "You won't need to anymore," I said. "You don't ever have to be anyone but you,

320

ever again." I paused and looked up again. "Unless you decide that you want to."

"I won't want to."

"But if you do—"

"No. This is it for me now. I will be Will Mallory, and I will be with you and love you and worship you, and eventually I will grow old with you, and that will be that. But," he added, "if *you* change your mind. If you ever feel like you've made a mistake, tell me and I'll go. Just throw all my things on the front lawn and you'll never see me again."

"It'll never happen," I said. "This is it for me, too."

"Good. Then it's settled."

"Can I kiss you again now?" I asked. His answer was not verbal.

We stayed there until the librarian threw us out.

We spent the evening in my kitchen, and for once I was glad that Liv had to work late. It was wonderful to be alone with Will, and I wasn't ready to share my attention with anyone else just yet. I had dinner sitting on his lap, but truthfully neither of us ate much; we were too occupied with other things to even think about chewing. Afterward, he helped me straighten up the kitchen.

"Are these all your college applications?" he asked, rifling through the drafts I'd printed of my essays. I had them in a file on the kitchen counter.

"That's all of them," I said. "Unless there's someplace I missed. Didn't you have any place in mind that you'd like to go, since you'll be starting over as an undergraduate?"

He shook his head. "No, I've lived all over the world already. Wherever you want to go will be fine."

"Oh, no," I said. "Don't make me responsible for your happiness. There must be *someplace* you would rather go."

He was thoughtful for a while before he answered. "Okay, then. I'd like to be someplace near the ocean."

"That's all?"

"That's all."

I sifted through the packet of essays and pulled two of them out. "Neither of those was high on my list anyway."

"Are you sure?" he asked. "I don't want you giving up a school you wanted just for me."

"Positive. I kind of wanted to stay on the West Coast, anyway. I think I've moved around enough for one lifetime."

He came up behind me, wrapping his arms around my waist and leaning down to rest his face against my ear.

"Isn't there anything else?" I asked. "Anything else you need to be happy?"

"Nope," he said, kissing my temple. "To be with you is better than any dream I ever had for myself."

It made me smile, to know that I could be the dream as well as the dreamer. I reached up and locked my fingers behind his neck, basking in the love that radiated from his face. For some reason, at that moment I remembered the fat, bumbling caterpillars we'd raised when I was thirteen, and I finally understood them. To be able to grow wings, you have to be willing to open yourself up to the world, to your dreams— dreams bigger than you think you deserve. My dream was staring down at me, and my heart was wide open.

Will loved me, he came back for me, and we were together. I closed my eyes as I reached up to kiss him, and deep inside me, my soul was flying.

End of Book One

The Metamorphosis Trilogy

Acknowledgments

A number of people have helped with the writing of Caterpillar, since its first chapter was penned in the summer of 2010. Thanks are especially due to Kathy Walden Kaplan, who is always my first (and best) reader, and to Dave Callahan, who so diligently edited this work. I also want to thank Eva Soulu, who created Caterpillar's amazing cover art.

Thanks also to Brett Thelen, for giving me hints as to the kinds of things Liv might have been up to in her grad-school adventures, and to all the many military and Foreign Service Brats I have known and loved, who helped to inspire the characters of Cara and Liv.

And, finally, to my children, for inspiring me to write a story about sisters, and to Paul, for his endless support, and who keeps me from forgetting to feed myself for a week and subsequently starving to death.

About the Author

Born in Santa Barbara, California, Kate Oliver has lived most of her life just outside of Washington, D.C., where she grew up in the company of many Foreign Service brats and the occasional FBI agent. Having worked as everything from a professional statistical programmer to a professional student to a professional parent, she now splits her time between wrangling her three kids and writing books for children and young adults.

Visit her online at kateoliverbooks.blogspot.com

13247195R00195

Made in the USA
Charleston, SC
26 June 2012